To Heather —
Drink wine, read
books —

A Tainted Finish

A Sydney McGrath Mystery

By Rachael A. Horn

www.BarrelAgedPublishing.com

ISBN-10: 0-9861966-1-4

ISBN-13: 978-0-9861966-1-4

A sweet darling man put up with countless nights of insomnia; the noises in the kitchen, lights being turned on to find slippers and the endless click of computer keys. Questions about murder, motives and human psychology were answered with patience and interest (with only a little suspicion). And encouragement? Loads and loads.

This book is dedicated to Todd, my keystone.

Acknowledgments

Of course, there are many people involved in writing a book. I would like to thank my husband Todd for his endless technical support in creating an eBook. I would like to thank Chris at Open Book Editors for editing. Thank you Jon Davies, my insurance guy, for not reporting me to the police when I asked about murder and life insurance policies. Thanks to all of my early readers, who gave me insightful feedback (Mom, Allison, Brittany, Rat, Monica, Talia, Tom and Anais!).

As odd as it is, I would like to thank wine. Wine has taught me the patience required to allow an idea to unfurl and slowly morph into something on its own volition. Wine has secrets and questions unanswerable, a destiny of its own. But mostly, wine is a work of human ingenuity bent on pleasure...it is a lovely release to know that wine and fiction save no lives or script no treaties. But wine and story offer a momentary escape, and this is what I offer you.

Prologue

A yellow haze drifted over the glorious basalt walls of the Gorge in subtle illumination, the gray-green of dawn slowly dissolving to the light. She stood outside her car at the Cape Horn looking east some fifty miles downriver. The tiny turnout near the hundred-year-old bridge cantilevered a thousand feet above the Gorge. She stopped to stretch and feel the cool air on her face. It was no coincidence that she stopped here, at his favorite spot. He used to terrorize her by hopping up on the Civil Conservation Corps-era rock wall, pointing his camera towards home, only steps away from a perilous fall. When she was really little he made her sit in the truck. Or on the rare occasion that he uncovered his shiny black Austin Healy, she would sit in the sun-warmed red seats, gripping the leather next to her thighs with white-knuckled fingers. He would jump back into the car and say, "God lives here," with a wink and a rough tumble of her thick dark hair. Then he would start the cantankerous engine and set off down the S-curves of the Cape at a snail's pace.

She threw her arms up wide in the air, trying to open up her tight chest and back. Deep cool breaths filled her lungs, and she rolled her head around her shoulders. She had been driving through the early hours of the morning. Instead of being tired, her mind stormed with memories of fights and deeply regretted words said over stupid things that now seemed so flimsy, so silly. They were wispy, paper-thin reasons for being estranged for so long. She had loved him fiercely and this spot reminded her of how she felt as a small child; he was her only family, *the most important person.*

"God lives here," she said meekly, whispering to no one but the picture-perfect red and orange sunrise.

She got in her car and felt a momentary sense of peace. She drove the remaining fifty miles thinking of a day when they hiked Mt. St. Helen's during one of its active stages. Her uncle got in an argument with a ranger after their hike. The trail had been closed, but he had dodged the signs and proceeded to lead her to a view of the caldera. He feigned ignorance to the angry ranger when she confronted him at the end of their descent. He proceeded to argue his case in perfect Argentine Spanish for a long time, gesticulating wildly up at the trail head and ending in mock genuflection, pleading for forgiveness. The ranger believed his ruse, and he winked at Syd when they turned to walk away.

Earlier, they stood looking into the moonscape crater, a cinder cone in the far side of the caldera that puffed out 300-foot plumes of white cotton ball smoke.

"The only things that matter, Sydney: truth, beauty, love," he shouted into the volcano, his voice gruff and hoarse after hours of silence and walking.

She pondered the predictably cryptic declaration during the long hike down, realizing that he had planned the day, the hike and his words like a six-move chess play. She knew she wasn't supposed to comment or discuss it, but somehow he expected her to know the meaning of his words and follow them like a compass needle. She was thirteen and completely annoyed.

Now 32, and sadly complacent in a relationship with her only parent figure mired in strife and misunderstanding, she pondered his proclamation into the mouth of the volcano half a life-time ago. His *raison d'etre*. Now she knew he was giving explanation and asking forgiveness for his future trespasses and the inevitable foibles of their lives to come. The poignancy of it stuck in her throat like a shard of basalt.

Chapter 1

She turned left off Highway 14 onto the Cook/Underwood road cutting in front of a flatbed truck loaded with half-ton fruit bins stacked two high. She watched it disappear in her rearview mirror. But as she turned into the driveway and entered the gorgeously forged iron gates laced with hand-blown glass flowers, she noticed that the truck turned onto the same road behind her. Theirs was the only winery on this road.

It must be coming here, she thought, frowning.

She stopped her car and watched the truck struggle up the steep climb of her road. It slowed and signaled left. She accelerated her car ahead of the truck, up the long, steep gravel road to the winery, and parked it out of the way.

The truck pulled around the narrow gravel drive with expertise, just inches from the rock island in the turnaround. It backed into place and stopped near the deserted strip of concrete, the crushpad.

In her rearview mirror she watched a dark, young man rush out from the side of the winery. He had his hands on his head in exasperation. He approached the driver who remained seated high up in his cab and discussed the obvious error. He looked down at his feet often. His hands moved over his mouth and chin as he listened. Even from the distance she could see that the young man was distraught.

She got out of her car and crunched across the gravel toward the two men. They were silent now, with faces frozen in deep thought. The driver had his hands on his head too. She knew him but avoided his eyes.

"No one called the vineyard then?" she asked, shouting over the diesel engine.

"Pardon me?" the young man asked. He looked up, startled, having just noticed her.

"No one stopped the fruit from coming," she said, louder and oddly annoyed.

"Uh, no. No," the young man answered, bewildered and thick, his hand on his head in confusion.

"I'm sorry," the driver said. He glared at her with pleading hands.

"Horse Heaven Hills today, Jimmy?" she asked. She chose to take his apology as an admission of his error.

The driver nodded and rested his head on the steering wheel.

"Well, then, this fruit needs to be processed," she said, bounding to the end of the truck. She loosened the straps on the tie-downs, her hands expertly working the cranks and latches with the heavy bar she had found in the toolbox at the front of the flatbed.

The dark young man approached her slowly. He was tall and classically handsome, and he walked with familiar grace.

"You're Sydney?" he asked in a lilting tongue. His face bore the haggard, bereft terrain of a stranger, but his thick eyebrows and nearly black eyes pierced her in a familiar way.

She nodded and rolled up the straps into the crank. He watched her while she sidestepped to the next strap.

"We can do this another day," he said in the same thick voice. *Maybe an accent*, she thought.

"This fruit is $2800 a ton," she said, counting the bins on the truck. "We have eight ton of cab here? We'll process it *today.*" She sounded as authoritative as her uncle ever did. She felt a sudden pain in her chest and gasped. She willed her heavy feet to move and carry her hands to the next strap.

The young man followed her around the truck, watching her remove the straps. She worked in silent fury until all of the straps were rolled up. She brushed her hands off in a white cloud. They were covered in a white dust specific to the silty loam of Horse Heaven Hills. Both men stood silent and stared at her.

She looked down at herself. She was still wearing her clothes from the night before. Her black crêpe Armani pantsuit was now dusted with the chalky dirt from the straps. She had changed her shoes before heading down from Seattle. Her running shoes peeked out from the too-long draped slacks that were meant to be worn with four-inch heels.

She raised her eyebrows at the staring men. "Okay, then!" she said, and disappeared into the winery.

When she returned the men had their heads together, whispering a plan. She donned a pair of rubber overalls far too large for her and a bright yellow rubber slick jacket. She couldn't find any boots in the lab, so her running shoes remained hidden under the huge pants. She made her way over to Hulk Hyster.

The old battered forklift desperately needed a coat of paint. She had painted it in a multi-colored flower-power motif with her best friend Charlie during Crush 2000, back when they worked their summers and harvest at the winery. But her uncle would have never painted over the weathered artwork of her adolescence, and the patina looked so much like a beloved timeworn fresco that he couldn't replace it with a new model. His sentimentality was lost on Sydney, however. She dismissed it as a sign of his renowned frugality.

Hulk Hyster started up right away. *A bad omen*, she thought. *But the worst has already happened.*

She grimaced at the two men staring at her in helpless despair. A stabbing pain gripped her, and her hand move involuntarily to her chest. She closed her eyes and took a deep breath. *We can't let this fruit get warm*, she shouted in her head, pushing all other thoughts out. She put the forklift in reverse and the back-up beeping echoed through her head.

She had successfully unloaded two bins off the truck when the dark, young man stepped in front of the forklift and waved his hands.

"We can't do this today," he said.

She lowered the forks and put the machine in neutral. She looked down from her perch and sighed.

"Who are you?" she asked. He opened his eyes wide and she felt instantly annoyed.

"I am Olivier. Olivier Ruiz." He gestured with a stiff politeness that didn't fit his age. He couldn't be older than she was. She thought he might bow. She raised her eyebrows, another relic of her uncle's preference for silence.

"I am Olivier," he repeated stupidly. "The assistant winemaker".

"An intern," she said dismissively. She knew she was being rude and felt a sudden surge because of it. He looked offended.

"And why can't we crush today?" she asked.

He blinked at her. "I have called off the crew," he answered in stiff, perfect English. The grief and despair evaporated from his face for the first time. He met her raised eyebrows with a steely stare.

She got off of the forklift wearing a frown and walked over to the harvest bins. She leaned over a bin and buried her face in the cold clusters of blackish grapes, inhaling deeply. She stood up and brought several clusters to her face in a gentle intimate gesture, something like a kiss. Her eyes shut as she smelled each cluster. After inhaling the aroma of many bunches – rummaging through the depths of the bin – she started to pop berries into her mouth. She spit seeds into the palm of her hand and inspected them as her teeth ground up the skins. She spit out the skins and proceeded to attack other berries with the same concentrated fury. She held them up to the light and inspected them in the early morning sun. The small clusters looked straggly and airy; tiny black grapes on reddish stems.

"Can you sort?" she asked, still inspecting the clusters.

"Of course."

"This fruit is gorgeous. Clean and cool. We'll dump straight into the destemmer-crusher and sort as we go. But keep an eye out for ladybugs. This vineyard once had them everywhere. Yuck."

"We run with a crew of five," Olivier stated, attempting to gain some ground. No intern would tell this arrogant female about their crushpad operations, Clarence's niece or not. He was not going to back down.

"And we sort *always,*" he added, parroting her uncle's standard of procedures.

"Yes. Always," she said, climbing up into the forklift seat again. "Just not always on the tables."

~

Sydney and Olivier worked side by side sorting and pushing fruit through the machine. The destemmer-crusher sat in a metal cradle in a frame over one-ton fermenter tanks. Sydney loaded the harvest bins onto the forklift and turned the forklift head. The heavy fruit bins pivoted twelve feet in the air over the machine and rested near the hopper so that grapes could move easily into the mouth of the machine. Olivier was busy with the pallet jack, moving filled fermenter tanks in and out from under the frame and staging Syd's next harvest bin. They worked well together, falling into step in a silent dance of two people expertly doing a job with multiple tasks reliant on the other's skill. They worked in the din of two machines, each thankful for the roar that excused their silence.

Once the fruit bins were all emptied, Syd took samples from the tanks Olivier had carefully lined up in the full winery. She entered the lab with averted eyes, trying not to see too much. But she couldn't help herself. It smelled liked *him.* This was his domain. The concrete lab counters were littered with beakers, pipettes, and every kind of glassware needed in a mad scientist's workshop. Chaos was the only obvious theme. She forced herself to search the metal cabinets for the chemicals and reagents she would need to start testing the juices. After several minutes spent searching for the right glassware, she began her basic analysis of the juice, a process she was taught when she was six.

After an hour of running the pH and titrating for acids in each sample, she stood up and stretched. She knew she ought to run the spectrophotometer tests for nutrients but she had forgotten the procedure and her brain was foggy. A nagging pain in her stomach began to demand notice, followed by a growing headache. She felt as if a tight metal band was being screwed around her head. The buzzing fluorescent lights in the lab didn't help. A noisy clock on the wall reminded her that it was 6:40 pm. They had worked for the last ten hours. She hadn't eaten anything since the night before, and she could hardly call that a dinner. She had a tiny foie gras appetizer refused by a customer and hurriedly swallowed in the wine alley at the restaurant where she worked around 9 pm. The headache required less sleuthing; she hadn't had her requisite pot of french press that morning.

She shuffled out of the back room through the labyrinth of barrels and equipment, all miraculously crammed into a climate-controlled space. She found Olivier hosing down the destemmer-crusher on the crushpad, finishing just as she arrived. She turned the water off for him and began to roll up the hose on the overhead rollers.

He stood next to her as she finished, both of them leaning against a tank. Together they scanned the winery for incomplete tasks with expert eyes. She began to take notice of the changes in the winery. The back pegboard with all of the sanitary fittings was organized by size and machine. All of the cleaning materials were on labeled shelves, each in the right place. The barrel room had been rearranged with the handiwork of a mind much different from her uncle's. She had learned from her uncle to sanitize and keep tools immaculately clean, but her uncle had no sense of organization. All surfaces and shelves would remain cluttered under her uncle's direction. She knew with embarrassment that she had inherited her uncle's penchant for chaos. Apparently, the man next to her had not.

She absently rubbed her head as she cataloged the subtle changes in the winery, childish resentment building up in her chest. Olivier abruptly left her side for the lab, while she noted the bright red SOP manual on the chemical shelves. Another one was clipped to a new whiteboard that listed tasks. She had always thought her uncle needed a whiteboard. Olivier came out of the office with a jar of Advil in one hand and her suit neatly folded in the other. She couldn't remember folding it. A whiskey bottle was deftly tucked under an arm. He set the suit gingerly on the clean counter and handed her the Advil. Then he handed her the half empty bottle of Buffalo Trace.

"For your headache," he said. He smiled sheepishly, flashing a white-toothed-grin that shocked her out of her fog.

They hadn't spoken in ten hours, other than the necessary grunts for directions during crushing. His tone with her had changed. He was clearly more relaxed now. He watched her closely as she threw back four Advil with a bourbon chaser and handed the bottle back to him. He took two long pulls from the bottle and wiped his mouth with the back of his hand.

"Nice suit," he said, nodding to the tidy black bundle on the counter.

She smiled sheepishly. "Yeah. Armani. Cost me nearly a month's pay." She paused. "Thanks for folding it". She just remembered that she had stepped out of it and left in on the lab floor.

"Clarence told me that you were a gifted winemaker," he said, crossing his long legs and leaning against the tank. His eyes fixed on his feet.

"I'm not," she said, aping his stance against the tank deliberately. "I'm a sommelier."

"But you have the instincts of a winemaker."

"Clarence never wanted me to be a winemaker. Doctor. Physicist. World chess champion. But not a winemaker." She smiled wryly.

"I would have never sorted that way. I would have never just dumped the grapes into the machine without a sorting table. I am used to having equipment and a full staff. But you were right, the fruit was perfect. If we had waited until we got our crew together we might have had some issues. It got warm today." His accent reappeared in rolling r's, soft w's, and tongue-dampened t's.

"We could have just called them back." She shrugged, a little embarrassed now at her bull-headedness over getting the fruit processed immediately.

"Maybe. Alejandro and the crew would have been drunk. They were pretty torn up last night. It could have sat for days. We would have had to find refrigeration, and the fruit might have soured." He glanced down at her, checking her reaction. He was offering a flimsy argument, but she appreciated the gesture. She had been an ass by any standard. She grabbed the bourbon from him and took two more pulls surveying the tidy counter space in front of them.

"This your handiwork?" she asked, waving at the organized shelves. The fraternal prodding of the whiskey was beginning to loosen her tongue.

"Clarence is a genius, but I have no idea how he works this way." He smiled at her, but his expression changed slowly as he realized his blunder. Her face blanched. A simple tense change could mean so much.

Sydney looked down at her feet, suddenly feeling an immense gravitational pull on her chest. Her head whirled and her knees collapsed under her as she slid down the side of the tank onto the cool concrete floor. A violent *Guh!* escaped from her chest, and she began to weep loudly, heaving grotesquely. She curled into a ball and pressed her wet face against the concrete, surrendering to the grief that had stalked her all day.

Olivier tried to wrestle her into some kind of comforting embrace, but she was taken in a wave of loss so violent that he knew she wasn't aware of his presence. Instead he stroked her thick black hair and finished off the bourbon, eventually letting his own tears fall freely.

Chapter 2

Syd jumped out of bed wearing only a sheet that she wrapped around herself in a blurred hurry. She cursed the quiet, persistent knocking on the kitchen door. She opened the door to see Jim Yesler in uniform, hat in hand and a bereft look on his face. She stepped forward instantly and hugged him, burying her face in his chest. Something about seeing a man like Jim Yesler overwrought with grief was heartbreaking. When she finally let go of him his choked sobbing had abated. She slowly realized by his growing embarrassment that she was hardly dressed.

"I think I left my bag in the car. Up at the winery," she explained, tugging on the sheet above her chest.

He nodded without a word, turned on his heels, and made out of the door on a welcome errand.

Syd rummaged around the kitchen for a french press and coffee beans, still holding onto the sheet with one hand. She lit the huge black enamel AGA stove and started the kettle. Next to the stove sat an expensive Italian espresso maker, her uncle's preferred mode of morning caffeine. The hundred-year-old farmhouse kitchen was equipped with modern conveniences, but she preferred the rusticity of her childhood. She moved around the familiar old kitchen with muscle memory. Her bare feet on the cold wood floorboards felt safe and grounded. The smells of the house all emanated from the kitchen; from the subtle aroma of baking bread to the sourness of the current batch of pickled vegetables in the huge crock on the metro rack under the window. They were all familiar and comforting. A half loaf of bread lay on the cutting board on the island next to a colorful bowl of tomatoes. The kelly green walls glowed with a vibrant freshness and reminded her of the day when Clarence picked out the color. He had chosen a butter yellow. But she was feeling snarky that day and chose the bright green in a juvenile act of subtle rebellion. He quickly embraced it and learned to love it with the grace of a man who would sacrifice everything for love.

She moved to the stove and filled the coffee press with boiling water. From the window she watched Jim Yesler swing her heavy bag like an airy satchel, crunching down the steep gravel road from the winery in long-legged strides. His hat was back on his head and he wore the Sheriffs' uniform that she remembered as a child. He looked exactly the same.

He came into the house without ceremony and placed her suitcase in front of her in the middle of the kitchen. She raised the roller handle and rolled it into the back bedroom without a word.

When she returned she was wearing jeans, flip flops, and an old red WSU sweatshirt. Jim had already pressed the coffee plunger and was pouring it into the hand-thrown ceramic mugs she had set out. She heard the muffled chime of the Westminster mantle clock downstairs and patiently counted ten chimes.

"I need you to ID the body," Jim said after a full five minutes of looking for words in the bottom of his coffee mug. Syd nodded and smiled apologetically.

"I don't know where my keys are," she said. She looked him in the eyes with controlled despair. The terrible weight in her chest that had been nagging at her since she jumped out of bed felt heavier by the minute. She began to wonder if she could walk at all, let alone drive. She couldn't remember where she left her purse, her keys, or her phone. She vaguely remembered the day before; the work in the winery and her breakdown last night. The fogginess in her head was as consuming as the hole in her chest. She felt worse than hung-over. She felt wretched.

"I'll drive," he said paternally. He was the sheriff now. She looked at him curiously, wondering how difficult it must be for him to regulate his emotions at a time like this.

"But how will I get back?" she asked. She was surprised by how young she felt when he used this voice.

"I'll take you back, Siddy-biddy," he said. He smiled sadly and pulled her to his chest again.

~

The half hour drive to the coroner's office gave Jim plenty of time to explain the details of the night before last: the 911 call, the response time, the list of people who were at the winery when he showed up. He was on duty and he was the first responder. He had always kept a special eye out for Blackwell Winery and the folks who lived there, so he wasted no time getting to the scene. But Clarence was already dead when he arrived. There was nothing he could do, he said helplessly. The assistant winemaker had found her uncle submerged in a tank of red wine, drowned. He kept the worst details to himself. He called her around midnight after two torturous hours spent trying to figure out what to say.

She looked at his dry rough hands on the steering wheel while he talked. He fit in the cruiser like a puzzle piece, all six-foot-four of him. The cruiser smelled like leather and sweet male sweat, a smell she always thought belonged to the man. She was a little afraid of him as a child. He was her best friend Charlie's father and the only source of envy she had for her friend. Charlie and Jim were extremely close, especially after Charlie's mom died of cancer when they were teenage girls. He was just as attentive to his adult daughter. Jim sent Charlie notes and gifts, and traveled the 240 miles to Seattle almost monthly to take his daughter to the opera or a Mariner's game. She would occasionally tag along with Charlie and Jim, although he invited her to almost every outing they had. She loved them dearly, but lately she began to define the strange feeling she had when she was around them as envy. It embarrassed her to feel that way toward her best friend.

"I talked to Charlie this morning," he said as he glanced at her, almost reading her thoughts.

"I didn't call her," she said, her voice flat. "Actually, I did, but it was at 2 am, from the car. But I couldn't talk. She kept saying *hello* and she was getting mad, like I was some kind of creeper."

She smiled sadly at him and swallowed back a sudden wooziness.

"Yeah. You're lucky she couldn't taze you through a phone line," he said halfheartedly. He was always proud of his tough little girl. Syd nodded silently.

"She's coming down tonight. She told me to tell you she'll do the arrangements for you."

"I'm. . . I can do it." She realized as she said it that she really couldn't do it herself. Suddenly she felt desperately alone. She wanted Charlie with her so badly. Charlie was like a sister. She was family. Charlie knew her issues with Clarence. Charlie knew about every fight and challenge Syd threw back at her uncle. She understood what Syd faced with his cryptic, eccentric efforts at parenting. Still, Charlie understood her uncle like no one else. She admired Clarence with quiet awe and always defended him, even during the worst storm – when Syd left her Fulbright scholarship at Oxford to attend sommelier school. It infuriated Syd that Charlie could empathize with her own hurt but still maintain an unwavering reverence for Clarence. But Charlie was special like that.

"Have you heard from Marcus?" Jim broke the silence.

"Who?" she asked.

"Uh, Marcus. It's Marcus, right? You two still together?" Jim looked ready to backpedal out of unsteady ground. Boyfriend issues with his girls were always hit or miss.

"Oh. . .Marcus. Yes, we're still together." A feeling of wretchedness swept over her. She was unsure if it was coming from her head or her stomach.

Jim squished his face in hesitation. "Charlie says you might want to call him. She says he's frantic."

"Oh." A moment later she squealed, lurched forward, and vomited on the floor at her feet.

~

"It smells nothing like the movies in here," she said, feigning humor to Jim. He looked at her with concern. "I've never been to the morgue."

He wanted to ask her if she had ever seen a dead body before. He knew she was pre-med in college. He certainly didn't want to cause another bout of nausea, so he decided to keep his mouth shut. Besides, it wasn't just a dead body. It was her uncle she would be looking at, and he wouldn't look like she had remembered. Honestly, Jim was a bit haunted by the transformation of Clarence Blackwell.

"This is the coroner's office," he said, gently guiding her by the shoulder into a small room adjacent to what looked like a reception area. Her wet flip flops squished in conspicuously vulgar sounds on the linoleum tiles. They had to wash the vomit off her feet and pant legs with a hose they found outside the county buildings. Her jeans were wet almost to the knees and she was trembling. He wrapped his arm around her shoulder tighter, hating his job. He felt utterly helpless.

They stepped through the next door with trepidation and Sydney squished into a room filled with an odd mix of smells: wine, something earthy and woodsy, terpenes, and a kind of chemical sweetness. She was surprised at how comforting the aromas were at the same time that her sterile surroundings seemed so surreal. She looked at the form on the table in the middle of the room, astonished.

Clarence was purple. The deep lines in his 64-year-old weathered face were traced in dark purple that looked like dried African mud. He was bloated, like most drowning victims. Thankfully his eyes were closed, which Jim saw as a blessing. He had seen his eyes when the EMTs had shown up at the scene, and they were so deeply stained that they were almost solid black. His thick white hair was now stained reddish purple, and it stuck strait out in tufts like a gruesome troll doll. He reminded Jim of a Marvel comic villain.

Syd stood anchored three feet away from the body, eyes wide and mouth agape. She stared for what seemed like an eternity to Jim, but may have been only a minute. Then she stepped forward and laid her hand on the nearest large purple hand resting on the cold stainless steel table. She was used to purple-stained hands; a winemaker's hands were almost always stained in various shades of purple. She lifted it to her face and examined the palms, tracing the calluses and lines with her finger. She turned the hand over and noticed a swollen knuckle protruding outward over the index finger. She ran her finger over it and pressed into the lump.

Signs of bruising had begun, but there was a surprisingly little amount of swelling.

"He dislocated his finger," she whispered to herself.

"His hands aren't always like that?" Jim asked quietly.

"He's left-handed, like me. He was doing punchdowns. How could he do that with a dislocated finger?" she asked flatly.

"Maybe it happened during the, uh, drowning?"

Syd stepped back and stared at the gruesome face and body in front of her, a steely look in her eyes. Every trace of the desperate little girl she had been a few moments ago were now gone.

"Why would my uncle drown in a tank of wine, Jim?"

~

The car ride back seemed to take forever, and Syd couldn't stop fidgeting. She ran every possible scenario in her head and bounced a few of them off of Jim in a breathless stream of theory and anecdote. She sat picking the skin on her lip, a nervous tick she had when she was deep in thought. Was it a heart attack? An aneurysm? Did he fall and hit his head?

"Who found him, again?" she asked, picking the skin off her lip in a fury.

"The foreign . . . uh, the Argentinian kid," Jim answered, hesitant to indulge her in her new state of mind.

"Olivier? The winemaker?"

Jim nodded. She sat hunched in her seat, silent for a while. Her brows furrowed as she worked her nails on her bottom lip.

Half-way through the drive, she let out a deep sigh, "Why would my uncle drown in a tank of wine?" But this time the question was couched in a tone of deep curiosity that Jim found utterly disarming and dangerous. He shuddered involuntarily.

Chapter 3

Clarence held the punchdown tool with the deftness of a swashbuckler. He twirled it overhead and lunged it at imaginary foes for her amusement. She would hang her head over the side of the tanks and watch him as he deftly walked barefoot on their edges, the aromas from the fermenting wine singeing her nostrils. The long stainless steel pole was attached to a welded flat disc. The disc had four large holes that let the skins seep through the flat surface of the tool like a giant potato masher. At first he would cut into the fresh cap of skins in the tank at an angle and pull upward to make a hole. Then he would plunge the punchdown tool deep into the skins and churn them under the juice in a swirling jerking motion, like the dervish dancers she had seen the previous summer. Sometimes he looked like a circus performer or a dancer himself, wielding a tool from side to side and walking a tight-rope above her. He was graceful and confident, and she loved him best during punchdowns.

"Punchdowns are an art form," he said one evening when he was pleasant and playful. "The skins have to be agitated and engulfed in juice, but never damaged or bruised." He stood poised high above a tank of Mourvedre, waiting to have its first

punchdown of the fermentation.

She stood on a stool, barely able to look into the tank. She was only six. A sudden waft of gas hit her and she pulled back with a contorted face.

"Yes, Sydney. That's gas burning your nose. Carbon dioxide. CO2. The yeast eat up sugars and nutrients and produce CO2. Taste it." He squatted on the edge of the tank and reached down with a beaker from his pocket. He handed her the beaker of half-fermented wine. It tasted sweet and fizzy.

"CO2 makes pop fizzy too. But we can't breathe it. It's a poison to us. This is why you aren't allowed in the winery without me during Crush. This is why we can't go into the winery right away when the doors are shut. Do you understand?" He nodded toward her. She nodded back, bored.

"How many times do you have to tell me this? Geez!" She bopped her head with her hand.

"I'll keep telling you until you stop sticking your nose in the tanks right after I open the lids," he said, mocking her girly voice.

"Then how do the yeast live in CO2?" she asked after a minute, her fingers working at the skin on her lower lip.

He stopped the punchdown tool and smiled down at her.

"They can get poisoned too, actually. And they can breathe oxygen in the wine or live for a while without oxygen. Aerobic versus anaerobic. Yeast are remarkable organisms."

"Can we breathe aerobic or anaerobic?" she asked.

"We can only breathe air. Aerobic. Oxygen mostly. We're certainly inferior to yeast in a vat of wine." He smiled and she knew it was a good question.

"But what if a person got stuck in there?" she asked, her dark brows furrowed.

Clarence raised his brows at her in one of his wordless answers.

"Do people die doing punchdowns?" she prodded.

He openly winced at her childish voice - still echoing a recently outgrown lisp - asking such an adult question. Her casual relationship with death was a painful vestige of her orphaning that often jarred him. He grimaced through the tight knot in his throat.

"Sometimes, yes," he said soberly. "But only because they

made very stupid mistakes. And no one at Blackwell's would ever do such a thing." She smiled a toothless smile up at him as he leaped over to another tank and plunged the tool deftly into the cap, releasing more noxious gas into the air around her.

Chapter 4

Sydney asked Jim in for lunch when they got back to her uncle's place. She busily gathered the ingredients for something easy and found enough prosciutto and cheese to make a grilled sandwich. The last of the garden tomatoes sat in a bowl on the island in the middle of the kitchen. Clarence was an avid gardener and grew obscure and delicious heritage varieties. These were brown, purple, and yellow tomatoes, the size of baseballs. A delicious loaf of Clarence's famed country bread sat on the counter, donning a crumbling black crust nearly a quarter-inch thick.

In fifteen minutes, Syd set a table with open-faced grilled bruschetta, fresh tomato slices, some fermented vegetable pickle, and pear slices drizzled with blue cheese crumble and honey for dessert. She served a local bottle of semi-dry Gewurztraminer. She smelled it as she opened it, reflexively-grapefruit, lemon peel, and a hint of lychee.

Jim paced the deck outside, grunting in a low tone into his cell phone on official business. She popped her head out the kitchen door. “Soup's on!” she said, feeling surreally cheerful.

Jim ate like a big man with a purpose. She knew he was hungry. It was already past 2 pm and he was a man sized to make every meal count. Charlie used to joke about her dad being a perpetual teenage boy in his appetite. The man consumed 4000 calories each day. She watched him thoroughly enjoy two giant slices of bruschetta with melted triple cream brie, prosciutto, and fresh mayonnaise piled high with the veggies. She silently poured him another glass of wine when he had drained his. She noted that he had never been much of a drinker; at least he certainly never drank wine while in uniform.

He eyed the other two bruschetta on the plate and looked at the nearly empty plate in front of her. She had been chasing the same battered slice of tomato around her plate since they sat down.

"You need to eat, Siddy-biddy. When was the last time you ate?"

"Um, Sunday night at work, I think," she said. The last 48 hours were a broken jigsaw puzzle of distant events.

He moved to put food on her plate, but she refused it, pushing her plate away. Preparing food made her almost happy just now, but the thought of eating brought on a new wave of nausea. Instead, she reloaded his plate. He gave up and tucked in to his seconds.

"Charlie will be here around six tonight," he said, dabbing his mouth with the yellow cloth napkin she gave him. He stared into her with his large dark eyes. He had deep purple circles under his eyes, dry skin, and deep creases beneath his bushy dark eyebrows. He was getting older too, she thought. His thinning brown hair stuck up off of his head in tufts, an occupational hazard of his sheriff's hat. He looked completely worn out. He had a dollop of honey on his stubbled cheek. She took his napkin and wiped it off.

"Charlie and I'll make the arrangements with Jack Bristol. Don't worry about anything. Get some rest." He spoke with paternal force, his giant hand pressed on hers. For a medium-sized woman she could feel tiny next to him.

"I will," she lied. He frowned at her.

"You don't need to get up to the winery, Sydney. I've talked to Olivier. He has it covered."

She pulled her hand away and rose to start cleaning up.

"No, Sydney. Go rest. Now!" He escorted her to the back spare bedroom and stood at the door.

“I have to go. But I'll be back tonight. Charlie and I’ll bring dinner.” He raised his eyebrows at her and she surrendered with a nod. She felt grateful for his concern, but his mothering was overbearing and she suddenly wanted to be alone. She smiled weakly and hugged him. He held her and rocked her for a few minutes in silence before she moved away.

“Thank you,” she said, feeling weak and tired. She moved her feet slowly to the room she left so abruptly that morning.

The room was cool and dark. It smelled like some kind of wood resin and tobacco. The mixed leathery smells of Jim and the woody smells of her uncle's reading room made Sydney feel safer than she had felt in as long as she could remember. She climbed into the daybed as Jim watched.

“Jim,” she said, stopping him as he turned to go. “There will be an autopsy?”

“Oh, yes,” he nodded. Something in his voice revealed his determination. She fell asleep almost instantly, knowing that he was as puzzled about her uncle's death as she was.

~

Syd stirred as Charlie climbed into bed with her. She rolled to spoon Charlie, wrapping her legs around her and burying her face in Charlie’s think blond hair. She smelled like Charlie; a mix of cumin and applesauce, a comforting smell from their earliest sleep-overs when they snuggled together and whispered over dreams of becoming queens and sorcerers in their own fantasy land. Syd moaned and rocked Charlie when she felt sobs take over her long body. Her best friend spilled her sorrows onto the soft feather pillows covered in Belgium linen.

~

It was past 9 pm when Syd woke up again. She crept out of the room and into the bathroom. Her pants were sticky and wet, and when she peeled off her jeans, her underwear and pants were completely covered in blood. She felt heavy and weak. She moved in slow motion as she stripped and got into the shower. She was so weak she could barely lift her leg over the edge of the clawfoot tub. She let herself give way to the gravity trapped in her throat and muscles, reflexively sobbing while the hot water beat against her head and back. The full force of grief surprised her not for its weight so much as for its inexplicable continuity; a slow leak of an ethereal substance into her cells, and her lungs and her being. Her body pulsed in a slow gyration with sobbing. But with no relief from the crushing pull. She understood in a moment of despair that crying would not relieve the pain at all. She got out when the water began to run cold, feeling more light-headed than before. She wrapped a towel around herself just in time. The bright blue walls of the bathroom rapidly faded to darkness in the midst of twinkling stars. She frantically grabbed the side of the tile counter to ease herself onto the floor when she lost consciousness.

She woke with the sensation of cool tile on her cheek. Then she felt a throbbing pain on her head above her right ear. She sat up slowly, using her arms to push her body from the floor. She felt the bump on her head with her fingers and brought them to her face. No blood. She stood up carefully – feeling only a little dizzy – and filled a glass of water. It was deliciously cool and almost instantly improved her fuzzy head. She drank another and another, sitting on the toilet, assessing what happened, feeling foolish.

She wrapped herself in the thick white terrycloth bathrobe hanging on the back of the door that smelled like Clarence. She threw her long wet hair into a towel knotted on her head. She shuffled into the dark kitchen, lost in an eerie thought. Losing consciousness and falling onto the floor gave her a large knot on her head. *But if you lost consciousness and fell into a tank of wine, what would happen? How would someone dislocate a finger?* She had no time to ready herself for impact when she fell, but she was able to avoid hitting the counter. If Clarence had fallen during a heart attack he would have avoided the tank altogether. But what if the CO2 overcame him?

She was so lost in thought that she was unaware that the kettle was already on. Steam spurted out of the pot and began to whistle. Olivier bounded into the dark kitchen and they both jumped, startling each other. He moved to turn on the light.

"Good evening," he said in polite formality. Again, she almost expected a bow. She stared unabashedly at him and he grew uncomfortable. He was remarkable. He had deep blackish eyes and black hair curling to his chin that looked wet in the kitchen light. His nose was high-bridged and straight above full lips. He looked larger than she remembered, more than six feet tall, but she had been feeling small all day.

"Tea?" he asked her politely, retreating from her deliberate eyes. He brushed by her, smelling like sandalwood and lemongrass.

"Yes," she answered, wanting to help get mugs, but her feet felt like lead.

He moved with cat-like grace and in a vaguely familiar way that disturbed her. She watched dumbly, transfixed. The bump on her head began to pound.

"Chamomile?" he asked. She nodded as he filled the tea pot with loose-leaf from an ancient tin canister. He dragged the cast iron kettle off the stove with industrial scraping and filled the tea-pot. He found a creamer pot in the mug cabinet and filled it with half and half. He set the two mugs on the table, along with some sugar, honey, and the creamer dish. She watched him gather napkins. He finished with a flourishing gesture that resembled a bow. She smiled and sat down. Apparently, they were having tea together.

"Clarence and I did this every night," he said to her after he fixed her tea to her liking. Honey and cream.

"High tea?" she asked, pretending to look baffled.

"We discussed the winery operations. Yes, sometimes over tea." His English was perfect tonight. He sat up straight and brushed his longish hair back behind an ear. She saw that it *was* wet. He had just showered.

"Clarence discussed winery operations with you?" she asked, narrowing her eyes. "*You?*" She knew her uncle well enough to know that he was secretive and elusive when it came to winery operations. She watched Olivier stiffen and realized she had offended him yet again. Touchy ego, she thought to herself. Apparently the intimacy of the night before - her sobbing in his arms - was a thing of the past. She found herself thankful for his memory loss.

His face grew expressionless. "I want you to know that I am taking care of everything in the winery. You do not need to worry about Crush while you do the funeral business." He was cutting to the chase again. Not a man for small talk.

"How gallant of you," she muttered into the steam of her mug.

He looked at her sharply. "Jim Yesler told me it would be best this way."

"Jim Yesler thinks I'm a fragile wilting flower right now," she said. He looked at her with eyes filled with concern and pity, but offered no argument.

"*I'm alright*," she shouted back at him, furious at his expression.

He visibly jumped and raised his eyebrows with a nod.

"Sure, sure."

She could tell he was confused and perhaps in over his head. She watched his face change with every thought, working his way through her outburst. She softened her frown a bit, feeling bad for yelling at this stranger in her childhood kitchen.

"We can still have these meetings every night, okay?" she said with a nod. He nodded back at her. "You do the winery work. Just keep me informed. If there's a problem–anything from an off-nose on a ferment to a vineyard sample–keep me informed, right?" He nodded again and she half smiled. "We're almost through harvest?"

"Yes. We have only the Petit Verdot and Mourvedre from Rattlesnake Hills left. We are at the end," he said quietly. This woman was worse than Clarence or his own father. He would need to handle her carefully, but he was no stranger to navigating the inner workings of a complicated mind. For now he would do things her way.

He proceeded to fill her in on the details of Crush; issues with growers, schedules, and trucking problems. Thus far, they had no equipment failure, which was an unusual blessing. Olivier had an astonishing memory of Blackwell Winery's general operations, which surprised Sydney. He recalled the names of vineyard managers, last week's Brix reports from growers, and row numbers of contracted fruit in specific vineyards. He recalled the yeast strains used in ferments, even the yeast blends.

"I used to collect data on our yeast blends," she said absently. Memories of working next to Clarence over petri dishes and five-gallon buckets of fermenting grapes in test batches seared in her head.

"I know," he said with quiet respect. "I've read your data."

"You knew I experimented with yeast blends?" she asked. She had published an article on her findings when she was only 19.

"Yes. You are famous for it, apparently. Francois Bertrand told me about it first." He looked down at his folded hands on the table.

"Ah, *him*," she said, smiling. Bertrand was her uncle's famed rival winemaker from across the river, "I'm sure he was all praises." She followed his eyes to his forearms. They were long, brown, thinly muscled, and covered in silky black hair.

"No, he was derisive. But with men like that the source of contempt is often the source of envy as well. I knew he was on to something so I asked your uncle for the data." Olivier rubbed his stubbled chin and looked away. His fingers were long and brown, with lovely long nail beds miraculously white for a winemaker. She caught herself staring at him and shook her head.

"So you and Francois are tight? Go out for beers? Maybe troll for local yoga babes? Or are you more into the board head type?"

"Francois courted me when I first arrived here in July. He isn't subtle. Apparently he is used to buying favors and information from assistant winemakers and interns with beer. We had *one* beer." He held up a finger.

"Thanks for that. Uncle never saw him as a real threat, but he's always up to some mischief. Something recent too. Uncle alluded to it on his last visit to see me in Seattle. That was in August." She frowned and thought about her cryptic lunch with Clarence that day. "Funny, he didn't mention you that day." She lied.

"He wanted us to meet in person," he said quietly.

She arched her eyebrows, and he threw up his hands in feigned defeat.

"And I don't like women who smell like B.O. and neoprene or obsess over their gluten and lactose-free diet in over-priced lycra. Spandex is for exercise, not to wear in public. Besides, I have a girlfriend in Buenos Aires. She teaches politics at University."

"And *she* has a boyfriend who teaches wine marketing at college in Seattle!" said a booming female voice from the kitchen doorway. Sydney turned around to see Charlie filling the door frame with her six-foot tall lankiness and golden hair back-lit by the kitchen light like a lion's mane. She held a phone up. "A boyfriend who left 22 messages on your phone, mind you!" She waved the phone at Sydney.

Olivier stared at her and Charlie tugged on her leggings in an awkward curtsy. "Spandex," she said. She walked forward and pulled the towel off of Syd's head. Olivier blushed. Charlie ignored him and began to run her fingers through Syd's hair.

"I hope you two had *separate* showers," she muttered, working knots out of the ends of Syd's long dark tresses. Charlie missed nothing. "Yes, alas. Considering the *Death* I decided to forego the hazing and seduction of interns this year. I spared the young neophyte his mortification. For now." She winked at Olivier.

"Actually, I think we showered at the same time," he said, clearly trying to maintain his composure. "Mine was freezing, and with an 80-gallon tank, her's must have lasted for a half hour. I am Olivier, by the way." He rose and extended his hand to Charlie.

"Charles. Charmed." She took his hand and smiled genuinely, with only a hint of suspicion in her squinting eyes. Olivier sat down confidently, and Charlie continued running her fingers through Syd's hair.

"What's this?" Charlie asked, frowning at the bump on Sydney's head.

"Oh. I passed out in the bathroom."

"*What?*" Charlie hollered, turning to look her in the eyes.

Syd arched her eyebrows and shook her head.

Charlie wrapped her arms around Syd's head.

"*Fuuuuuck!*" she growled, cradling Syd's head against her body. She began to slowly rock her. Olivier stared into his hands.

A moment later Syd untangled herself from Charlie and moved to get up. Olivier sprang out of his chair, scraping its legs against the floor.

"*I'm fine!*" she yelled, tossing her hands up in exasperation. She turned and walked into the kitchen. Olivier gasped when he saw a giant blood stain on the back of Sydney's white bathrobe.

Charlie and Olivier exchanged a look of shock and then they both came to a silent understanding of Syd's current plight at the same time. Their eyes locked again in silent agreement and collusion. They would work together to help Sydney get through this crisis.

~

Syd and Charlie ended the night with a few slices of pear and some cheese and the rest of the Gewurztraminer from lunch. Syd choked down some pear but couldn't manage the cheese and bread. Charlie offered to heat up the burritos her dad had picked up earlier for the dinner Syd slept through. But she could never have eaten them.

They made plans for the memorial while they ate and Charlie took notes. She would make phone calls in the morning while Syd met up with Jack Bristol, the family lawyer. Syd promised she would be up to it. She also promised to call her boyfriend Marcus the next day, since Charlie was beginning to field all of his calls. He threatened to leave Seattle during his last call and come down the next day. That was the last thing Syd wanted, so Charlie convinced him to wait for Syd to call him in the morning. She told Marcus that Syd was resting after taking Valium. Syd whispered a teary *thank you* as her friend lied to her boyfriend.

"You know, it's a little weird that you don't want to see him," Charlie said after hanging up.

"I do want to see him. Just not like *this*." She gestured at herself, at the train-wreck she had become over-night.

"He's really concerned," Charlie said, surprised that she was arguing in favor of Marcus. She was never a big fan of Syd's boyfriend. "He just wants to be here for you."

"He wants to get closer. He's been pressuring me to move in and spend more time with him."

"So soon? But you've only been dating for, what? Six years, Sydney. *Six years!*"

Sydney winced and rested her head on the table. "I know, I know. He's perfect. I'm an asshole."

Charlie reached over to stroke her disastrous hair, still damp from the shower.

"Wait a minute. You don't even like Marcus," Syd said,

pushing her hand away.

"He insisted that I tell you how much he loves you too," she said, shrugging. "He made me promise to say it just now. Yes, he is a pretentious white boy with perfect teeth and perfect hair and an encyclopedic recall of every fucking opera ever made. And he never says *fuck*, by the way, which is weird. You notice that? And he wraps his stadium dogs in the deli sheets like a burrito. He actually *asks* for them. And he doesn't know how to–"

"Okay, I get it. He's not like your dad. He's not like us." she interrupted what could have been an endless litany of Marcus's faults in Charlie's one and only opportunity to catalog them out loud. Normally the subject was out of bounds.

"But you're in need right now, and he wants to support you. He's working hard at not feeling really hurt that you've completely ignored him."

Syd knew she had a point. Leave it to Charlie to defend someone for whom she is entirely indifferent.

"Honestly, I don't know if he could handle it," Syd said. "He only met Clarence once, you know. And Clarence was his usual charming self. My life here is so different from my life *there*. I've worked hard to keep it separate."

"Oh really? I hadn't noticed," Charlie said, mocking a British accent. Syd rolled her eyes at Charlie, who got up and disappeared into the kitchen.

"Well, it's all bullshit anyway, Syd," she bellowed from behind the liquor cabinet. "They all know who you are. You're in the wine industry, and like it or not your uncle's fame is going to rub off on you. His infamy too."

"Well, Marcus didn't even know I was related to Clarence for a long time after we met."

"And when he found out he was weird about it, remember?" Charlie plopped back down in her chair and opened up a bottle of liquor. She took a swig and set it down.

"That's only 'cause he knows Joe Donner," Syd said. "And Joe hasn't been exactly quiet in building a case against Uncle Clarence. And how was Marcus supposed to know Joe was such a sycophantic prick anyway?" She grabbed the bottle from across the table and took a thirsty pull.

Charlie clapped her hands in mischievous glee. "Bravo!" she said, pleased at the whiskey pull and Syd's rant. She pointed at the bottle and read Whistle Pig Bourbon on the label. She got up and disappeared into the dark kitchen again, returning a moment later with two snifters. She poured the whiskey out and wiped the lip of the bottle with her sweatshirt sleeve out of new-founded reverence.

Each woman swirled the brown liquid from the base of her snifter and buried her nose in the glass. Syd took a deep sniff while Charlie took her famous triple sniff, taking a deep long draw with the last one. Then they took sips.

"Wow," Charlie said. "A terpene rye. Clove. Fennel. Fresh caramel. French vanilla bean."

Syd sucked air into a sip she held in her cupped tongue, aspirating the aromas up into her head before swallowing. "Yeah, I get the rye. Marshmallow. Is it *French* vanilla bean? Something herbal too," she said with a sigh. "You were always better at whiskey than me. How do you even smell it through all that oak and alcohol?"

"You've got wine, I've got spirits," Charlie said with a wink. She cupped her snifter in her hands to warm it up.

But Charlie was excellent with wine too. She had a remarkable nose, even for a sommelier, and she could rattle off unusual attributes without apology. *Baby Poop* was her nick name in sommelier school, as she called out a particularly stinky Rioja in the first weeks of class. Luckily, it morphed into *Baby* as the months wore on, taking on a new meaning for the tall blonde rock star sommelier. She and Syd were the pinnacle of their class, and each landed an excellent placement in a boutique Seattle restaurant. Charlie had recently garnered modest fame as a somm who specialized in boutique spirits and extraordinary mixology using her home brew of bitters. However, Syd took the traditional route as a quiet sommelier building a reputation for finding excellent craft wines from the Pacific Northwest. Both young women were part of the up-and-coming talent flooding the industry in urban America.

"This is one that Marcus would like," Syd said, still swirling and smelling for the mysterious terpenes.

"Really? Why's that?"

"Because it's expensive." They cackled but Syd felt terrible. She winced at the thought of her unkindness. Why was she working so hard to push him away?

"Just promise me you'll call him tomorrow morning. He deserves a call." Syd nodded obediently, suddenly feeling very tired. A few minutes later Charlie tucked her fragile friend into bed with a Valium and a few minutes of sobbing into one another's hair. They held each other long after the sobbing had stopped, and each could sense the other's mind working on her own pressing dilemmas.

Syd broke away from her suddenly. "You should have seen him, Charlie," she said, choking out of her tight, painful throat. "He was purple."

"Dad told me," she said, pulling Syd back to shoulder and stroking her head. "Kind of poetic, right? He was always stained with wine."

Chapter 5

Syd awoke to the whining of a vacuum cleaner somewhere in the house. It was still early, but Rosa must have already started her Wednesday morning routine. Rosa always began downstairs next to her old bedroom at the crack of dawn. It was a memory so deeply lodged in Syd's mind that she often found herself dreading Wednesday mornings. Her first few weeks away at college she slept in late in secret defiance of the tyranny of an early rising house cleaner. This morning she found the sound of the vacuum deeply comforting and dozed back to sleep to the lulling sounds of the living.

A few minutes later a terrible whining din came from somewhere closer by. Syd woke up startled and grumpily shoved herself out of bed. Some kind of heavy machinery was operating in the kitchen, and people were talking in hushed voices. She dragged herself into the well-lit kitchen.

Rosa was shoving whole carrots into an industrial-sized juicer. Olivier was standing next to her, handing her some apples and sliced ginger. Syd could smell kale and spinach too. Olivier leaned down and said something in Spanish, and Rosa smothered a sad chuckle, apparently trying to keep her voice down. Syd laughed undetected. She approached Rosa from behind and put her arm around her.

"There's no need to whisper," she said. "I'm awake."

Rosa turned around and gasped. She hugged Syd with a mother's ferocity.

"*Mi hija, mi hija. Oh, mi hija!*" She trembled against Syd's chest, squeezing her and patting her back. Syd held her against her and stroked her short black hair. She rocked back and forth with Rosa in slow dance of two women grieving. Syd's nose filled with a deeply familiar smell of Dove soap and bay leaves. Rosa pulled away first and squeezed Syd's shoulders with her strong hands.

"I make you a juice," she said in a stiff Mexican accent. She handed Syd a tiny glass of green liquid. Brown foam floated on top of a six-ounce jam jar. Syd grimaced.

"Sí, *comprendo.* Pero it is muy importante that you eat s*omething,*" she shoved the glass against Syd's lips and tipped it into her mouth. Syd had no choice but to drink it. She swallowed obediently while Rosa poured the green-like sludge into her mouth. It wasn't so bad. Still she was thankful that she could finish it in a few gulps.

Olivier stood near the women, watching with interest. He studied their intimacy and was intrigued by the deference that Syd showed Rosa. This tiny Mexican woman had a good deal of influence over her and they clearly cared for each other deeply.

Syd saw him staring and stepped back. She was wearing a black silk slip, which was a little too revealing for the bright light of the kitchen. She blushed, and then grew irritated at her own embarrassment.

"Good morning," she said coolly.

"Good morning," he said, looking down. He shifted his weight and reached for a glass of the green goop. His was a pint jar that was filled to the brim. He lifted his glass to Rosa in salutation and downed it without stopping for breath. He gently placed the jar back on the concrete countertop, turned on his heels, and skulked out of the kitchen with feline grace, frowning.

Syd watched him make his way to the winery out the kitchen window. She relaxed. "Thanks, that made my head feel better," she said to Rosa, who started cleaning the many parts of the juicer. Syd watched Rosa's familiar plump back in front of the sink. She had missed Rosa, and the sting of her absence over the last few days was fresh.

"Where have you been, Rosa?" Syd asked quietly.

"I have my day off on Monday and Tuesday and Alejandro came by Monday night. Borracho. I don't have no cell phone. I didn't know. And yesterday I stay home. Alejandro tell me to stay home for one day. Now I am here for you." She was still crying silently, her tears streaming down her cheeks while she washed the machine parts without interruption. Life rarely intervened with the work of the house. Rosa never stopped moving, even for grief. She poured the remaining juice into a mason jar and pushed it across the counter to Syd.

"Drink it all day. You need the medicine. I make this for the *Jefe* every day." Her voice was untouched by the tears streaming down her face. Syd nodded obediently.

"Your life will never be the same," she said suddenly turning to face Syd. She pushed a flat palm against Syd's chest. "He is here, next to your mother and father. Your heart will always be heavier." Rosa had a long history of telling Syd the gravest truths with startling brevity. Syd swallowed a knot in her throat.

"It hurts," Syd whispered, relieved to express the unexpected physical manifestation of grief. "Like someone hit me."

"You *have* been hit. We all have. We were preparing but not so soon." She shook her head angrily. "And I do not believe he did it on purpose."

"What do you mean?"

"Nada, nada." She put her hand up and turned away. She held up a jar of green juice. "You drink this today." Syd watched as Rosa bustled out of the kitchen, lost in a frown and free flowing tears.

Syd stood with her feet bolted to the floor. Rosa's words washed over her in a wave. Her eyes darted to the bowl of heirloom tomatoes on the island counter and the half loaf of bread under a white linen cloth. She stepped toward the kitchen window that looked up at the winery. The giant red doors of the winery were open wide and she could make out the fermenter tanks, even at a distance of nearly a hundred yards. So many wines had not yet finished fermentation; so many still needed pressing. She lingered in the kitchen, looking for proof of Clarence's intentions. Everywhere she looked she found evidence of unfinished business. Still, Rosa's words resonated in her head like a piercing tinnitus. They filled the hole in her chest with sickening doubt.

Chapter 6

Syd sat in Jack Bristol's office cupping a mug of black coffee in her hands. The door was ajar and she could hear his muffled voice while he gave instructions to his assistant, a woman Syd recognized from school. They were not to be disturbed. The voice that she had grown to love as a child – the voice of Uncle Jack – had never held the kind of authority she heard through the crack in the door. She felt unsteady sitting in his office on official business. She was not going to cry, she told herself with resolve. She had questions and she wasn't about to spend another day feeling like a lost child. Surely an adult woman could grieve with dignity.

Jack walked into the room and shut the door quietly behind him. "Syd, I'm so sorry," he offered and embraced her like an uncle. His familiar smell of expensive cologne clung to his freshly shaven face, which now hovered close to her own. Syd was the first to pull away. She moved to take her seat again and picked up her coffee, wielding it like a shield in front of her.

He took his seat behind his desk, which was an inexpensive Scandinavian light wood office desk, uncluttered and unadorned. In the center of the desk sat a red folio, the kind Clarence used for his official papers. The room was lined with neat bookshelves in the same blond wood as the desk, and the walls were a pale purple. It seemed more likely to be a woman's office. But its smell was distinctly male, permeated by the more subtle aroma of Jack's cologne. A set of golf clubs leaned up against a wall and scattered baseball paraphernalia peppered the landscape of the bookshelves self-consciously dispelling any misconceptions about the gender of the occupant.

"You redecorated your office," she said, looking out the window. The only remarkable thing about his office was the spectacular view of the Columbia River and Mt. Hood. His building was prime real estate, poised on the bluffs of White Salmon.

He nodded at the door. "Becky did it," he said, defeated. He clearly was not on board with the make-over, but he was living with it all the same. He was either a compromising, kind man or a coward. Syd hadn't decided. She was surprised at her need to make an adult assessment of the man. Clarence had sown a seed of doubt earlier in the summer, and she marveled at the power of suggestion her uncle held over her.

"Do your clients like it?" she asked. She wondered how a lawyer could garner confidence in a mauve colored room.

"Most of my clients don't ever come to the office. Farms, wineries, businesses. I mostly make house-calls." He winked. She didn't smile. *Except me*, she thought. Why didn't he meet her at the house?

"I have Clarence's will here, and his important papers," Jack said, shifting in his chair.

"Uh huh," she said into her mug. She crossed her legs.

"Have you read his new will, Sydney?" He asked warily.

"No," she answered. He looked crestfallen. "But he did tell me he was changing it. He visited me in Seattle in August. He said he was making changes."

"We changed it in August. Honestly, I was against it. In fact, we fought over it. I advised him to go a different direction." He was distraught now, looking down at his hands. Syd squirmed in her chair. She wasn't going to feel badly for him until she had some real answers.

"Is that why he was so angry with you?" she asked, looking him in the eye for the first time.

He looked startled. "No, there's more to it. Lately his life had become a bit complicated. What do you know about the buyout?"

"Only that it went bad. That the investor was planning to sell out the winery to a big corporation behind our backs. Hell, everyone knows that. Thanks to the weasel Joe Donner. At least we have him to thank for that."

"Except I'm pretty sure his intentions were anything but noble," Jack added with surprising contempt for the critic, "I'm certain he intended to out Clarence as a sell-out, among other things."

"Well, that was obvious, Jack," she interrupted him. She had no intention of discussing the infamous rivalry between her uncle and the insipid pop culture wine critic. She had to work closely enough with Joe Donner in Seattle, occasionally running into him for judging events or openings. His dislike for her was never far from the surface during their encounters. In fact, she discovered that he had gone out of his way to discredit her expertise in Sommelier school, whispering malfeasance in the ears of her instructors. In the end she had to agree with her uncle's assessment of the man: he was a sycophantic, self-promoting chauvinist. Clarence once had an altercation with Donner years ago when he revealed a nauseating tendency toward misogyny. Clarence was an avid feminist and a vocal believer in the talents of female winemakers. He defended the work of a well-respected, up-and-coming colleague after Joe Donner published a ridiculous review of her wines. Clarence wrote a scathing open letter in the *Seattle Times* about the review and the nepotism surrounding what he called the "fraternity of bottom-feeders", people who prey on the talent and hard work of creative winemakers. He pointed out Donner's history of refusing to review the wines of female winemakers with fairness. Joe Donner countered with a litany of despicable attacks on his blog that were dangerously libelous. However, Clarence accepted the response as being a childish one, and wrote off the critic as a fool. Their rivalry began many years ago, and Clarence paid little attention to it except as the butt of an occasional joke. But Syd suspected that it was at the forefront of Donner's mind and it carried over to herself. While Clarence dismissed him as a fool, Syd saw him as far more nefarious than her uncle ever did.

"The buy-out was all but complete, Sydney." Jack said. "We had to do some fancy footwork to get your uncle out of it. And frankly, I'm not sure it was such a great idea."

"His life's work? He was supposed to just cash out and hand over the winery to some corporate label?"

"He was burned out, Syd. He was tired. Didn't the man deserve a retirement? He busted his ass for thirty years on that winery. And he had no one to hand it to." She heard the bitterness in his voice.

"That wasn't my fault," she said through clenched teeth. A surge of anger and guilt rose in her throat.

He threw up his hands. "I know, I know. He discouraged you. And I know why, and I never agreed with it. But you know how stubborn he was. We argued over it for years. As odd as it sounds, it was out of love. And respect for your talent and intelligence. He was in awe of you. He always said you were meant for bigger things."

"But all I ever wanted was to make wine, like my mother." She said flatly, the tragedy of her conflict with Clarence staring her in the face.

"I think that was the crux of it. Honestly, Syd, I think you always reminded him too much of your mother."

"I've always known that," she said, feeling the old resentment well up in her chest. She strategized a way to take control of a conversation going in a dangerous direction. "Anyway, the buyout? What happened?"

"Well, thanks to Joe Donner, Clarence changed his mind. The contract was tight. I drew it up myself. Clarence was supposed to work as the winemaker and maintain all proprietary decisions for at least another five years, with an option to renew if he had not found a replacement winemaker by that time."

"What would the investor get? Who is he, by the way?"

"A man named Hans Feldman. He's fairly new to the area. From New York, but he lives in Hood River. He would've had 75%

ownership of the winery, and Clarence would be under salary. We included a clause to allow Clarence to live in the house until his death. Clarence would get a big cash out and the winery would get some new equipment and a general manager. Not that Clarence needed the money. He saved everything. He just wanted to make wine and not do the business end of it any more. It was a sound investment for Feldman. The winery's been fully allocated for decades. But in the end he would've almost doubled his money immediately. An easy $20 million."

"The corporation would have bought it for $20 million? Did they offer it to Uncle?"

"Several times. In fact, their hounding him is what gave him the idea to sell to begin with. By selling it to a small investor he thought he was staving off the possibility of a sell-out to the big boys. Naively. Feldman had other plans from the beginning, it seems. He could've easily fought for control of Blackwell's. After getting to know the man, I suspect he intended to batter Clarence with bullying and undermining him until he broke down. Clarence was tired, Syd. His heart wasn't in it anymore." He looked down at the red folio in front of him, "in the end it would have been better for everyone if he just sold it to the highest bidder."

"What do you mean?" she asked, taken aback. Jack folded his hands on the desk in front of him.

"What do you know about Olivier Ruiz?" he asked. There was an edge to his voice.

~

Syd left Jack's office holding the will and the nullified papers related to the sale of the winery. The bump on her head began to pound while Jack expounded on the mystery of Clarence's adventures in Argentina long before Sydney was born. Jack mulled over details, never having received the full story of Clarence and her mother in South America. But he could piece together fragments of the story that he culled from Clarence over the years, and he was nothing short of suspicious. The sudden arrival of Olivier Ruiz and his connections to the family in Mendoza that caused so much tragedy for the Blackwell's gave Jack considerable pause. Sydney's head was swimming by the time she left, but she felt that she was under control of her emotions for the first time since she arrived home. The intrigue was a welcome distraction.

Charlie was busy in Clarence's office when Syd entered. The desk was cluttered with crumpled tissues, and she was cooing soothing sounds into the phone. She looked up at Syd with tears rolling down her puffy red cheeks and shrugged. The person on the other end of the phone line was obviously sobbing. Syd left to make some tea with a lump in her throat. Charlie was the best friend a girl could have.

Later they sat at the kitchen table, sipping their tea. Charlie had recovered sufficiently for another round of phone calls, informing loved ones about the death and memorial service for Clarence Blackwell.

"The things I do for love," she said, rolling her eyes at Syd. She squeezed Syd's hand.

"Thanks," Syd said. She was truly grateful for Charlie, but more than a little preoccupied with what Jack told her.

"How was Jack, by the way?" Charlie asked, playing with Syd's hand.

Syd pondered for a moment. "Weird, actually. And angry. At Uncle, I think. Did I tell you that they fought this summer? Jack didn't want Uncle to back out of the sale. Even after he found out about the corporate buy-out. And he rewrote Uncle's will, which he didn't want to do either. He wouldn't tell me about the will. He wanted me to read it myself before the reading of the will, whatever that means. And, you know, Charlie? I don't think he was even that broken up about Uncle's death."

Charlie frowned. "But they were best friends, Syd. And everyone has different ways of grieving. Trust me, after today I could write a book." Syd frowned and picked the skin on her lip. Charlie patted her hand and got up to make more calls.

Syd stared at the thick red folder on the table, trying to not make out the syllables of Charlie's phone calls in the other room. The fine red linen paper folio donned a wax string that wound around a bone button. The elegant simplicity of it struck her as a perfect symbol for the man she loved so dearly. While others might see a simple pocketed folder for important papers, Syd could see what it really was; a carefully detailed enticement of something precious inside, withholding secrets and offering a defense built entirely on the assumption of common decency and restraint. Clarence crafted a reality in which the details of hand-made paper and a hand-hewn bone button might thwart the ugliness of the world. Punishment for upsetting his eccentric reality was swift and Earth-shattering. It was the thing that Syd feared the most in her lifetime; his disappointment.

Chapter 7

She hardly remembered her uncle when she came to the States to live with him at five. He had been in Argentina with her family when she was a baby, but he left when she was four. She had not seen him since. When she first came to his house, she was frightened and alone, and he scared her most of all. She only vaguely understood the circumstances of her life's upheaval, but she was aware of the tragedy of her parents' car accident, their deaths, and the untethering of her feelings.

Her uncle spent most of his time up in the winery, smelling like everyone she ever loved. He worked all hours of the day, and when he came back down to the house he barely looked at her. Once, when she first arrived, he sat at the kitchen table with a nearly empty bottle and wept while she spied on him from the darkened doorway. He got up abruptly and strode into her room, and she scurried ahead of him and jumped into bed. He sat on her bed and hugged her, squeezing so hard that she gasped for air and hit him in the face to make him let go. He pulled away and left, leaving her frightened and alone. He didn't speak a word, and he hardly ever hugged her since.

As time went on, she and her uncle grew comfortable with each other, in spite of their idiosyncrasies. He was quiet and gruff, and he wore his grief like a mantle weighing down his shoulders. She busied herself with information, reading books and gathering erroneous data to keep her mind occupied. She was a precocious five-year-old. She spent her time shadowing Rosa, the nanny he hired to help him with his unexpected parenthood. They shuffled in their individual self-preservation for over a year, until the day Syd pulled out the chessboard in Clarence's office. It had been buried in a cabinet of papers and books.

Clarence taught Syd how to play chess on his lovely reproduction Isle of Lewis Chessmen set, with four queens. He had carved the board as a young man and purchased the set one piece at a time through a monthly subscription service. They were made of fine ivory, though not walrus bone like the 12th century originals. The board was a work of art as well, with inlaid burled maple and black walnut, made with hand tools over the course of several months. Clarence hand-carved vines along the border that vaguely looked like grapevines. Later he confessed that they were imaginary flora, and not true to any particular species. But they looked like wild grape leaves to Sydney.

Clarence's passion for chess was almost as deep as his passion for wine, although he had laid aside his chess board for years. He had played chess every day with his sister Floy – Sydney's mother – when they were teenagers. He told Sydney that she was better than he was, and it was true. But she often grew impatient, and he almost always beat her in the long games. Frequently they played with competition timers and she would prevail. But then she would want a slow game and let her mind wander. She was a gifted abstract positional chess player, while he played in more calculated moves. She engineered vast and complicated conundrums for her brother's more methodical defensive playing. Floy never bothered to study opening strategies, controlling the middle of the board, or castling in the first three moves. She had been using black's Grundfeld defense for a decade before she knew it had a name. But Clarence studied and loved the chess games codified in the newspapers. He analyzed their meaning in his own journals. He jotted down her moves and strategies, and tried to capture her apparent chaotic style of playing. Secretly he knew her talent wasn't in the careful analysis of long game strategies, but rather in the relative positioning of the team. She had an intuitive sense of the probability of play as a function of synergy, while he saw individual pieces in positions with their own set of odds. Even worse, she never cared about winning, a trait that baffled her brother.

Syd played almost identically to her mother. When Syd was seven she and Clarence played a match in candlelight for an entire afternoon and evening. The power had gone out during a particularly severe winter storm, and they moved their chairs and the chess set near the wood stove. The match was drawn out and leisurely. Syd held his captured pieces in her hands, her small fingers moving over the ivory absently. She sat gazing at the fire, mesmerized.

"Why do you do that?" he asked softly, pointing at the berserker rook she was holding in her hand.

"Do what?" she answered self-consciously, jolted out of her trance.

"Hold the pieces like that," he said. He paused before continuing softly. "Your mother. She used to do that."

She stared at him for a long time. "I like the smoothness of the pieces, but I like to feel the bumps of the carving too. I can feel where the knife has been." A hint of a lisp hid in her tongue, a repository of the slowly filling hole where her two front teeth were growing in. She was startled to see his eyes fill with tears. He dropped his head in his hands and wept quietly while Syd watched him.

Over time Syd began to equal her uncle in play. She began to understand sacrifice when she was eight, and played with relentless ferocity that bordered on recklessness. When she was ten she played with sacrifice, but often to soften her uncle's mood or appease his desire to teach her something of value. She was his superior in play from that point on, but it took him a few years to figure it out. The chess board was the classroom, and Clarence never tired of the metaphor. To his masculine mind he could teach her the ways of the world through well-planned strategies and maneuvers. But she could see the inherent flaw in his lessons; in the end life is unpredictable.

At fourteen Syd played chess to suit her mood. She could

beat her uncle or not. She rarely played the game for puzzle anymore. They played less frequently by then and she only wanted to play when she wanted to talk to him about something. She understood that Clarence knew that his lessons were no longer her guiding compass, but they danced the dance of teacher and pupil all the same. Besides, they could fight their battles on the chessboard and still understand the rules of the game. However, they managed to avoid their primary sources of conflict while always fueling the growing sparks between them that flew just beneath the surface.

Syd wanted to be a winemaker. Like her mother. Like her uncle. Clarence all but forbade it. But Syd had winemaking in her blood. Clarence confused her desire to make wine for rebellion and he dismissed the possibility of her ever becoming a winemaker. He told her that winemaking was a man's world. He did not mean to say that women don't make excellent winemakers. In fact, he believed just the opposite. But the industry was infested with megalomaniacs; self-important, posturing men with little intelligence and no imagination. Clarence expounded on the experiences of so many women colleagues who had to work so much harder than their male counterparts despite having more talent and finesse. But the fraternity of mediocre male winemakers was never better bolstered than when they silently mustered against the ultimate threat; a superior female palate and nose. His opposition was vehement in a way Syd could hardly understand. His reasoning always seemed to miss the mark for such a violent opposition. Her own experience with the winemakers she met revealed little of what Clarence believed. She certainly could see that they treated women differently, but no differently than the way men treat women in every other role.

They had their final blowout – the big fight over her future endeavors with the Isle of Lewis pieces – when she was seventeen. It was an October day, and they waited around for the first fruit to come in, itching impatiently, static electricity in the air. Harvest was weeks late and impending poor weather loomed in the minds of everyone deeply dependent on weather and seasons. Clarence was in a rare state of anxiety. Syd goaded her uncle into a conversation about the virtues of harvesting based on pH and the phenolic sweet point relatively independent of Brix, or grape sugars. She had taken to reading all the back journals of the American Society of Enology and Viticulture *and she craved some kind of discussion about harvest parameters. She hounded all of the local growers, begging to get her hands on clippers and discuss every aspect of vineyard management. But they grew tired of her questions and felt secretly threatened by her insatiable curiosity. In the end she made friends with the vineyard crews and slipped in the lineup of workers who pruned, hoed, and harvested fruit. She found that the pickers knew far more about the vines anyway. The view is always closer from the ground than from the seat of a tractor, or behind a desk.*

Clarence stroked his beard while she prattled on about mid-season leaf stripping for pyrazine management. He tried to change the subject.

"Did you talk to the counselor about your trip to Harvard?" he asked.

Syd stopped mid-sentence and mumbled no.

"I thought he might be interested in helping you with your essay."

"Actually, he said I should have at least five schools picked out," she said. Clarence scowled at his knight on D3, pursing his lips. "I'm thinking about Harvard, Wesleyan, Cornell, WSU, and Davis." She moved a pawn in a stupid but appeasing move, exposing her bishop. She wanted to stall the game, anyway.

Clarence looked up at her and glared with dark eyes. "Why Cornell, WSU or Davis?" he asked in low gravelly voice.

"You know why," she said through gritted teeth. "They all have excellent Enology programs."

"Well, I won't pay for it," he said. He moved his queen out, ready to take her bishop.

"I have my own money. From Mom." She took his knight on D3 with her rook. Clarence scowled at the board.

"Not enough for an Ivy league school." He shook his head angrily.

"I'll get loans, and my grades are good enough for scholarships," she replied through a sigh, drumming her hands on the board in feigned concentration.

"What you'll get is disappointment," he roared. Syd sat up with mouth and eyes wide open. "Why not be a secretary? Or a stripper? Why not squander all *your talent!" He pushed over the chessboard and stood up, knocking pieces on the ground. She stared at the man who never showed emotion while he paced in front of her. He held his hands on his head as if to keep his head from exploding. After a torturous moment he stopped pacing and jabbed a finger toward her. "*You *are brilliant. You have so much to offer to the world. You can do whatever you put your mind to, Sydney. Very few people can say that. Your natural talents, your IQ, your privilege of living in North America, of being white, for God's sake! You have a great responsibility. And you want to squander it all and be like* me!*"*

He sat down in the chair opposite her again, his fury melting into disappointment. They sat in silence for an eternity. Clarence fumed as Sydney put the chessboard back together.

"What's wrong with wanting to do what you do? What Mom did?" she asked timidly, tears streaming down her face.

He threw up his hands. "What I do is meaningless, Sydney. Ultimately unimportant."

"You're an artist and you give people joy."

"In the end I produce piss, Sydney. Any greatness attributed to wine is a function of status and ego and all kinds of the worst human attributes."

"But I love that it's simple and humble and transient. You taught me that."

"Being a winemaker isn't about art, Sydney. I've known far too many women who are eaten up in this industry. It's heartbreaking. Even dangerous." He mumbled into his hand, staring at her slack shoulders.

"Don't tell me it's 'cause I'm a girl" she spat. She slammed the pieces back in position.

"No, it's not just 'cause you're a girl. It's all of it, Syd. Wine is unimportant and you can be anything. Don't you see that?"

"So it doesn't matter what I want?" she asked, placing the last pawn back on the board, creating an exact replica of the game they had been playing.

"It matters, Syd. But you're seventeen and you can't possibly know what you really want at seventeen. Trust me. I wanted to be a lawyer, for Christ's sake!" He waved at his working clothes, long hair, and beard, a subtle stab at humor.

"Mom knew what she wanted at seventeen." She moved her castle forward. "Check. Mate in two moves."

Her uncle sighed. She watched his eyes cloud over. He worked to control his emotions with deep breaths. She felt sharp stabs of guilt in her chest, seeing him so defeated.

"In the end it was wrong for her," he said, eyes fixed on the white queen in his hand. He turned the piece over and over, caressing it with his thumb. The man who Sydney had grown to know as distant and unemotional now looked so vulnerable. For the first time Syd saw her uncle for who he truly was; a defeated man plagued by the tragedy of losing the people he loved the most. The realization washed over her while she righted the pieces for another match. She gestured for him to make the first move, but she knew he had already won.

Chapter 8

Syd spent the remainder of the day avoiding the red folio on the kitchen table. Charlie made some phở earlier and managed to get Syd to eat some. Her first real meal in a few days strengthened her enough to take care of something she had been avoiding. She sat out on the deck looking out over the Gorge and the river with another bowl of phở broth in her hands. The crisp autumn day was beautiful. The angle of the sun cast a lovely green light on the tree branches and shrubs. The river glimmered in the afternoon sun, and the sky spread a vibrant periwinkle blue. She sighed and picked up her phone.

Marcus was a mess. She could read it over the phone. He was worried, then frantic before eventually becoming dejected. Syd felt terrible that she left him hanging so long. The hurt in his voice was painful to hear. She placated him and apologized, hoping to quell his feelings of rejection with less than genuine excuses. But he went on about it a bit too long, and she grew irritated. Which made her feel guilty, and finally angry that she had to call him to begin with.

"Look, I didn't get the manual on how to bury a parent," she said in frustration through her clench jaw. He grew silent on the other end. She knew it was unfair, but she also knew that

Marcus did not.

"Sorry, Syd," he said softly. She sat in silence, listening to him breathe. She bit her lip and drummed her fingers on the arm of the chair. "I'll be down Friday. Charlie said Friday would be best. Unless you want me earlier? I could come earlier, Syd?" He whined slightly and Syd jumped out of the Adirondack in frustration.

"No, Friday's best. You have classes."

"I could help with arrangements."

"Charlie and I have it covered." She paced the deck, furious at herself for calling and unsure why.

"Okay," he said, sounding defeated. "Should I book a hotel?" His tenuous whine tipped the scales.

"No. You'll stay *here!*" She was almost shouting into the phone.

"Syd, I'm sorry…" His pleas only made her angrier. She hung up on him and paced the deck. A wave of anger overtook her and she squeezed her fists into a ball. She screamed, desperately wanting to hit something or someone. Instead she slammed her way back into the house, quickly changed into sweats, and running shoes and ran up the road into the forest.

She ran for a few miles, sprinting and screaming a piercing fury heard only by the startled crows watching from the trees. She ran hard until she was dizzy and wet with sweat, her face streaked with tears. She spent her energy running out into the woods and she found she had none left when she finally turned to make her way back home. She walked back slowly, feeling empty and blank, and oddly refreshed.

Charlie and Rosa were seated at the kitchen table nursing mugs of Mexican chocolate when she stumbled into the house past dusk. They exchanged worried glances and a sigh of relief when she walked in. Syd brushed past them and made a beeline for the shower.

~

Syd woke up before dawn the next morning. She made a pot of french press and sat down in the worn leather chair next to the picture window that looked out to the river. The lights from the bridge between White Salmon and Hood River sparkled in the chilly morning air. After her first cup of coffee she got up to retrieve the red folio from the kitchen but found a note on the table. It was written in a tidy back-slanted cursive, a left-handed smudge of ink smearing the page along the script in an all too familiar way. Syd was left-handed, but she hadn't noticed that Olivier was as well.

Sydney~

You were asleep when I came in for our meeting. ~Here is an update~

We are receiving Petit Verdot from Horse Heaven Hills on Monday, I think. I drove out today for samples. The PV is at 26 brix, pH of 3.7 and TA of 4.5g/L. A little overhung, I think, for your liking? I was not trusting the grower's numbers and it turns out I was right. It needs to come off ASAP.

We are pressing the Grenache tomorrow. 5 ton. The crew will be here. No need for you to come up.

~I started the malolactic inoculate, will pitch tomorrow.

Ollie

She sat back in her chair with the note in her hand. Jack Bristol's words filled her head; his suspicions about Olivier. She grew resentful and ashamed that she had a scheduled meeting with him and had missed it. She felt light-headed after her shower the evening before and lay down for a few moments. She woke at 5 am the next morning.

She worked the note in her fingers, mulling over the loose ends of her uncle's life. She had inherited a tangle of a mess and was not sure if she could ever unravel it. She wondered if everyone's lives were so messy and undone. Her uncle lived what seemed to be such a boring life. His daily routine was mundane. But underneath it all boiled complex layers of conflict, love, and secrets. And it would all burn up with the man tomorrow.

"Why didn't you tell me?" she spoke out loud to the glowing orange and purple sunrise outside.

She got up and fixed herself some toast from the last of Clarence's famous bread. The smell of the toast dripping with butter made her smile. He would eat toast daily for morning breakfast, butter and crumbs getting caught in his reddish beard. Coffee and toast. He was not the gourmand people assumed. He was not so complex.

~

It was chillier than she expected when she stepped outside a few minutes later. Her boots slipped a little on the deck boards, a slight frost glimmering in the early morning light. She wore an old pair of double-fronted Carhartt's, a flannel from the mudroom cupboard, and her old muck boots, a mere sampling of the clothing left behind for her sojourn to a city life in Seattle. She welcomed the androgyny of work clothes; they were comfortable, loose-fitting, and snuggly warm. Still, she cupped her mug of steaming coffee in both hands for warmth while she made her way up to the winery.

The smell of Crush beckoned her at the bottom of the hill and grew more intense and inviting as she walked up the gravel road. Fresh herbaceous aromas hit her nose first, and she breathed in deeply. Her eyes welled up with tears. The overflow of emotion the smells elicited were complex and inexplicable. She smiled through the tears as she opened the large red doors of the winery. She moved around the building and opened the side doors. A wave of CO2 gas and fermentation aromas washed over her as she stepped back. She would have to wait to go inside. CO2 had built up in the winery all night long, and there was little air movement to expedite the evacuation of the gases.

She decided to wait it out in the vineyard and hiked farther up the hill. The slightly frozen gravel crunched under her feet, and the smells of the vineyard began to overcome the fermentation aromas from the winery below. She walked by the compost pile, which was smothered in a cloud of fruit flies. The frenzied compost was unthwarted by the frost, protected by the heat of the decomposition. Fresh stems and skins steamed in purple and green piles, and she scrunched up her nose to avoid sucking up tiny flies into her nostrils. She pushed farther up hill, beckoned by the view from the top of the vineyard. She stepped off of the gravel road and took a shortcut through a block of thick of vines. The vineyard was head-trained gobelet style, so her progress was unimpeded by trellis wires or rows. The stubby vines gnarled up from the ground like two-foot-long contorted arms, with hands cupped in supplication to the sun. These vines of Picpoul and Roussanne were harvested at least a month earlier, and the leaves were mostly yellow and brown. She frowned at the patches of red leaves intermittently peppering the vineyard.

At the top near the fence line Sydney stretched her arms up over her head and inhaled several deep breaths. The view was nothing short of majestic. To her right triumphed the tip of Mt. Hood, with its white peak still shedding the pink hue of sunrise. Directly to the east the sun hovered over the river in a vibrant orange. The black basalt cliffs of the Gorge cradled the sun on either side, reflecting an array of purples, grays, and pinks. She stood mesmerized, filling up her lungs with the sunrise, closing her eyes.

She jumped at the sound of the rifle shot fired from the vineyard next door. She followed a cloud of birds rush up from the vineyard as the gun reported another round. A half-dozen more shots were fired, each sending up a clammer of birds in different areas of the vineyard. She used to feel terrible for the birds until she understood the ruin they could cause a single vineyard in just a few short hours. Now she simply felt bad for her neighbor and wondered why he opted to forego bird netting this year. Bird shot was far less expensive, but it could make for some cold mornings chasing down the pesky marauders. Not to mention dealing with grouchy neighbors. She had never grown accustomed to gunshots in the early morning and she was even less so after her long stint in the city.

Movement caught her eye and she looked down to the Airstream parked below her neighbor's vineyard on her uncle's property. A man walked out and stood outside the trailer in the universal posture of a man urinating. He finished his business and arched his back into a long, elegant bow shape before bending and reaching for the ground. He lifted his arms to the side and then up again before arching his back further. Syd watched his morning ritual with the guilty pleasure of a voyeur, riddled with the kind of shame experienced by an onlooker who fiercely guarded her own privacy. Still, she watched him as he trudged across the north vineyard and down into the draw. She stood several hundred feet above him across the ten acres and mapped his way into the deep V of the landscape while he strode up to the winery. She started back down through the vineyard as she watched him. They met up outside the winery in front of the open large red doors.

"Good morning," Olivier said, surprised to see her.

"Good morning," she said with a nod and a modest smile. She found it unsettling that she meant it. She knew it meant she was feeling good.

"Did you do punchdowns?" he asked.

"No. No, I just got here, I opened the doors ten minutes ago."

"Ah. I'll get started." He walked into the winery, turning on lights and disappearing into the cool depths of the building. She listened to sounds of running water and the scraping of a ladder on the concrete floor.

Syd sat out on an Adirondack outside the winery, drinking in the remainder of the sunrise. She sipped her lukewarm coffee and pondered her own resilience. She felt fine for the moment. Somehow the sun, the vineyard, and the winery filled her with an unexpected buoyancy. She still felt the devastating pain in her chest, but her head somehow felt detached from it. She was awed by her sense of suspended grief. She became aware of the gracious gift of patience she had for herself; an acceptance of her own process. She invited the grief to settle in her chest and found a kind of comfort in the weight of it.

~

The day of pressing red wine passed similar to the day of crushing fruit when she first arrived. She and Olivier worked side by side in a graceful rhythm; two experienced winemakers falling into sync. Three other cellar hands busied themselves with cleaning and storing the tanks, and wrangling hoses and sump pumps. Two of them were familiar to Syd. Alejandro was the primary connection for cellar hands in the winery, and he often found help from his cousins and friends. Clarence was always better at working with the cellar hands than she had been. Most were Mexican or Salvadorian workers who lived permanently in the area. He spoke fluent Spanish and he managed to maintain a universally casual nature, with little need to flex his authority. She always felt awkward at the deference the workers showed her. She was never sure if it was because she was the niece of the *jefe,* or because she was female, or just because she was white. The racial disparity between Mexican and Salvadorian workers and white workers was not as obvious in the fields when she worked alongside them. But in the close quarters of the winery she was always aware of social stratification, and always deeply uncomfortable with it.

But now things had inexplicably changed. She felt more at ease with the cellar workers than in the past. She joked and flirted her way around the cellars hands. She could ask them to do a task without feeling bossy, and they clearly respected her decisions. She was grateful for this. She noted that Olivier was more aloof with the workers than she was. They stayed clear of him, even though she never observed him say or do anything unkind or dictating.

Alejandro disappeared in the vineyard after he realized he was not contributing much with Sydney on the forklift. He nodded at her when he entered the winery and avoided her eyes. They had known each other for years. Alejandro had loved her uncle like his own. He had strong feelings for her too. Many summers ago, they had a fling that caused a temporary rift between Alejandro and Clarence. But that was almost a decade ago, and she had all but forgotten about it. But she suspected that he didn't dismiss their romance as easily as she did. Whenever she visited it took him a few days to warm up to her. She would sometimes catch him glancing at her out of the corner of her eye. Still, she wanted to talk to him.

She finally got her chance to corner him when the other workers began to clean equipment at the end of the day. She was outside, stretching and staring at the view. Alejandro drove down from the vineyard on an ATV, and she stepped out in front of him.

"Hey! You dodging out of work?" she asked, teasing him. Her question forced him to look her in the eyes. He shut off the 4-wheeler.

"Only one seat on the forklift, *senorita*," he said. His smile was so full of sadness that it struck her in her sternum. She wanted to embrace him and hold him against the pain in her chest. But he stoically kept his composure. His dark eyebrows pulled together in a squint. His full lips stretched thin in a face meant for laughing. He swung his leg over the side of the ATV and stood up, staying as far away from her as he could muster for polite conversation. He looked down at his feet.

"We're finished now, anyway," Syd said after a long pause. He nodded at the ground like a soldier waiting for orders. He looked like a young lost boy. "I went up in the vineyard today," she said. "Do we have leaf roll in the Picpoul?"

"No. Not leaf roll. Red blotch. It is similar. A cousin virus." He turned and walked up the hill in big strides and Syd followed. He had the graceful stride of a well-proportioned man, not too much taller than Sydney. His dark hair was curly and shined around a gorgeous brown face with nearly black eyes. She watched him in admiration as he trudged ahead of her. They stopped next to the block that puzzled Syd earlier that day. She was winded and dizzy from the steep climb up the hill, and she steadied herself on his sleeve reflexively. He was breathing normally and smiled as he glanced at her hand on his sleeve.

"They don't have Stairmasters in Seattle?" he teased.

"Looks like you could use a Stairmaster *here*," she retorted nodding at his growing belly. Alejandro had easily gained 25 pounds since she saw him last. "You're looking prosperous."

"Hey, *gordita, mi novia* is a good cook," He clutched his paunch with two hands and jiggled it proudly.

She smiled at him gratefully. He used to call her *gordita* as a term of endearment. He was the man who taught her to embrace her curves and size-10 hips and D-cup bra while she lambasted herself in the mirror with the cliché self-torture of young women everywhere. Her hourglass body didn't look anything like the emaciated photoshopped models she saw in magazines. But Alejandro gently taught her about her own rare beauty over the course of a long summer in the hot Airstream under the stars.

He reached out and plucked a dry, reddish leaf from a vine next to him.

"No curl, see? The leaf is flat. Also, the veins are red here. With leaf curl, they are green." His calloused index finger traced the veins in the leaf.

"What do we do? Pull them out?" She looked down at the entire vineyard. She figured maybe two percent of the vines showed red leaves.

"It is the only thing we can do. But it won't save us from infecting the entire vineyard. Everybody up here has it. I was up in Ted's lower block this weekend. They have it much worse than we do. But it is only a matter of time before it takes over." He frowned, his black eyebrows arching together.

"What are they doing about it?" she asked.

"*Gringos*? Nada, as far as I can see. But I think they are worried. When I was up in Ted's vineyard I saw a group of them walking around up there. Some kind of secret meeting, you know? A *jefe* meeting." Alejandro feigned a half-mocking Chicano accent when he talked about the *gringos*. They had a long understanding about the differences between Mexican-Americans and white folks in these parts, especially with respect to the vineyards. Alejandro referred to the owners as *gringos*, and his Mexican and Salvadorian friends as the workers. Ownership was always defined in racial terms. He made no attempt to hide his contempt of the *gringos* and their lack of expertise with the vines. But Syd knew there was much more to the management of the vines than their health. Ripping out vines meant delayed production, and growers lived on short margins as it was.

"Why do you think it was a secret meeting?" she asked.

"They all looked around suspiciously to see if anybody was around. And they parked their Beemers behind the trees. Over there." He pointed to a copse of Douglas firs that separated the two vineyard blocks from one another a couple hundred yards from the fence line.

"They didn't see you?"

"I'm invisible, Grasshopper. I move with the wind." There was a long-standing joke between them about the ubiquitous and thus invisible nature of Latino workers and being completely ignored by the *gringos*.

"What were they doing?"

"They mostly just stood around and pointed at the vineyards. Come to think of it, they didn't really look at the vines. They just stood and pointed out the easements and roads. They didn't walk around much. *No one had boots*." He shook his head in derision. "I was too far away to hear them. But Jack was the one leading the conversation."

"Jack Bristol?"

He nodded.

"Who else was there?"

"Francois."

"Francois Bertrand?"

He nodded. "And The Feldman guy, the one who almost bought us out. And that little fucking weasel prick, the wine critic."

"Joe Donner?"

He nodded, waiting for her reaction. It dawned on him that the meeting of the *jefes* must have had little to do with red blotch. He watched as she paced back and forth with her hands on her hips. She paced for a full five minutes.

"Why on Earth would Jack Bristol, Francois Bertrand, Hans Feldman and Joe Donner be skulking around behind our winery, Alejandro?" she asked softly. "When was this?"

He thought for a moment. "Sunday, around four," he said. His eyes grew wide at Syd's furrowed brow. She turned silently and wandered down the path in a trance while Alejandro fought a superstitious tingling at the back of his neck. Clarence was found dead only a few hours later.

~

The sun was sinking fast by the time Syd got back down to the house. She realized she was starving. Charlie was waiting for her on the deck in an Adirondack rocker, cupping a large snifter of caramel-colored liquid. Syd plopped down next to her.

"Long day?" Syd asked. She took the glass from her and smelled it. She swirled and gulped without further ceremony.

"Yeah, you could say that," Charlie replied with uncharacteristic melancholy. She reached over and snatched back the glass.

Syd reached for her hand. "Thanks, Charlie."

Charlie sighed deeply, sipping the scotch tenderly. They sat quietly for a half hour, passing the snifter back and forth. Charlie refilled it twice.

"All of the arrangements are done," Charlie broke the silence, startling Syd out of her troubled thoughts.

Syd nodded.

"Dad came by with the autopsy report. And some tampons

for you," Charlie delivered in her usual deadpan. Syd smiled at her and chuckled. Charlie caught her eye and smiled back. They surrendered to the crescendo hysterical humor and cackled, bending over and gasping for breath. Charlie fell off her chair and thudded onto the deck.

Syd toasted to the air. "To Jim Yesler, the father I never had!"

"Here, here!" Charlie said, threatening to pee her pants.

Chapter 9

Friday started with a severe headache and a bout of nausea. Syd sat naked in bed with her work clothes balled up on the floor. She had no recollection of going to bed, let alone undressing. The night before had dissolved into a foray of Clarence's liquor cabinet. A tall glass of water sat on the nightstand. She picked it up and drank the entire glass in one go.

A dry cleaning bag with her Armani suit in it hung on the door. She sat up and tested her body slowly. She wrapped the old quilt from the bed around herself and shuffled out of the room to meet Olivier in the doorway. He held a small glass of fizzy water.

"This will help," he said, shoving the glass in her hand. He turned on his heels and left before she could feel embarrassed.

She crawled back into bed and drank the fizzy water. She slowly tried to piece together the day ahead of her. She would have to meet with Jim Yesler. He had the autopsy report and he wanted to discuss it with her. She had an appointment with the insurance agent in the afternoon, a new guy she had not met before. And she was expecting Marcus late that afternoon. *Marcus*. She threw herself back on the bed, and burrowed under the sheets.

Charlie burst in a few minutes later and flung open the window. The room filled with head-pounding light. Syd threw a linen pillow at her.

"It burns, it burns!" she yelled, burying her face in the other pillow.

"You need to get up, lazy bones," Charlie said. She flopped down next to Syd and stroked her hair. Her fingers probed for the bump from a few days before. Syd knocked her hand off playfully and they held hands behind Syd's head.

"What time is it?" Syd asked, rolling over and kissing Charlie on the lips.

"*Geez!* Time to brush your fucking teeth," Charlie said. She recoiled in feigned horror and bounced toward the door. "9:15," she shouted on her way out.

~

Paul Renquest sat at the table, absently spinning the mug of tea she had placed in front of him a few minutes before. His other hand sat protectively on a file in front of him. He waited patiently for her to emerge from the kitchen with her own mug, flip flops snapping on the hard wood floors.

After the usual apologies and condolences – which Syd was growing accustomed to by now – she watched as the middle-aged man paused to collect his thoughts. He bowed his head and fiddled with the file in front of him. He was bald and bespectacled, but his obvious fitness bulged out of his tight-fitting fleece. He was a member of the wind chaser tribe that was so prevalent in the Gorge. Being a kiteboarder and windsurfer required the kind of job that left time for a quick jettison to the river when the wind kicked up, which it did every afternoon during the windy season like clockwork. Middle-aged adrenalin junkies were a dime a dozen here. She watched as he cleared his throat, unaware of her scrutiny.

"Your uncle had a life insurance policy that left you enough to be comfortable for life," he said. "We had been talking about different ways to set up a policy to give you more. Unfortunately, we had a meeting scheduled this week to consider other options for you. Too late. I'm sorry. But I think that you'll find he was thinking about your future."

He slid the file to her across the table. The grief hung in his eyes, but his face was charged with an odd excitement. Her stomach churned as she stared at the file. She opened it and read it slowly, a blank expression on her face. *Enough to be comfortable* was a gross understatement. She took a deep breath.

"It will fund soon after you file the claim. Within the month, in fact. In the meantime, are you able to cover the funeral expenses?" He searched her face for some kind of response.

"Hmm? Oh, yes. Uncle had savings. And his plans for the funeral have been set for ages. He was very particular about the wake. No funeral. He wasn't religious. He always said he wanted a good old fashioned party. The memorial will be short and sweet." She smiled at him demurely, a foreign gesture for her. Her head was still rolling over the figures on the papers in front of her.

He nodded and folded his hands on the table. Syd watched the powerful muscles in his forearms when he moved his hands. They sat in a charged silence for a few minutes. He began to drum his fingers on the table.

"There's one more thing," he said with averted eyes. "I'm not sure I should be telling you this, but there was another policy. It was taken out for a business contract between your uncle and an investor. It's called a key man policy. It's normal for an investor to take out a policy on a person of talent when that person is the primary source of the investment. Like your uncle was to the winery. These policies were drawn up when his winery was being purchased by an investor. There are two recipients in the key man policies. The potential business partner and a smaller policy for the lawyer who drew up the contract. Both policies are still current." He glanced up at her, over his glasses.

"Current? Why weren't they stopped when the buyout fell through?"

"I'm not sure. Most of these kinds of policies aren't kept when escrow falls through or when a deal goes sour. Considering your uncle's age and his risk habits, the policy is expensive. He was lucky to get insured at all."

"Why are you telling me this, Paul?"

"These kinds of policies are fixed monetary sums intended to make up for the loss of the talent in the event of death and to facilitate business continuity. A business is usually the recipient, but this policy claimed Hans Feldman as the primary recipient." He sighed and fidgeted with the corner of the folder. "I was with your uncle when his plane nearly crashed last June, Syd. I was on the tarmac. We've been flying together for years. Your uncle was an excellent pilot."

"And?" She felt a nasty lump caught in the back of her throat.

"And I'm not comfortable with what I know. I'm not so sure that the plane malfunctioned accidentally."

"I understood that he was in a stall during a dive. And he couldn't pull out of it, correct?" Syd asked through a dry throat.

"Have you ever known your uncle to not recover a stall?" he asked quietly. She stared at him. "Listen, I'm not saying this to frighten you or stir up any trouble. But before he went up that day we had coffee and he was pretty pissed off. He told me about the buyout and that he was backing out. We talked about revamping all his policies to make up for the loss of business I would incur from his backing out of the contract. He was fair like that. But the hospital after the accident and the busy summer got in the way, and we never got together to redo his insurance plans. He got lucky that day. It's only because he is, was a damned good pilot that he could recover that dive at all. And his love of that old plane, I suspect." He winked at her.

"So what are you saying to me, Paul?" she asked, suddenly feeling exhausted.

"I'm just giving you information, Sydney. Your uncle was a friend of mine. I respected him. He was a good man." He bowed his head. "And I can't imagine anyone paying those kinds of premiums for a policy on a man who's no longer a business partner."

"Who paid the premiums?"

"Hans Feldman paid one of them."

"So, you're telling me Hans Feldman had something to gain by Uncle's death? And that he may have been complicit in the plane crash in June?"

"I'm just saying that the circumstances are curious," he said in a whisper, raising his eyebrows. "About the lawyer too."

"And who's the lawyer?" she asked incredulously.

"Jack Bristol." He lowered his voice and inspected the back of his hands.

Chapter 10

Jim walked through the door holding a greasy paper bag. He wore a red plaid Pendleton button-down flannel, jeans, and old Danner mountain boots. His out-of-uniform attire made him look like a handsome lumberjack. He strode across the kitchen in two steps and embraced Syd in a protective embrace.

"Hey, Pop," Charlie said from the open fridge. She tossed a beer bottle at her dad. He caught it in his huge hand and released Syd, who looked as lost in thought as ever.

"You're late." Charlie added. She lunged for the bag in her father's hand. He dodged her and held it high over her head, nearly touching the ceiling. He dwarfed his very tall daughter.

"Hold your horses, little piggy!" he yelled back at her, spinning his giant body in the cramped kitchen.

"Where you keep the plates, Syd?" he asked, opening random cupboards. "If I don't find plates now the vulture will eat over the kitchen sink!" He jabbed a thumb in Charlie's direction.

Syd navigated a path between a father/daughter game of keep-away to gather the plates and utensils they needed for dinner. She grabbed a few beers from the fridge and walked into the dining room to set the table, smiling to herself. Sometimes these intimate father/daughter moments filled her with envy. But today she was simply grateful that she could be near it. They had a loud, rough-and-tumble kind of love.

It was soon apparent that Charlie had gotten hold of the greasy paper bag. She hopped into the room and jumped into a chair at the table triumphantly, where she began divvying out burritos and rationing containers of hot sauce. She glanced with purpose at Syd and nodded at the red folio that was pushed aside for their plates, still waiting to be read.

"You might want to read that soon," Charlie said, ripping the paper off her giant burrito. "Before tomorrow?"

'I can't right now," Syd replied, feeling a tinge of shame. She was going to have to find the courage to read the will and face all the secrets inside another day. Her grief was enough to bear, and yet she was still bombarded with information that tore away any sense of closure she could have about her uncle's death. Her head was still spinning from her conversation with Paul. She knew she needed more time to process it all. She knew she would have to talk to Jim about it. After the memorial, she told herself.

They were all hungry and they tore into dinner in relative silence. Syd had very little to eat in almost a week, and her appetite was returning to her. She was ravenous. The burritos were her favorite, and the beer was cold and delicious. She looked up to see Jim watching her, his eyes filled with tears. Syd looked down, unable to bear his naked empathy and grief.

"Pop's sad to see his girls eat like wild women," Charlie said, noticing the looks they exchanged.

"Well, at least Syd *chews* her food," he joked. He wiped his own mouth and his eyes with the crumpled napkin in his lap. He paused, looked at Syd, and took a deep breath.

"I've got the autopsy report," he said, soberly. "We should talk about this, Sydney."

"I think I need to talk you too, Jim. But maybe after tomorrow."

They were all startled when the kitchen door slammed a second later.

"Sydney?" a man yelled into the darkening kitchen. They all exchanged looks. "*Sydney?*" The voice called again, louder this time.

"In here!" Charlie yelled back. A moment later a good-looking, tall, toothy blond man filled the doorway.

"Sydney!" he said in something like an exasperated sigh. Syd slumped down in her chair. He moved to hug her in an awkward embrace while she stayed seated.

"Marcus," she said into his shoulder. Her voice was muffled in his death grip of a hug. She shrugged at Jim, who took a cue and got up to leave. Charlie cleared the table and left them to work out their troubles alone.

Chapter 11

The day of the memorial was filled with a gorgeous, crisp, autumn sunshine. Syd awoke to the sound of trucks driving around the house to the lawn on the north side of the property. A stream of bright light filled the guest room upstairs Syd now claimed as her own. She lay listening and followed the sound of the trucks around the house, up past the lower vineyard to the Green. The Green was a half-acre of flat field, the only flat ground on the property. Clarence called it the Green, as he was not inclined to maintain a lawn. But he did mow the wild grasses when they browned in the summer and cast out meadow seed mixes every spring for a gorgeous wildflower field in June. Now it was clumpy and brown, and would endure a good many feet later in the afternoon.

The first truck delivered a fancy vault toilet in the far north corner of the field. The second was noisier and delivered a giant tent along with four loud and burly young men who set to work quickly on erecting the large white structure.

Syd got up, made some coffee, and watched the tent go up from the deck. She wore an old oilskin coat of Clarence's over her black silk nightie. The tinny clanking of mallets driving in tent stakes sounded thin and far away.

"Good morning," Marcus said as he dragged a heavy Adirondack chair next to her.

"Morning," she said, flashing a lazy smile. "Looks like a good party." She said ruefully, gesturing with her mug at the scene in front of her.

Marcus looked uncomfortable. He had slept in her old bedroom downstairs and she knew that he was feeling untethered from her. He had wanted to sleep with her, but she couldn't bear the closeness. She needed to steel herself and she knew his clumsy empathy would only soften her and make the day more difficult to bear. But he looked miserable now, and she felt sorry for him in spite of herself.

"I met Olivier," he said. "Any reason why he waltzes into your bedroom like he owns it?"

She stared at him. "Beats me." She said, trying to stifle a smile. *Jealous*. She was barely holding it together and Marcus was jealous?

Olivier walked out of the kitchen door a moment later holding a bundle of dark cloths. He walked over to them and nodded formally.

Syd raised her mug to him. "Good morning," she said, flashing her friendliest smile. Olivier blushed with embarrassment and nodded again. Marcus's eyes narrowed.

"My apologies," Olivier said. "I had to get my clothes for today. I assumed Sydney was using the room upstairs."

Syd looked at each of them. "No problem," she said with a wave. She could see Marcus's shoulders relax at Olivier's sense of formality and submissiveness.

Olivier inched closer to her chair and spoke softly "I was planning to speak a little today. I wasn't sure if Charlie told you. Do you mind?"

She felt an immediate lump in her throat. *Oh god*. "Why would I mind?" She answered flippantly and swallowed hard. She looked back at him and saw that he was hurt. "I appreciate your consideration. Really."

Olivier looked defeated. She felt a deep stab of empathy for him, comprehending for the first time how much he must have loved her uncle. She knew now that he was devastated. And perhaps confused. Maybe even as confused as she was. She was a little ashamed that she was only now figuring out that he had been living in her old bedroom until her arrival. He must have moved into the old Airstream for her comfort, and she was clueless about it. He was close to Uncle Clarence, close enough to be living in the house. His grief was obvious. And she had only been thinking of herself in her own grief. She realized how strange and uprooted his situation must be, and how much he must despise her. She had been self-important, petulant and rude to him. And he held her when she sobbed. He held the winery together through his own grief. He even dry-cleaned the suit she would wear today, for lack of anything else. She thought of the Alka Seltzer and the glasses of water by her bed.

She grabbed his hand and squeezed it tight. "Thank you," she croaked out of a dangerous throat, not sure of what she was thanking him for. He looked away and stepped back, looking for an escape route, but she jumped up and embraced him. Tears streamed down her face. They stood in quiet agony together, letting the tears flow freely. When they finally broke apart, they smiled at each other and averted their eyes.

"No more tears today," she said, wiping her nose on the stiff sleeve of the old coat. "I promise."

"No," he said, nodding. He took a sharp breath. "I have work to do." He turned on his heels and strode across the deck to his trailer in the vineyard.

Marcus strained to watch him walk up the vineyard path and enter the trailer. He sat and stared at her in confusion.

"Who is that guy?" The suspicion in his voice betrayed his feelings, though he kept his hands in his pockets in the practiced relaxed posture of a confident man.

"Honestly, I don't really know," she answered. Marcus looked alarmed. "He is the working winemaker now. From Argentina. An old friend of Uncle's." But she knew she had no idea who Olivier really was or why he was here.

Chapter 12

Charlie had outdone herself with the flowers. There were huge urns of sunflowers and dahlias in a cacophony of color at every corner of the tent. Each table was adorned with a tall vibrant centerpiece featuring brown, black, orange, yellow and red sunflowers, more fitting for a wedding than a memorial. But Clarence had always loved sunflowers, and she had chosen his favorite things to theme the memorial. It was fitting that these blooms were the last of the season from his own garden. Sydney sat in a black satin-covered folding chair that looked out over the sea of empty chairs and tables under the tent. A young man was working on the PA system in the corner, but the scene was otherwise deserted. Clarence would have hated the fuss of this day. But he would have understood the ceremony, the rites of passage a death facilitated, in a philosophical way. Clarence was always fascinated by the human need to mark important events in life in a form of social acknowledgment. He loved to study wedding traditions, birth traditions, and death ceremonies. But Clarence was an atheist, and he had no spiritual traditions of his own to follow. He always told Sydney that he would like his wake to be a bawdy party, featuring loud music and drunken souls. It was not an easy recipe to deliver for a man who was something of an eccentric recluse. Charlie's answer was a superbly stocked bar and a classical guitar and cello duo. She knew that Clarence's fantasy was more hyperbole than genuine desire, and as usual, she was dead on.

"You look lovely," Charlie said sardonically, plopping down next to Syd. She offered a tumbler filled with ice and a rare bourbon. Syd took her drink obediently. "I mean, you look like a somm. Or a lesbian. I'd date you." She lewdly ran her hand up Syd's leg and feigned bedroom eyes.

"You'd date anyone," Syd said. "Besides, I didn't have anything else to wear. I'm lucky I had this suit. I was wearing it when I got the call and drove down here without thinking about clothes. It's a little big on me right now." She pulled the Armani suit jacket back to reveal a loose waistband. Charlie reached over and bounced a lock of freshly curled hair that rested on Syd's collar bone.

"No, I mean it. It works. Your hair looks great. You have a kind of androgyny in that suit that you might need today. How you holding up?"

"Well, I'm not going to cry today, Charles. If that's what you mean."

"This thing might blow up a bit, Syd," She offered, apologetically. "I called all the key people, but I saw some other folks at Backwoods Brewery last night. They were in town for the memorial. Dad and I went there after Marcus showed up. There may even be folks you don't want here at all."

Syd heard a bitter note in her voice. "Well, I'm wearing my suit of Armani. I can handle it." She paused and looked at her. "Who is it you're worried about?"

"Joe Donner, for one. I saw him last night at the brew pub."

"Figures. Hell, maybe he'll write up a retraction of all of his nastiness? But I bet he won't be the most unsavory guest we have the honor of entertaining today." Syd drained her glass and got up to walk up into the vineyard, deep in thought.

Charlie watched her make her way up through the vines, absently touching the leaves and inspecting them. She marveled at her friend's strength, but there was something in Syd's behavior this morning that alarmed her. She *was* in full armor. She was calm and held herself in a suspension of emotion with the kind of brevity she possessed in a crisis. Before tests and during emergencies, Syd was always able to collect herself with a crystal clear head, taking over whenever necessary. Charlie realized she was preparing for battle. She was biding her time. Charlie had been looking at the memorial as the end of something; something to slowly move away from. A day of closure. But she suddenly realized that Sydney was waiting for this day to be over so that she could start something, and whatever that something was filled her stomach with sinking dread.

~

More than 250 people showed up for the memorial service. The street was lined with cars all the way down to the main road, and folks who dressed up in their fine suits and dark dresses walked upwards of a quarter mile to the service. The tent sheltered nearly 150 black satin-covered folding chairs, all lined up in tidy arched rows. Every chair was filled, and the rest of the group stood around the tent, holding their thin coats around their bodies in a solitary embrace. The sun shone brightly. The view of the river was particularly clear, but the air was chilled. The crowd remained somber in spite of Charlie's best efforts to force cheerfulness with color, booze and Vivaldi.

Syd paid little attention to the attendees. She sat still, in the corner up front, bolstered by Jim on one side and Charlie on the other. Many people got up one at a time and spoke of their memories of Clarence. Most of the stories were pleasant and spoke of fond memories. Syd frequently found herself fighting back her emotions when a familiar face offered a story of how Clarence helped or influenced them in one way or another. She thought she had steeled herself for the memorial speeches, but her gratitude for the kind words and obvious grief of so many people challenged her resolve. In the end, she managed to keep herself in check. She knew that if she gave into the emotion of the day she would fall apart. Her grief was a bottomless well that she could stay clear of for the time being. Her grief was also an intensely private thing.

Olivier was one of the last speakers. Syd had been waiting for him to get up and make his way to the microphone. She was aware of his presence, behind her and a few seats to the left, sitting beside Rosa. Each time a speaker left the microphone she noted the stillness in his chair. She was beginning to wonder if he had lost his courage. When he finally got up, she had been distracted by a question from Marcus. She looked up to see Olivier standing at the microphone, his face calm and elegant.

"I have known Clarence Blackwell for my entire life," he began in perfect English, a formality in his address. "He has always been something of an uncle to me. Clarence taught me to play chess, and to study soils in the vineyard. He taught me how to dance the tango of my own country. He taught me how to love." He paused and took a breath. "His visits to Argentina were the hallmark of my childhood, although they often gave him grief." He swallowed and paused again. "He taught me so much. I came here this summer to learn more from Clarence. No longer a child, I was able to learn from the man as a man. I found him to be honorable and steadfast, kind and patient, the best of men." He paused again, looking down at his hands. "Knowing him has been a great honor." He locked eyes with Sydney and gave her a quick nod before he turned to leave. The bitterness of his address struck her. She watched him disappear behind the group of nearly one hundred people who were standing in the back of the tent. He vanished.

The remaining speakers regaled the group with personal histories and anecdotes that buzzed around Syd's impenetrable head for the next half hour. She sat mesmerized by Olivier's words. They were simple sentiments told with such remarkable bitterness. She attempted to meet Charlie's eyes as he left the microphone, but Charlie appeared unaware of what he said. The mystery of his relationship with Clarence filled her head, and she dissected his short eulogy in search of hidden clues. The man who had embraced her that morning in a moment of honest grief was a complete stranger to her. *And yet Clarence had known him all his life.*

Syd was jarred out of her musing when Jack Bristol spoke. He was the last speaker. He talked for a long while, remembering a dear friend with a fondness that quelled some of Syd's misgivings about him lately. He spoke eloquently. He was a natural speaker with a gift for intonation and timing. She wondered if her suspicions were a figment of her imagination or a product of grief that had nowhere else to go. He ended with a call for a toast. The crowd rose at once and moved toward the bar in a quietly buzzing swarm. Clearly everyone was ready for a drink.

~

It took Syd nearly an hour to find the strength to get up and make her way to the bar on her own. Jim and Charlie waited patiently with her in the front row after the service. Marcus was busy fetching drinks from behind the bar, not bothering to wait in line with the rest of the guests. Charlie entertained Syd with an ongoing narration of the guests, pointing out the people she knew and making things up about the people she didn't, sparing no one. Her game of gently poking fun at the mourners wasn't exactly kind, but Syd knew she was just trying to keep her buoyant. Syd suspected that if Charlie came up for air she might be overwhelmed by her own grief. Her incessant chatter was as much for self-preservation as it was for Syd's.

Small clusters of mourners began to form shortly after the first round of drinks, as people searched for their own tribes. Charlie's running commentary didn't fail to mention how odd humans could be in their desire to search out their own people. The winemakers and growers found one another and stood loosely around a few wine barrels, with more space between them than that of other groups. They talked shyly and fiddled awkwardly with their pockets or nervously side-stepped to the classical music from the string duet. Syd knew most of them. They were all men; a veritable who's who of the winemaking world. But these men who she had witnessed for the duration of her life as arrogant and self-assured – these men who hardly noticed her presence other than stealing a look at her face or breasts – now stood stripped of their confidence in the face of a respected colleague's death. Now she was seeing the posture of men who were overtaken by sadness and humility. For once she felt an odd camaraderie with her uncle's peers.

The workers – who were a mix of Salvadorians and Mexican – had gathered on the fringe of the field and perched themselves on the old wood stumps that lined the perimeter of the Green. They talking softly to one another with the unselfconscious intimacy of a family. Alejandro stood among them and occasionally wiped tears from his face. An attractive, plump young woman stood next to him and absently rubbed his back in quiet consolation. Another man, Juan the cellar worker, cracked a joke and brought a smile to Alejandro. Rosa sat on a log in a lovely black chiffon dress and a veiled hat. A small group of young men and women who Syd recognized as vineyard workers hung on her words as she gestured toward the blue sky and shook her head.

A smaller group of stiff business suits stood in the middle of the lawn, holding their drinks woodenly in front of them, each posturing with fixed wide stances and steady gazes. They hardly spoke to one another, and studied the gathering with purposeful analysis. Each man felt the eyes of the mourners with narcissistic self-consciousness, nodding and shaking hands with the kind of practiced ambivalence of important people. If they were truly grieving, it was lost behind a shield of the fabricated pretense scripted in business magazines and television. Although Syd found these men repugnant, she realized that she was donning a similar kind of mask.

One group of guests who attracted the majority of Charlie's sharp wit was a motley mix of some of Syd's favorite people, and some of the most despised. They had pulled chairs together around a table and a wine barrel and snatched a few bottles of scotch from the bar. A woman Syd knew to be a critic for a Portland newspaper meandered over with an ice bucket she sneaked from the hired bartender, who was quickly losing control of his bar. The group was comprised of writers and critics who were known to Syd at first from her uncle's work. Lately she had grown to know these folks as colleagues and peers, and as an excellent source of information on current events in the wine industry. Although she held her uncle's beliefs about the critics, she was far more tolerant of the writers and bloggers who exploited the more newsy aspects of the industry. There were only a few women. Most were white men who carried themselves with the casual manners of the self-important and entitled. A few men stood around a larger seated group. Syd was certain they had managed to find the best scotch and whiskey at the bar and had not bothered to bribe the bartender for it. This group was used to drinking free liquor. They had no qualms about holding court in the back-yard of a dead man they previously used as fodder for their work over several decades.

"Vultures have to pick the bones too," Charlie said, leaning into Syd.

"Or maybe they're honoring him, Charlie," Jim Yesler said, correcting his daughter's vitriol. He watched Syd carefully.

"And what better way to honor him than by drinking his best scotch and taking notes on who gave a revealing eulogy?" Charlie asked. She pointed out the busy pens and notepads flipped open among the circle of critics.

Syd shrugged. "I better go say hello to Michelle though," Syd said. "And Joe." She drained her third bourbon and sucked on the ice.

"What on Earth do you have to say to that weasel?" Charlie said with a thickening tongue. She may have been on her fifth scotch.

"Joe *Mitchell*, Charles," Syd said. "He writes for a few magazines. A pioneer in Washington, really. Clarence was good friends with him. A good man." She looked at Jim, who seemed alarmed by his daughter's outburst. "He's the big guy in the Adirondack chair. The one with the beard".

Syd's legs felt heavy when she finally got up. The whiskey had certainly reached her head by then. She steadied herself, aware that a few eyes from each of the tribes were keeping a careful watch on her small posse in the corner. She strode confidently to the bar and waited in line with a few folks, chatting them up and shaking hands. She realized that her performance would be the highlight of the memorial when the energy in the Green changed as she entered the arena. She would have to feign a confidence she didn't feel at the moment, but she knew she could summon it if she needed to.

She approached the group of writers like a queen entering her court. The group parted as she entered their circle as if they had been waiting for her. She knew she had to be careful about what she was going to say. She wasn't going to let them have the last word or leave them to their own devices. All of the side conversations hushed as they waited for her to speak. She stood silently in the middle of the group for a few moments, her face calm. She cleared her throat and made eye contact with each as she spoke.

"Thank you all for coming. My uncle owed a good deal of his success to many of you who took the time to notice his work. A good many of you acknowledged his artistry when it took courage to notice. I'm grateful for your condolences." She gave a small gracious smile and nodded. A woman next to her stepped forward to hug her. A few other writers approached her, offering a warm hand or an embrace, whispering words of sympathy. When the throng of people dispersed she moved over to Joe Mitchell who sat in his chair, beckoning her.

"Sorry, I'm finding it difficult to get up out of this chair," he chuckled sonorously, his flushed face wet with tears that landed in his beard. He took her hands in his. "I am so sorry, Sydney. I loved your uncle. He was such a remarkable man. A true artist and an honorable man. I was so shocked to hear of his accident." He spoke thickly through choked tears and a sad kind of laugh. A young editor friend named Michelle stood at his shoulder and rested a gentle hand on his arm. Joe Donner hovered behind her. His back was to Syd but it was clear that his ears were straining to hear the conversation. She caught sight of the back of his receding red hair clipped close to his scalp and a tweed jacket with leather elbow patches. He had not bothered to turn and face her, or even join the others in offering sympathy. The few others who clustered around Joe Mitchell's chair patted his arm or nodded at his words.

Syd kneeled down at Joe Mitchell's knee. "Thank you, Joe. Uncle loved and respected you too. You were good to him." She pulled his hands closer to her chest in a kind of embrace and smiled at him. She stood up to leave as the man gave way to new tears. But she stopped and turned to look at him over her shoulder.

"And Joe," she said softly. "It was no accident. My uncle was murdered."

She turned and walked through the long stretch of field, over to where Alejandro and Rosa were sitting at the periphery. Alejandro gave Syd a play-by-play of the activity going on behind her once she walked away from the media circle. Complete silence had grown into a buzz. She was anxious to know how the information was circulating. Alejandro pointed to the same group of businessmen he had seen in the field the week before. He had been watching them carefully. He told her to turn around when a man unknown to Syd walked quickly over to the bar. Within a minute, the entire line at the bar turned to look in her direction, heads drawn together in a strange intimacy. Jim Yesler was standing at the bar when news began to spread. He strode across the field toward Alejandro and Syd while a man in the group of suits hustled over to apprise his friends about her announcement. Tribes disbanded and began to mingle with one another. By the time Jim was standing next to her, almost everyone in the field was turning his head to steal a glance at her.

"I suppose you did that on purpose," Jim Yesler said, clearly exasperated.

"All the persons of interest are here, Jim." She turned to look at him and stole a sidelong glance at the crowd.

"Persons of interest?" he asked, eyebrows raised. "We should have talked about this first, Sydney."

"I know," she whispered. "But you agree with me."

He paused before answering her. "Yes, but I would have spared you this drama."

She turned to observe the field of people, who were now stirred up like bees. "I think someone *here* killed my uncle, Jim. I'd like to know who."

Chapter 13

Jim Yesler stood for a full hour observing the memorial guests as Sydney made her way through the crowd, accepting handshakes and embraces. Alejandro told Jim about the meeting he witnessed the previous Sunday after Syd requested that he do so. He pointed out some of the same men in suits looking intensely at Syd from across the lawn. The winemakers and growers stood with heads hung low and hands tucked in their pockets. Alejandro and Jim watched an unkempt, portly middle-aged man cross over from the group of winemakers. Jim recognized him as Francois Bertrand and watched him meet up with Hans Feldman, a balding birdlike man in an expensive suit and lifts. Jack Bristol stood next to them. Francois looked nervous and agitated while the other two held their emotions in check. Hans Feldman stood with one hand in his pocket and the other cupping a glass tumbler with scotch. Even from a distance, Jim found his cool arrogance disturbing under the circumstances. His body language was almost glib; he appeared to enjoy the discomfort of the winemaker. Jim wondered what he was saying to match his triumphant posturing. At one point Hans patted Francois on his back and leaned in to say something into the anxious winemaker's ear. Francois then stormed off and left the memorial. Jim could hear the ringing of Hans Feldman's mocking laughter from across the lawn, and he witnessed Jack Bristol bristle with contempt and turn his back on him. It was clear that Hans was enjoying himself.

Soon after, Syd walked away from the group of nearly thirty winemakers and growers, leaving them to stare into the ground. She strayed over to Marcus, who had not left Charlie's side all afternoon. He was clearly inebriated, and his face was flush.

"Hi, baby," he cooed, offering Syd a wet kiss. Syd side stepped to dodge him and grabbed his arm around her shoulder to hold him up.

"Whoa, big fellah," she said, bracing to hold him steady. "Maybe it's time for you to call it a night?" she asked. She exchanged glances with Charlie, who looked less empathetic. She had been babysitting him all afternoon.

Olivier showed up out of nowhere at Syd's elbow as she tried to pry the tumbler out of Marcus's hand. "I can help with this," he said softly. He patted Marcus on the shoulder and put an arm around him, ready to bear his weight. She hadn't seen Olivier all afternoon and now he was coming to her rescue again. Syd watched them walk away. Marcus was taller and had a larger frame. She thought they looked like a panther and a St. Bernard. Olivier deftly managed to lead Marcus down the stone steps and onto the garden path. After thirty seconds, Marcus suddenly stopped, almost falling over.

"Hey Syd!" he called out, slurring and turning back at her. "Joe Donner said he wanted to talk to you today."

She waved him off and Olivier took him into the house.

"I bet he does," Charlie hissed. "Succubus." She was obviously not sober herself. Syd hooked her arm and led her away.

They made their way to the bar for a glass of water for Charlie. She already pointed out the exchange of cash between the bartender and guests for bottles that had already been purchased for the *open* bar. "Corruption is everywhere," she said, winking when they saw one of the business suits bribe the bartender for a bottle of scotch. Jack Bristol stood patiently in line to place an order for another gin and tonic, following the rules of the game. He looked sideways at Syd. He was talking softly to a red-headed critic who eyed Syd with unveiled loathing as she approached. Jack rocked back and forth, looking agitated.

"Nice speech," Charlie slurred, sarcastically.

Jack looked at Syd and ignored her. "Will I see you at the reading of the will Monday morning, Syd?" he asked.

"Mmmm," She nodded, trying to convey her reluctance to talk in front of Joe Donner.

"You have read the will, of course?" he asked tentatively.

"Nope," she said, shaking her head. His mouth opened in shock. Next to him Joe Donner feigned indifference, his blue eyes searched the sky in boredom, but Syd sensed him hanging onto to her every word.

"Uh, well you might want to read it before Monday," Jack stammered. He turned to Joe Donner with distaste. "He has left something for you as well, it seems."

Joe Donner raised his auburn eyebrows incredulously. "Really?" he asked in surprise. He looked back at Syd with wide eyes.

"Maybe a thank you for all of your kind words over the years," Charlie snarled at him, reaching for a glass of water from the bartender. Syd saw him glance sharply at Charlie in a flash of loathing and then recover his expression, wearing the same fake smile he had before. Syd thought he only reserved his dislike for herself. She remembered her uncle's old fight with Joe Donner years back. He noticed her staring at him, and his eyes flashed again, this time with a triumphant amusement.

"What is it?" Joe asked, turning his back on Syd and Charlie.

"I'm not privy to the contents of the envelope, Mr. Donner," Jack said, his voice dripping in disdain.

"It's an envelope," Joe Donner said. He smiled charmingly at Jack. Jack bristled and frowned.

"Yes, but this is hardly the time or place to discuss this," Jack said. He glanced at Syd near his right elbow.

Joe Donner shrugged dismissively. He glanced at Syd and nearly snarled then recovered rapidly while she observed with interest. He looked comical to Sydney, like a troll. He was smug and triumphant in one moment and furious in the next, followed by a practiced mask of pleasantness. His micro-expressions transfixed her and she studied his face with newfound interest.

"You can mail it to my office in Seattle then. I'm going back tonight," he replied to Jack in a strained, high voice, his expression calm and pleasant. He turned to look at Syd.

"And please accept my sincere condolences. Clarence and I had our differences, but he's always been a person of interest for me." He bowed his head and turned on his heels.

"Marcus said you wanted to speak with me?" Syd asked, low and calm. The critic turned and looked back over his shoulder.

"It seems I've gotten what I wanted," he replied, not bothering with the courtesy of looking her in the eye. Syd winced at his oily voice, filled with triumph. He walked away bouncing on his toes and Syd forced down involuntary bile in her throat.

"Icky, icky, yuck, yuck!" Charlie exhaled out while they watched him disappear into the group of writers, charming them with handshakes and bidding them farewell.

Jack cleared his throat. "He's a silly man."

"A snake," Charlie interrupted with a contorted face.

Jack ignored her again. "But he's not someone to worry about Syd. Your uncle thought he was ridiculous. Anyway, I'm quite concerned that you haven't read the will yet. Had you read it you may not have made your. . .uh. . .announcement today." He sighed wearily through a furrowed brow.

Syd looked at him and chose her words carefully. "So you believe that something in the will would shine light on my uncle's death?" Her voice was treacherously low, anger and frustration bubbling into her mind as she endured his patronizing tones and implications. She swallowed hard.

"See, I'm not so certain that the will can reveal much about his death. I didn't read it, true. But I did have a nice chat with Paul. About insurance policies and their recipients who benefit from my uncle's death." She left him standing with his mouth open, Charlie stumbling at her heels.

Chapter 14

Sunday morning proved to be a day of recovery for everyone. Syd awoke a little before nine, and the house was quiet. She knew Marcus would be sleeping it off, but she half-expected the buzz of the day before to fill the morning. Instead, the house was silent and the kitchen clean, thanks to Rosa, no doubt. She was left to make her own coffee. She had taken an Ambien the night before, more as an excuse to repel Marcus's drunken, affectionate advances than for sleep. But she was glad she did. She woke up feeling more focused and alive than she had since she arrived.

She sat on the deck nursing her coffee, with a quilt from the spare room upstairs wrapped around her. On her lap she held the red folio she had been avoiding all week. The morning was eerily quiet, no bird song or distant engines. No neighbor's shotgun fire or worker chatter from nearby vineyards echoed in the morning air. A thick layer of clouds moved into the Gorge overnight and she could hardly see to the bottom of her neighbor's vineyard, let alone the river. The chill made her shiver, and she huddled herself closer under the quilt and drained her mug. She mulled over the surreal events of the day before.

Jim had agreed with her. He had the autopsy report and he

was certain Clarence was murdered. He had come to the same conclusion without knowing anything that she knew. He hadn't known about the insurance policies, the mysterious meeting in the vineyard behind their winery, or the plane accident in June. She was meeting with Jim later that afternoon to discuss everything with him. The last thing he said to her before he left the night before was that she needed to wait for him before she did anything else. He was concerned for her safety. She shivered again under the quilt and jumped suddenly at the sound of the scraping of the chair next to her.

"Sorry, I did not mean to frighten you," said Olivier. He reached for the empty mug she held. "I thought you heard me in the kitchen." He poured steaming coffee into her mug from a large french press and followed it with a splash of cream from a porcelain creamer dish. He turned and set the french press and the creamer down on the ledge next to him. He turned back and sat with his elbows resting on his knees, holding his coffee silently. She felt an urgency to say something, like he was waiting for her to speak. They sat in silence for minutes before he cleared his throat.

"Your mother's quilt," he said, nodding at the old quilt she had cocooned around herself.

"What?" She looked down incredulously at the blanket wrapped around her.

"Oh, um, I believe that your mother made that quilt. We have a few of them at home too. She was a talented woman."

"My mother made this quilt? *My* mother?" Syd felt a wave of resentment and frustration wash over her.

Olivier realized he was on shaky ground but didn't know how to recover. "Yes. I had one like it on my bed as a kid. The Uco Valley can get chilly."

"Unbelievable," she said, shaking her head. She was suddenly furious. How could she not know she was sitting huddled under a quilt made by her own mother? Did Clarence keep everything from her?

"You have read this then," he said, gesturing at the red folio.

"Why do you say that?"

"Well, you are clearly angry. At *me*, it seems." He paused, looking down at his hands. "I have been expecting it."

"Actually, I haven't." He looked up at her, astonished.

They locked eyes, each trying to read the other. He stood up suddenly, exasperated.

"Well, when you have, please come and discuss it with me. I won't be there tomorrow for the reading. I have to get that Petit Verdot myself. No trucks are available. Everyone is rushing to get fruit off before the rain. We will have to process it in the afternoon. Alejandro will have the crush pad set up so you don't need to do anything." He spoke stiffly and turned on his heels. She didn't watch him go, but she followed the clacking of his boots on the gravel road until they vanished.

She stared a good long time at the files in her lap before she found the courage to open them.

~

Jim came over later in the afternoon with the autopsy report and a list of suspects. He also explained that he may not be the lead detective on the case. The sheriff was concerned about his closeness to the family and he was unsure if he was going to be forced to hand over the case to the only other detective in the department, the man who happened to supervise Jim Yesler. As a deputy detective, he might not have a choice. But for the time being, he was going to help out as best he could while he still was in charge of it. He had mixed feelings about including Syd in the investigation. It wasn't exactly up to regulation, but his instincts told him she would be a valuable asset, and the case could be reassigned at any moment. At least he would have better access to information without having to cull through as many lies as he usually faced in an investigation. He was also aware that her eagerness to find the murderer was fueled by a suspended grief, and the sooner she could find resolve, the sooner she could move on.

Syd shared the information she gathered from Jack and Paul Renquest and compared it to Jim's list, crossing people off who were not around or who had little motive and adding a few others who stood to gain from her uncle's passing. She sensed that Jim was reluctant to include her in his investigation, but she found he was more eager to get information that only she could gather to get the case solved efficiently.

“Not Alejandro or Rosa,” she said, pointing at their names on his list. She picked at the skin on her lip and he raised his eyebrows. She reached over and slid the list across the kitchen table and crossed their names off.

“But *he's* at the top now, Syd.” He wrote Olivier's name at the top.

She scowled and shook her head.

“He has the most motive, Syd. He discovered the bod...he *found* him. He was here the entire time. The will makes it kind of obvious”.

“It’s impossible, Jim. I'm mad as hell about the will, but I've watched him and he loved my uncle. I’m certain of it.”

Jim drummed his fingers on the table. He was beginning to regret including her.

“I know it looks obvious but there's more at play here.” She made an effort to keep her voice steady. “What about the plane? That happened before he arrived this summer.”

“We don't know that yet and we don't know that the plane accident was sabotage. And we don't know anything about his connection with your uncle. What we do know is that someone held Clarence down in that tank of wine with the intention of making it look like an accident. A person with strong hands. A person who knows something about winemaking. I'm going to start questioning him first. And no, you can’t come with me.”

Syd scowled, but felt she had gained some kind of leeway by keeping Rosa and Alejandro out of the investigation for the time being. She watched Jim leave and head up to the winery. She knew he was going to question Olivier and that it wasn’t going to be pleasant. But she found herself giving in to the logic behind Jim’s argument. He who stood the most to gain was the obvious first suspect.

Syd spent the remainder of the day in a chair by the window, reading over Clarence's harvest prep lists and his notes of the summer blending trials. She found them scribbled in a notebook in his desk. She read Olivier's name more than a few times, with comments in the margins about his excellent nose or his talent for developing a perfect finish in a blend. Apparently, Olivier had been a part of almost all of the winery's operations since his arrival. It was also apparent to Syd that the will was not a last-minute whim, but the product of a well-thought-out plan that included grooming Olivier for the job as the primary winemaker.

She remained silent and withdrawn through the dinner that Charlie and Marcus had pulled together from the leftovers of the memorial. An hour earlier she watched Jim and Olivier leave the winery and head down toward the trailer. She kept an ear out for Jim through dinner but heard nothing. Their interview had lasted for hours, and she knew that it must end soon. She lay her head down on the table and listened to the banter between Charlie and Marcus. She fell asleep almost immediately.

Charlie must have taken her to bed, because she woke up a few hours later to Marcus attempting to crawl into bed with her.

Chapter 15

The next day was as gray as the day before, threatening rain. Syd woke up with the familiar pain in her chest that she tried to ease with a few moments of meditation on the deck, but the oppressive gray only made her feel heavier. She knew the day ahead was going to be terrible. Charlie was in danger of losing her job if she didn't return to the city and had made plans to leave. Marcus had left late the night before after their worst fight, which happened when she shrugged off his attempts at intimacy again. He was hurt and petulant, demanding that she give him some sign that she needed him. She responded with a plea for independence and some time to figure out her uncle's murder without having to deal with his emotional demands. He wanted her to agree to leave the investigation to the police, but she refused. He begged her to return with him, and she told him that she might not be returning at all. It was news to her as well. She only realized what she was saying after she said the words out loud. She hadn't really come up with a plan for the future, but she also hadn't allowed herself time to think about what would happen next. The will and the insurance money certainly changed everything for her. She was financially set for life now and she wouldn't need to keep her job in Seattle; a job she knew she may have already lost. She hadn't checked in with the restaurant in a week. But more than anything she had the winery to contend with.

She sat next to Charlie on a damp deck chair under her mother's quilt with a steaming mug of coffee. It was still early, and the clouds rolled over the river and settled like clustered cotton balls. The air was thick and cool. It smelled of rotting vegetation and wet earth.

"How are you going to work this out?" Charlie asked, shivering.

"Well, I think your dad will do most of it. I'm just going to let him know what happens at the reading of the will today, I think."

"No, Syd. I meant how are you going to share the winery with this guy?"

Syd sighed. "I've got no idea. I haven't thought about it. Your dad didn't arrest him last night or even take him in for questioning. And he's gone now. The truck's gone, so I assume he left to get grapes this morning as planned. So he must have convinced your dad he wasn't a flight risk."

"Or he took the truck to leave."

Syd shook her head adamantly. "No, Olivier's invested. He cares so much about this winery already. It's so weird, Charlie, but this guy seems more in love with this place than I am. Like he belongs here." She thought of the scribbles in Clarence's notebook.

"He does *not* belong here, Syd. I mean, who the hell is he?"
Syd furrowed her eyebrows. "He's the guy who inherited my family winery. Half of it. With me. A guy who I've never met before and have never heard of. A guy who loved my uncle. A guy who had a quilt on his bed as a kid that my mother made. He's the guy who stands the most to gain by my uncle's death, according to your dad. He's the guy who's held me twice while I sobbed. He kept the winery running this last week during all the chaos. He dry-cleaned my suit and slept in my old room, but promptly moved out to the trailer during all the commotion, probably just so I'd have a place to stay. I have no fucking clue who he is, Charlie. But I'm pretty certain he didn't kill my uncle."

"But the police think otherwise, Syd. He's their primary suspect right now."

"Yeah, yeah. And I'm really pissed off that he inherits the airplane. Why on earth would Clarence do *that?* Olivier doesn't fly. Jesus, maybe he does."

"See? You don't even know him," Charlie mumbled into her mug.

Syd brooded in her own dark thoughts. She savagely pulled the skin off of her lower lip while Charlie chatted about her plans to return later in the week. She had a big gala event to attend in two days for the magazine launch of their mutual friend, Michelle. They had attended sommelier classes with Michelle and were often considered a trio in their debaucheries and schemes. But Michelle was a wonder-woman with ambitions to create a print magazine devoted to the world of wine and spirits in a time when print publications were going under by the week. She pursued her dream with dogged determination, and Syd and Charlie were looking forward to attending her launch party. The who's who of the industry would show up; a smorgasbord for Charlie's appetite for human folly. But Syd could see no way to return to Seattle any time soon. She was honored that Michelle attended the memorial, despite the fact that it was just a few days before her magazine launch. But Syd would have to miss the party, regardless of how much she was looking forward to it only a week before.

"You're thinking of staying here then?" Charlie asked.

"I don't know *what* I'm thinking," Syd said, sounding as jaded as she felt.

"You probably already lost your job, you know? Jackson's an asshole." Charlie always hated Syd's boss. As usual, she was right about his personality flaws.

"Yeah, I may not even bother to call him. It's not like I need the cash anymore."

"That's a lot of dough, *schweetheart*," said Charlie, offering her best Bogart.

"Yeah, I'm surprised I'm not a suspect." Syd smiled sardonically at Charlie.

Charlie looked down cagily in her mug.

"Really? *Really*?"

"It's police work, Syd. All persons-of-interest make the list. And you do stand to gain *the most*. Dad had to rule you out. Of course, he could never think it was real, but he had to eliminate you. He's under a lot of pressure. They lost several days in the investigation, thinking it was an accident. They might still reassign the case."

"Great, what'd he do? Call my work?"

"Yup. Apparently, you were serving some posh Japanese guys a very expensive bottle of Châteauneuf-du-Pape."

"All night, actually. The same bottle of band-aid wine too. I tried desperately to give them a remarkable Rhône blend from Washington but they didn't bite. Bastards." Syd was letting Charlie off the hook. She didn't want to be angry when she said goodbye to Charlie. And, of course, she knew that Charlie was right. Jim was protecting her. Still, she pondered how he could ever imagine that she was capable of such a thing. How could she ever kill anyone, let alone drown her own uncle?

"No accounting for taste," Charlie said, smiling in relief for her clemency.

Syd grimaced. She began to imagine how her uncle had died, and how the killer must have done it. The autopsy report was clear. CO2 Asphyxiation as a product of dry drowning. The bruising on the back of the head could hardly have come from a struggle in accidental drowning. She was suddenly overwhelmed by nausea. Bile filled her throat. Before she could think she leaned forward and vomited on the deck between her legs.

Charlie jumped up. "Woah! Geez! Are you alright?" She leaned down and rubbed Syd's back, trying to gather her hair and pull it away from her face.

Syd spit out the last of it and wiped her mouth with the back of her hand. Tears filled her eyes. She looked up into Charlie's face.

"Someone held him down, Charlie," she said, sobbing tears of anger. They turned her eyes bloodshot red. "Someone held his head down in a tank of wine. He fought. He fought back. He had bruises on the back of his head. And a dislocated thumb. *He fought hard.*"

Charlie used her sleeve to wipe the tears from Syd's face. She cradled her head and rocked her, making cooing sounds. "I'll be back on Thursday, okay? As soon as possible. And I'll take time off. I've got some vacay saved up. Fuck the Bahamas!"

Chapter 16

Jack's office looked more gray than purple without sunshine to light up the space. Sydney walked into the room just as Francois Bertrand was leaving. He brushed past her, avoiding eye contact and muttered, "Good morning." He clutched an oversized frame that was messily rewrapped in brown paper. Rosa was already seated in the office alongside Alejandro, holding his hand and sobbing. There were two more empty chairs in front of Jack's desk. Syd sat down in the one next to Alejandro.

"Good morning," she said to both of them. She leaned over and squeezed Rosa's hand. She realized that Rosa had been avoiding her. She had hardly spoken two words to Syd at the memorial and she had been like a ghost in the house ever since. Here in this office, she looked small and fragile. Syd felt a jolt of pain in her stomach for her. Rosa squeezed her hand in return and buried her head in a handkerchief that belonged to Alejandro.

Alejandro's eyes followed the winemaker out the door, looking more angry than sad.

"Framed article of his best scores," said Alejandro, nodding toward the door. "That's what your uncle gave *him*."

"Francois Bertrand?" Syd asked. "Really? A peace offering?"

"A haunting," he whispered, leaning toward her and winking. "It had a photo taped on the back of it."

"You saw it?"

"I took it," he whispered, cryptically, and leaned back. Alejandro was full of surprises.

"When was that?"

"Last March. I saw Francois with Joe Donner in the Elk's Club parking lot. I was coming out of the Post Office, getting my mail, and I see him get into a Jeep. He gave Donner an envelope. Right there in broad daylight. I recorded it on my phone..."

"It's five minutes after," Jack interrupted as he entered his office. He sat ceremoniously behind his desk. "Should we wait another five for Mr. Ruiz?"

"Oh, he's not coming," Syd half-whispered, realizing that the last seat was for him. "He had to pick up fruit. Some Petit Verdot needed to come off before the rain."

"*Sí*. And I have to get back to set up the crush pad," Alejandro said loudly, clearly anxious to get things rolling. Rosa's sobbing was wearing on him, and he had to force himself to distraction.

"Okay, then," Jack said, looking disappointed.

He proceeded to read aloud what Syd had read four times the day before. Clarence had bequeathed a small financial fortune to both Rosa and Alejandro, which came as a complete surprise to them. Rosa stopped sobbing in her astonishment, and Alejandro could hardly contain his own tears. He got up shortly after the reading to step outside. He spent the remainder of the meeting pacing the sidewalk in the cold, trying to catch the unraveled emotion that escaped his best efforts in the hand that covered his mouth.

Jack's voice settled in a monotone cadence when he read the details of Clarence's estate; the dividing up of the winery between Olivier Ruiz and Sydney McGrath. Clarence had not forgotten his lawyer friend either, and Jack visibly squirmed when he read his own name in the will. Clarence had given his airplane to Olivier, which Jack read with particular bitterness. He regained his composure as he read on, ending with the reference to the mysterious packages that Clarence had bequeathed to several people. There was the one for his "friend", Francois Bertrand, whose mystery was revealed when Syd entered the room. Another was for Hans Feldman. It sat wrapped in brown paper on Jack's desk, a package roughly the size of a boot box. Jack read the last line of the will while he unlocked his safe and recovered two plain manila envelopes, sealed with red sealing wax. One was for Sydney and the other was for Joe Donner.

Jack opened an accompanying letter in a plain envelope clipped to the larger envelope addressed to Sydney, per instructions of the will. Syd could see it was handwritten in Clarence's left-handed script. Jack read it aloud.

"Dear Sydney, You may review the contents of this envelope or you may throw them away. Its mischief has given me some amusement, although you may find its malfeasance tedious. Either way, it's yours to do with as you see fit. I have played with it long enough. Signed Uncle Clarence. Joe Donner gets the other copy," Jack said, looking up to her. Syd could certainly guess what it might be.

"Was Uncle blackmailing poor Joe Donner?" Syd asked, both sardonic and inquisitive.

"No, no." Jack shook his head emphatically, which only added to Syd's concern. "He asked nothing for these documents, I assure you," he paused. "He was toying with him. Understand? Donner was an ass at every turn. But Clarence felt he owed Donner something at any rate. Donner was the one who revealed the corporate buyout, after all." Jack added the last with a note of more bitterness. "There's one more thing. Another sealed letter." Jack turned and retrieved it from the safe. He read it aloud.

"I hereby bequeath my *Isle of Lewis Chessmen* set and carved chessboard to Olivier Ruiz. Signed Clarence Blackwell. Dated August 30th".

Syd heard a sharp gasp before she realized it came from her own mouth. Rosa stared at her while she tried to recover from her shock. Of course she had assumed the chessmen were hers as her part of the estate. The chessmen *were* hers, by every right. She grew angrier when she realized that Clarence had written the letter just days after her last lunch with him, the last time she saw him in Seattle.

Chapter 17

Clarence sat waiting at the table for her. He had already ordered the wine and bruschetta to start. She was only a little late, but with Clarence a little late was as bad as not showing up at all. She was expecting a reprimand when she approached the table, but she was pleasantly surprised to hear his unexpected praises.

"You look wonderful, my girl," he said, rising to embrace her. He squeezed her for longer than usual, in a way that showed his genuine affection for her. She immediately noticed that he felt thinner through his clothes. She took in his familiar smell like a hungry person, in spite of herself.

"Thanks," she said, a little shaken by the generous compliment and display of affection. After all, he was a man who hardly said anything to her. He gestured for her to sit and informed her that he had already ordered for her. He poured her some of the rosé he held in his hand.

"This is Martha's rosé. An intentional rosé blend. Not that nasty saignée. I was pleased to see they had it on the menu." He chatted on in uncharacteristic enthusiasm. He mentioned the carpaccio bruschetta and the menu options while Syd sat staring, nonplussed. Sydney felt more than a little ambushed by the new

man in front of her and his incessant prattle. He was clearly twenty pounds thinner now and he looked older. But his smile made his face handsome and his skin was tan and healthy looking. His full head of white hair was trimmed neatly above his ears and his beard was close and neat.

"What are you staring at?" he asked after a few moments. He self-consciously ran his hand over his white beard to groom away any stray breadcrumbs.

"Nothing. I'm just...uh. Who the hell are you and what have you done with my uncle?" Her face broke into a smile.

He sat back and folded his hands on his thin belly. "I've had a change of heart, Sydney." He winked at her and stared, taking every bit of her in.

"Oh. Is it love?" she asked, teasing him. She was still a little uncomfortable with the candid nature of their conversation and his searching eyes.

"You could say that. And a brush with mortality. A cynic might find oodles of clichés here, really. The point is I've been wrong and I want to fix things. Ah, but our lunch has arrived." He made himself busy arranging the table for the dishes as they were set down in front of them. But Syd could see the glimmer of tears in his eyes.

They ate a delicious meal of mussels and pomme frites, seared ahi over grilled fennel, and roasted beet salad with goat cheese, hazelnuts, and oranges. They chatted over her recent adventures in finding the best Washington wines in her quest for an excellent wine list at work. He listened and gave her advice about a few labels and their winemakers. But he mostly just listened to her. The conversation grew comfortable and easy, and Syd began to enjoy her uncle's company for the first time since she was a teenager. It only grew slightly tense when he inquired about Marcus, which made her defensive.

"I'm only asking. He's stuck it out for so long. He has to have some redeeming qualities." He insisted when she bristled at his questions. She knew it was the closest thing to an olive branch that Clarence could offer when it came to Marcus.

He asked about Charlie, her apartment, and her daily schedule. He listened to her with a kind of attentiveness she rarely experienced with her uncle. It was clear that he relished every moment with her and she was deeply touched.

After a while, she pushed her plate back and rested her elbows on the table. She cradled her face in her hands. He was a darling man when he smiled and connected with others; when he was fully present and not sequestered away in some dark place in his mind.

"So, what is it that has you up here? What has changed your heart?" she asked softly. He looked at her with marvel in his eyes. She realized it was perhaps the first honest question she asked him in a decade.

He smiled sadly, and told her about his misadventures that summer. He explained some of the details of the buyout and how it went sour when he found out that the investor was planning to sell the winery to a big corporation out of California. Francois Bertrand was chosen as the winemaker after the buyout was completed and Clarence would be shunted aside. Francois was a crony of the investor. Worse yet, Joe Donner had revealed the inside scoop in a blog post on his weekly wine industry journal with the malevolent intention of outing Clarence as a washed out sellout. Of course, Clarence had been completely unaware of the investor's plans and he quickly pulled out of the deal. It was all information that Sydney already knew, but it was good to hear it from her uncle.

"And Jack and I have had a falling out over this," he said. "Jack is not in a good place financially and I suspect he was expecting a windfall from the deal. He was also going to broker the corporate buyout, apparently."

"Wait a minute. Your best friend Jack was going to help sell out the winery to a corporate investor behind your back? Why's he so hard up?" Syd processed the information slowly, trying to follow the story with three glasses of wine under her belt.

"Cynthia has a gambling problem, Syd. She's squandered away their savings, their retirement, everything. Jack's completely lost. She's gone for treatment, but Jack discovered the problem when it was too late. She handled all of their financials. Also," he added with furrowed brows, "he thought it was in my best interest."

"So why aren't you furious about this?"

Clarence exhaled deeply after sipping another glass of the port he had ordered. "Yes, Syd, he betrayed my trust. Yes, he stood to gain at my expense. But he is a friend, and he has done a recent good turn to make up for it all." He patted her hand. Syd sat completely perplexed. Forgiveness was not one of Clarence's strong suits.

"This all happened before the accident?" Syd asked. She remembered that the last time she saw Jack was at the hospital when Clarence had a near-miss in his airplane in June. Jack and Cynthia were in the waiting room when Syd arrived. Jack had been pacing the room for hours.

"Yes. And I was not speaking to him at the time, you remember. But the accident changed everything for me, Syd. That's all water under the bridge now. Although it's still a bit awkward between us." He leaned forward and held her hand. "Anyway, I have a new winemaker now. From Argentina. A friend, actually. I want you to meet him."

"So you won't be making the wine now?" She asked, completely dumbfounded.

"Of course, I'll be making the wine. I just need help now. I'm not getting any younger." Her mouth formed her next thought but he squeezed her hand. "Listen, I want you to come home this Crush. Can you do that? I want you to meet someone." He swallowed hard and looked her in the eye. "I want you to help with the wine this year."

"You want me to help with Crush," she said flatly.

"Yes! I want your input." He looked down sheepishly. It was another new gesture for Clarence.

"You want me to come help with Crush," she said through clenched teeth. "You want my input? After years of telling me to stay away?"

He nodded into his hands and sighed with resignation.

She shook her head in disbelief. "I've got a life here, you know? I have a home here and a good job that I do quite well, thank you." Her voice rose more than she intended, and the table next to them turned to look at her.

"Please, Sydney. Please come. This is so important to me."

His soft pleading was barely audible.

"A year ago you were planning to sell the winery to some random person, and you never even considered how I felt about it. You said you didn't care what happened to the winery. You refused to even entertain the idea of me taking it over. And now you want me to come down and help with Crush? Unbelievable!"

He threw his hands up. "I told you, I've had a change of heart."

"Well, so have I." She pushed back her chair and slammed her napkin onto the table. "Thanks for lunch." She left him staring at her as she stormed out of the restaurant.

Chapter 18

Sydney came back to an empty silent house, a hollow shell that echoed painful memories in every room. Still, she wandered through the house searching for the chess set. The old floors creaked in the usual places and the rooms smelled as they always had, but now the house felt dead and lonely. She spent an hour looking in every possible hiding place for the old Danner shoebox that held the chessmen. It was nowhere to be found.

She wandered into the kitchen to discover that she was quite hungry when the subtle smells of recently cooked food hit her nose. She made herself some eggs on toast and a cup of tea, and sat down at the table, still lost in thought. All week long she had pending tasks to contend with: the details of the memorial, the memorial itself, meetings, phone calls, and conversations. But now, at this moment, there was no pressing duty for her to perform. Her future loomed like an abyss in front of her, an ocean of regret and sadness that terrified her. Her stomach churned as she realized her fears. She shoved her plate away, having hardly touched it.

The haunting thoughts of her ominous indecision were interrupted by the sound of a diesel engine coming up the gravel road. She got up to watch the trailer pull up to the crushpad through the kitchen window, carrying twelve bins of grapes. She watched Olivier jump out of the truck and meet up with Alejandro. They began unstrapping the tie-downs. It occurred to Syd that neither man spoke. They each worked alone, rendered a silent prisoner by their worried minds. Without Charlie to help her through this day – without her compass – she knew she needed the company of someone, anyone. Even if it was next to the man who had inexplicably won her uncle's affection.

She rushed to get into her work clothes and bounded up the hill just in time to jump into the forklift. Alejandro stepped aside graciously and let her take over. She unloaded the trailer deftly, aware that she was being scrutinized by her new partner. Olivier didn't offer any clues of his opinion of her, but she knew he had been carefully assessing her skills on the crushpad. Of course, now she understood why.

They processed the Petit Verdot with more care than before, using the destemmer and the vibrating sorting table. Several workers stood on either side of the conveyor belt, examining the fruit as it traveled up the belt into the auger above. A good deal of fruit had been thrown onto the crushpad concrete when the day was over. Olivier was right. The fruit had hung too long. It suffered some shrivel and bird damage as a result.

"Was this netted?" she asked Olivier after an hour of sorting. They had only gone through one bin, and she knew this was going to make for a very long day.

"Yes. But the birds still got to it. I should have pulled it in last week." He was clearly disappointed with himself. He looked haggard and distracted. He had been grilled by Jim the night before as a murder suspect and left in the wee hours of the morning to get the grapes. Syd realized he may not have slept at all. His polite Old World veneer was wearing thin, and Syd felt surprising empathy for him, in spite of her anger over the chessmen and the will. She realized Clarence may have been right about him. He was committed to the winery wholeheartedly.

"We'll be here late with this sorting," she said. "Maybe you should get some sleep."

"Of course not," he said, dismissing her with a wave of his hand. He walked away with a tight frown. Syd bent her head to sort again, mulling over the complicated nature of their interactions.

~

It was late when they finished processing the Petit Verdot. The crush hands worked like silent drones, exhausted and ready for their beds. A few were still loading hoses back onto their hooks around ten, while the others headed for their cars down the dark gravel driveway. Sydney was spraying down the crushpad for a final hot rinse. She had let Olivier disappear into the lab for the tank analysis an hour earlier. She would have liked to have done the lab work herself, but he was in dour spirits and she sensed that he needed some space. She wasn't quite sure how the tables had turned so fast. Wasn't she the one who was supposed to be mad at him?

He emerged from the lab scowling beneath his protective glasses and holding a beaker of pink juice. "It's at 4.2 grams per liter in acid. Really low. I think we should bump it now. No danger of lowering the pH too much."

"Sure. The pH?" she asked, taking the sample from him and tasting it. She swirled it in her mouth and spit it into the strip drain on the floor. "Never mind. High. Soapy."

"3.9. I, *we* waited too long on this," he answered. He smiled at her through perfect white teeth and eyes that lit up. She realized he squinted when he smiled. Syd suddenly felt self-conscious. She was a mess, with her hair clumped in tangled braids and her Carhartts soaked. She still had sticky pomace stuck to her boots, pants, and hair. They faced each other in awkward silence.

"We should talk," she said, stiffening.

"I'm about done here," he said. "I'll make the acid adjustments in the morning after punchdowns."

"Down at the house then? I'm starved. I'll try to find some food, too. See you down there in about ten?"

She turned and strode downhill with a knot in her gut and a strange flutter of excitement. When she got back to the house she put on a pot of rice and hopped in the shower. She quickly stepped out a moment later and pulled on a pair of old jeans and a clean T-shirt. She felt rejuvenated from the hot shower and shampoo. She had been sticky all over from grape juice, and she was happy to have washed it out of her hair. Too often during crush time she found herself sticking to her pillow at night, too tired to shower before bed.

Olivier came down in his work clothes, which somehow appeared as clean as they were earlier that day. He was fastidious by nature, and the only signs of work she saw were his day-old beard and tired eyes. He immediately stepped in the kitchen and started working silently next to Syd, chopping vegetables for a quick stir fry.

Ten minutes later they were sitting silently next to each other at the table, eating their dinner with relish. Both of them were very hungry, and it occurred to Syd that Olivier may not have eaten all day. She watched him drain his beer and set the empty glass down.

"Long day," she said. She got up to retrieve another beer from the fridge.

He nodded and exhaled slowly. She watched him pour the new beer into his glass and drink half of it.

"This conversation can wait, you know," she said, feeling cowardice creep into her.

"No, now. I may be in jail soon enough, and you need to know where we are with the winery."

She winced and looked at him. "If Jim let you stay, chances are he's not convinced."

"He said he had no evidence to arrest me."

"Is there evidence, Olivier?" she asked softly.

He sighed and looked at her with dark tired eyes. "Are you asking me if I killed your uncle? No, I did not. But I would have if he asked me."

Syd stared at him and swallowed hard. Rosa had alluded to the same idea once.

"Why would he have asked you that?"

"Look, I understand that you are confused, and that you think someone killed your uncle. I know that I owe you an explanation. But I am honor-bound to be silent. Please understand that I made a promise and I have to keep it, regardless of how unfair it might seem to you."

Syd put her hand on her forehead and processed what he said. She was exasperated and exhausted. "So many fucking secrets," she whispered, shaking her head.

“Yes, but in the meantime we need to figure out how we will run this winery together. *For now.*” His face was stoney and assertive, a new feature of his.

“You think I’ll contest the will?” she asked.

“I'm not sure that it is not your right to do so. I might, if I were you.”

She shook her head. “Probate would take forever. In the meantime we could lose an entire vintage.”

“Exactly,” he said, expressionless. “Then you have decided to stay?”

“No, I'm not sure what I'll be doing.”

“Well, this conversation is useless if I cannot have some assurances that you will stick around to see through this Crush.” He couldn’t conceal his frustration any longer, though he was obviously conflicted.

“I’ll stick around through this Crush. I can do *that.*” She conceded, realizing that she always intended to stay and at least see the vintage get to barrel.

Olivier relaxed his shoulders, clearly relieved. “Good.” He sat pensively and she watched him. “Your uncle wanted us to share this winery. For his own reasons, certainly. I intend to respect his wishes. He fought to keep it as a family winery, and I feel that it would be a great dishonor to be responsible for breaking it up.”

“Are we family, Olivier?” she asked. It was the question that stirred in the back of her mind since she met him.

“In Clarence's mind, I think so.”

He stopped and swallowed hard. He pushed his chair back abruptly and stacked the plates on the table, carrying them to the sink.

Chapter 19

Jim sat with his arms crossed, his coffee steaming in front of him on the kitchen table. Rosa was making a clamor in the kitchen with the juicer. Syd was feeling more comfortable in the old house with a little more life in it in the morning. Rosa was a calming force for her.

"I asked him and he said he didn't do it," she said, knowing how it must sound to a cop. But she believed emphatically in what she was saying.

He narrowed his eyes and scrutinized her face as she sat across from him. He already regretted getting Syd involved at all. He should have sent her back to Seattle with Charlie after the reading of the will. Here she was, one day later defending his primary suspect, with obvious emotional attachment. He regretted not taking Olivier down to the station on Sunday too. Olivier had explained why arresting him would hurt the winery, which meant it would hurt Syd. He was convincing enough for Jim to let him go get his fruit and process it the next day. For whatever reason, he believed Olivier was telling the truth about not being a flight risk. He could see why Syd believed him. He had an old-fashioned sense of honor that Jim found compelling. Still, in his years of law enforcement he had come to the conclusion that the most obvious suspect was usually the correct one. And Olivier Ruiz was the obvious suspect.

"So tell me about the will Syd," Jim said, changing the subject. "What happened yesterday?"

"When I got to Jack's I ran into Francois Bertrand, who was carrying some kind of framed picture. He seemed angry. Alejandro told me it was a framed copy of the article that got him his best scores last year."

"Alejandro was there?"

"Yeah, and Rosa." She rolled her eyes at his raised eyebrows. She wasn't about to let his suspicions wander toward them again.

"Why were they there?"

Syd squirmed in her seat. "Uncle left them each some money. They're family, Jim. Rosa was practically my mother growing up, and Alejandro has been with Uncle for almost twenty years." She whispered back at him in a hiss, glancing at the kitchen door. Rosa couldn't know that Jim would ever think of her as a suspect. She was a proud woman and she'd be appalled. Besides, Rosa could hold a grudge for a lifetime. Jim's face and silence told her that he was annoyed but resigned. She took the opportunity to tell him nearly everything she knew about the will: the money bequeathed to Rosa, Alejandro and Jack, the mysterious package left to Hans Feldman, and the manila folders left for her and Joe Donner. She omitted the addendum about the chessmen. For some reason she suspected it might push Jim over the edge in his suspicions toward Olivier, and she needed him to stay out of jail. At any rate, she didn't trust her own emotions any more. She was still angry about the chessmen and knew Jim might react to her anger, which could be a disaster.

"What was in the envelopes?" he asked.

Syd rose silently and disappeared into the spare room. She returned a moment later with a large manila envelope while Rosa was filling Jim's mug with fresh coffee. Rosa bent over and kissed Jim's cheek before she left, with tears of gratitude in her eyes. Syd raised her eyebrows at him, accusatively. Jim shrugged and looked away. Syd sat down and slid the folder across the table. "Uncle's idea of fun, I think."

Jim opened the envelope and took out some 8x10 photos, a thumb drive, and a few letters. There were addressed envelopes too. He laid them neatly out on the table and eyed them carefully. The photo showed two familiar faces in the front seat of a car. The passenger was passing an envelope to the driver. His forehead furrowed, and his face exposed a new kind of worry. Syd was beginning to feel that they were not as harmless as she originally thought.

"Your uncle was blackmailing Joe Donner?" he asked while she held her breath.

"No, I mean he didn't ask for anything, I don't think."

"So it was a threat."

"I think so. It adds up. Uncle and Joe Donner hated each other."

"Francois Bertrand gets a framed copy of his accolades, and here we have photos and...is this a video of an exchange of *something* between the same winemaker and a well-known critic?" He held up the thumb drive, his forehead furrowed as he pieced it all together. "Joe Donner is a critic, right? Did Joe Donner give those scores to Bertrand?"

"I don't know," she said. But then she remembered reading the article in Joe's primary publication the year before. "Actually, yes. I remember now. The article was in Joe's primary syndication, and he had given Bertrand stellar reviews. And a full article about the changing of the guard in the Gorge. That kind of thing. It was an obvious slight toward Uncle. And Bertrand has always been intensely jealous of Uncle's scores and reviews."

'Where did this thumb drive come from?" he asked.

She shook her head, better to leave that one alone.

"These letters are addressed to the editors? Were these letters ever sent?" he asked.

"No. Uncle wrote me instructions to do what I liked with it. He said he had his fun with it. I wonder if this means Joe and Francois knew about it."

Jim deliberately collected the letters, photos, and thumb drive, and placed them back in the envelope. He slid them back across the table to Syd. It was obvious to Syd that Jim found the whole mess distasteful and sordid. She was surprised at her own feelings of shame and the embarrassment she felt over her uncle's behavior. She wanted to explain it to Jim. She wanted to make some excuses for Uncle, but she was as much in the dark about it as he was. She was almost certain that the letters and the photo were an indictment of sorts; her uncle's way of letting Joe Donner and Francois Bertrand know that he knew of their corrupt collusion. But she wasn't certain how far it had gone. Uncle had a wry sense of humor about these kinds of things. And she was surprised to find Jim so naïve about her uncle's cynicism. Clarence was no saint, although he always had an exacting integrity. Obviously he was not above holding a damning piece of information over a foe's head, leaving them dangling on the hook. But she knew her uncle well, and he would have had no compunction to expose Francois as a fraud, or Joe Donner as a critic for hire. She suspected it was far more entangled than it looked. Maybe Clarence hadn't sent the damning video as a gesture of gratitude toward Donner for revealing the nature of the buyout. Jack had alluded to something like that.

"Jack Bristol got some money?" Jim asked, interrupting her thoughts. He clearly wanted to move on.

"Yes. A good deal. $200,000. In spite of everything, Jack was uncle's best friend and he was having financial problems. I think uncle felt badly that he had cost Jack so much when he backed out of selling the winery. Jack would have made a bundle."

"Why does he have financial troubles? He's a successful lawyer." Jim asked derisively, revealing his own particular form of prejudice. He had little tolerance for fiscally irresponsible professionals. He had difficulties empathizing with the troubles of people who made their livings contriving contracts and agreements that could screw over an honest businessman like Clarence Blackwell. Besides, he really didn't like lawyers at all. He had seen too many of the wrong people serve time for minor drug infractions that were more a banner of poverty than malicious intent, while many criminal rich folk who could afford representation rarely saw the inside of the county jail. He had little patience for any manipulation of the legal system and the class of folks who benefited.

"Cynthia gambles," she said. "His wife."

"Hmm," he answered. "And he had a policy too, you say? So he clearly had something to gain."

"He and uncle were not on the best terms either. Because of the buyout going bad. Jack thought – he still thinks – that Uncle should have taken the deal. I think he shares your suspicions about Olivier."

"I might have to talk to Jack, it seems."

"Or you could just call Olivier's boss and check his alibi," Syd said sarcastically. "Oh, never mind, he's dead." She thumped her forehead, with a gesture Charlie used often. He reached over and rubbed her shoulder. It was a fatherly gesture and the only apology she would get from him.

"My job," he whispered.

Syd looked down at the papers in front of him. They sat silently while Jim looked over the notepad. Syd squirmed in her seat. She had no idea the Sheriff's investigation employed so much self-righteousness. But Jim was known to everyone as the incorruptible Sheriff's deputy. He had joined the department decades before and worked his way through a degree in Criminal Justice while he was in uniform. After a few years he became an investigator and moved to a desk job. He spent the better part of two decades investigating meth labs and marijuana production in the Gifford Pinchot Forest, which made up most the county. It was only recently that he put the uniform back on and drove a cruiser again. The department suffered budget cuts and Jim had volunteered to go back to police work. He was a part-time investigator, and the Sheriff was fully aware that the department owed Jim for his voluntary demotion. This was the primary reason Jim was allowed to continue working on the Blackwell murder case. He had little experience with homicide cases but he was the golden child of the department, the last bastion of trustworthiness in law enforcement. Still, Syd was unused to being on the receiving end of his judgment. She wanted to deflect the scrutiny from Olivier.

"So what about the guys in the vineyard on Sunday?" she asked, prodding him. "The guys Alejandro saw?"

"Yeah, I'll check that out too," he said, scowling at his

notes.

“Alejandro’s working in the vineyard today,” she said, trying to not sound too eager.

“Okay, I'll get up there now. Take it easy, Sydney.” He narrowed his eyes at her and pushed back his chair, draining his coffee mug. Syd slid the manila folder back across the table to Jim. He tucked it under his arm with the rest of his files and winked at her.

A moment later Syd watched as Jim took giant strides up the gravel drive in his uniform, his large hat bobbing up and down slightly. When she was certain he was veering away from the winery, where Olivier was doing punchdowns and lab work, she rushed to her room to get her boots on and she grabbed her car keys.

Chapter 20

Syd had to wait outside of Jack's office for ten minutes. She sat for a while, but found that pacing was far more comfortable. So she went outside and paced the same strip of concrete she observed Alejandro pacing the day before. The sky had been heavy with a steady drizzle earlier, but a breeze had stirred up a true autumn crispness that chilled her to the bone. She would have to ask Charlie to bring her some more clothes. She had rushed packing the week before and had little to wear for the sudden weather change other than the wardrobe of her youth that had been left behind in her closet. Eventually, Jack came out to beckon her inside.

"Getting chilly," he said as he escorted her into his office, closing the door behind her.

The office was the same as the morning before, but the box that sat on Jack's desk was gone. Syd sat down and rubbed her chilled hands together.

"What can I help you with, Syd?" Jack asked, with the confidence of a man who knew the answer to his question.

"I want to know about the insurance policies, Jack." Jack looked startled.

"I talked to Paul. Yours should fund within the month." He shifted his weight in his chair.

"Yes, I know that. I meant the other ones. The key man policies. The one you have."

He sighed and splayed his hands out on the table flatly. He stared at them for a moment before he spoke in a quiet voice. "Those policies will be nullified. I have a meeting with Paul later today."

"But Paul said they were legitimate."

"He thought so, yes. And they were paid for. Mine was paid for by Clarence."

"Clarence paid the premium on his own life insurance policy?"

"Through a retainer for my services held in escrow, yes."

"Why? He left you money, Jack."

"He did. I think he was trying to find a way out for me." He splayed his hands out further on the table.

"I don't understand."

Jack hung his head and shook it slowly. Then he took a deep breath and explained the nature of the rift between him and her uncle. Jack had been instrumental in the arrangements of the life insurance policies and all the other contract arrangements for the buyout of the winery over a year ago. He was eager to make it work out. He understood the arrangement to be a win-win for everyone involved, including himself. He was named a beneficiary in the key man policies as an executor of the estate and a manager of any transition in lieu of Clarence, in case anything happened to him. But the deal went sour when Clarence found out that Hans Feldman had inexplicably made arrangements to sell the winery to a large wine label out of California, news he had learned from the nefarious blogging of Joe Donner. Jack conveniently omitted the part about his complicity in the arrangement of the sellout. He explained that Clarence was furious, and pulled out of the contract that was very nearly ending escrow.

"Just a few days after we nullified the contracts, Clarence had his plane accident," he said.

"I saw you at the hospital. My uncle was still angry at you, I remember. What changed?"

Jack squeezed the bridge of his nose and exhaled. "Well, he was injured, of course. Just a broken rib and sprained wrist. Bruises mostly." He responded cagily. She nodded impatiently; she knew all of this. "And then they ran blood tests." His voice dropped off. Syd guessed at what he was getting at. "There was something else? Was he sick, Jack?" Suddenly some of the pieces of the puzzle fell in place. She remembered the last conversation she had with her uncle with a sickened heart. She felt like the chair was pulled out from under her, like she was falling.

"Cancer," Jack said flatly. "Pancreatic."

"Oh," she let out as a sigh through pursed lips. She digested what he said for a full five minutes. She recalled her recent encounters with her uncle, his sweetness and eagerness to make amends. She thought of his many phone calls she had ignored the past few weeks. Her mind raced through recent conversations with others and their lack of surprise at his death. It occurred to her that everyone must have known; certainly Olivier and Rosa. Jack was surprisingly level-headed over the loss of his best friend. They had all been preparing for it. Only she was surprised.

"I'm only telling you this because something occurred to me last night," he said at last, interrupting her thoughts. "So I went back over the original docs on the contract and I called Paul this morning. He faxed me a copy of the medical exam required for the key man policies on Clarence."

Syd sat silently with her hands in her lap. She was too preoccupied with her own pain to connect the dots. At the moment she didn't care what he had discovered.

"I think the medical report was tampered with," he said. "It gave your uncle a clean bill of health in January."

Syd was jarred alert. Her mind raced through the implications.

"So you think the policies were taken out on a man who had very little time to live?" she asked. Jack nodded.

"But you stand to gain from it, Jack. How do I know you didn't know about it before the plane accident?"

Jack threw up his hands. "I know how this looks, Syd. And I was in a terrible place, and I was not a good friend to Clarence at the time. I was furious with him. For years I watched him wallow in some kind of miserable self-pity, hardly getting excited about anything. He stopped going to Argentina. He gave you up for lost. He was beginning to lose interest in the winery, for God's sake. I wanted him to just sell the damned thing and move to South America. Maybe find a woman and retire. Hell, I would have encouraged him to go back to those people in Argentina who made him so miserable in the first place. Anything but waste his life around here in that dark mood all the time."

"Sure. You had his best interests at heart," she mumbled.

"I did, Sydney McGrath," he said defensively. "I always have. Clarence made sure that the premiums for that policy were paid out of the escrow funds. The other policy was let go, or so we thought. He was looking out for me. Of course, I have to come forward with the information I have now. My suspicions? It's insurance fraud, at the very least."

"Noble," she said in a hollow voice. "Fraud *and murder*, by the way."

"I very much doubt that," he said, his throat choking on the words.

"You think it was suicide?"

He nodded. "That was his plan. When it got too bad." He looked miserable. An old man disillusioned. Syd was disgusted. She could hardly drum up empathy for him, in spite of his self-pity.

"The autopsy report says otherwise," she said quietly.

She got up to leave, reaching the door before she turned around. She suddenly remembered the look of despair on Jack's face when he greeted her outside Clarence's hospital room months before. It was clear he had been crying in the palms of his hands. He loved her uncle and was trying to make amends by telling her about the potentially fraudulent medical report. She turned to look at the sad man, who sat with slumped shoulders at a cheap desk in an ugly room.

"You were a good friend to him, Jack." She walked out and closed the door quietly behind her.

Chapter 21

She pulled into the drive, almost running into the Sheriff's cruiser as it was turning out of the driveway. She pulled over and rolled down her window.

"You took off in a hurry," Jim said from beneath a mystifying pair of dark sunglasses. Syd felt more intimidated than she had earlier.

"Yeah, I went to see Jack again."

"Yup, I knew that." He drummed his fingers on the outside of the car door. Syd hated not being able to see his eyes. She scanned his face for cues. He spoke in a clipped tone but waited patiently for her to continue, drumming his fingers as both cars idled.

"Did you find Alejandro?" she broke the silence with more truculence than she intended. She found herself sinking under the oppression of Jim's authority and judgement, all played out in a nameless tune through thick fingertips tapping on the cruiser door. She felt like a guilty teenager.

He turned to look at her blankly. "Yup." He jutted his jaw forward. Syd figured he was angry. At her.

"Syd, I need you to listen to me. This is a murder

investigation. And I'm only now beginning to figure just what kind of people we're dealing with." He spoke quietly, his voice flat, but Syd could hear the condemnation sifting through the deep gravelly baritone. "You need to leave this to the police."

"I thought you wanted my help." she said, sounding more childlike than she intended.

"With the will, yes. But we got through that, and now I need you to stay home, okay? Just stay put."

"But I got a new lead on–."

"Stop!" he said through tight lips. He took off his glasses and leaned through the window, looking her square in the eye. "Syd, whoever did this to your uncle is dangerous. This is murder we're talking about. You will not interfere in my investigation. It's *dangerous*." His piercing blue eyes wore an expression that she had seen too many times in Charlie. Somehow she found it less intimidating. She found it patronizing, and it made her angry.

She leaned in to her open window and met his eyes. "Well, maybe you should investigate insurance fraud." She raised her eyebrows slightly and jutted out her jaw, nodding slightly. She stepped on the accelerator and passed him with more gas than she should have, leaving the cruiser in a cloud of dust.

She parked hard in the gravel, got out of the car, and slammed the door behind her. Her boots crunched the gravel up and down the length of the car several times as a white fury worked its way up her chest and into her throat. The frustration she felt with Jim transferred into a rage over the unwitting cloud of silence she was subjected to by her loved ones.

Why hadn't anyone told her? Why was she left in the dark?

She stormed into the house and yelled for Rosa. She had been with Clarence for years, but only recently had she been making him fresh juices every day. She certainly knew all along. In fact, Rosa thought Clarence had committed suicide. And she avoided Syd all last week. Syd slammed her way through the house, screaming Rosa's name. She ended up in the kitchen again, where her fury gave way to a lunatic rage. She picked up a pitcher drying on the counter and threw it against the wall, taking great pleasure in the smashing of ceramic shards skittering across the floor.

Rosa was not around. The house was empty, which left her

raging screams dampened to ineffectual tantrums by the indifferent walls and furniture. Syd felt smothered by ambivalence. It was like a nightmare in which she screamed as loud as she could, but no sound came out of her mouth. She was alone in her rage, and instead of feeling the fire burn out she was maddened by it. Who else knew?

She flew out the door and half ran up to the winery. The huge doors were closed, and she wrenched her shoulder flinging it open with a furious jerk of the handle. She yelled inside the dark winery, rushing into the black room filled with wine aromas and CO2. The distinctive smell caught her, and she stumbled back onto the crushpad. Even her delirious rage was tempered by the threat of the noxious gas, and she gasped for breath in the fresh cool air outside the winery. She stood a few moments with her hands on her knees, sucking in air and working to find traction in her rage.

"Deep breaths. Deep, deep breaths," she snarled to her knees. She wasn't sure if she was freeing her lungs of CO2 or fury. She paced the concrete with hands on her hips, mumbling to herself in a raving mantra.

After a few minutes of deep breathing, she found herself throwing her arms up wide to open her chest for air. She cleared her head while she took in the peaceful view of the river, the mountains, and the vineyards. The silent rolling countryside and the picturesque house held a kind of mesmerizing serenity that calmed her pulse. The place was a balm for her fierce anger and fresh wounds. She forced herself to take in the view and calmed down. She began to feel foolish and relieved that no one actually witnessed her tantrum. Still, she wanted some answers, and her anger was not extinguished. Her eyes caught the small Airstream trailer across the property.

Syd's feet seemed to move on their own as she made out a light on in the trailer. She tried to inhale deeply as she marched downhill and then up through the northern side of the vineyard. When she reached the trailer door, she felt in control of her anger enough to manage a civil conversation. She knocked.

Olivier opened it immediately. He was not surprised to see her. In fact, he had been waiting for her. He motioned her inside.

"Would you like some tea?" he asked politely. He ran his

hands through his hair self-consciously and flattened his shirt. He was clean-shaven and he smelled like cinnamon and sandalwood, but his eyes looked tired and worn. He seemed much smaller here in the trailer.

"Yeah" she answered gruffly. She sat down at the small table and watched as he started the electric kettle and searched for mugs and a teapot. The little trailer was well kept, which was a recent change. Syd had spent a good deal of time in the trailer many years back when she and Alejandro had their summer fling. Alejandro had been staying in the trailer as an intern, and he kept it in the state of disarray one might expect from a 22-year-old bachelor. While it was under Alejandro's care, the original linoleum floorboards were always sticky with spilled beer. The window blinds were mysteriously tangled and the few flat surfaces of the trailer were buried deep under stacks of mail and empty beer bottles. But now the vintage trailer was getting some gentle care. A small toolbox sat on the counter, and Syd noticed that one of the cabinet doors was resting on the bench at the table opposite her. The small trailer felt warm, and she saw the tiny space heater down the alley near the curtain by the bed.

"The trailer looks nice," she said, trying out her voice again.

Olivier nodded. "I have been working on it." He picked up the cabinet door on the seat and began to screw the hinge back into place.

She watched him silently as he methodically worked the screwdriver. The kettle whistled softly and he stopped to pour the water into the pot. He loaded a tea strainer full of loose-leaf tea from a canister. He finished screwing in the last hinge while the tea steeped, carefully putting his screwdriver back into the toolbox. He placed the toolbox in the upper cupboard above the small stovetop. He brought two large pottery mugs to the table with a bowl of fresh cream from the tiny fridge and sat down opposite her. A fabulous Darjeeling aroma filled the space around the small table. Syd felt herself sink into the bench cushion, and let the smells and the warmth of the trailer embrace her.

They sat drinking their tea together without looking at each other. She was still very angry, but she began to wonder how much she could justify being angry with him. She hadn't even known him before Clarence died. She had little right to feel betrayed by him withholding information about his death. He owed her nothing, really. And yet he sat patiently, waiting for her to speak. She began to feel embarrassed and pushed her mug forward in defeat. She was ready to go.

"Don't you have something to say to me?" he asked. He looked her square in the eyes. "You looked so angry up in the winery."

Her heart dropped like a rock. "You saw me?" she asked, covering her face with her hands.

"From the window here," he said. "I have a perfect view of the winery from this window." His face was placid and non-judgmental. Syd felt oddly reassured by his acceptance of her behavior. He seemed to expect her outrage and seemed to almost respect her passionate breakdown. Still he had witnessed a very private moment of unraveling, a moment that she would have never indulged in had she thought she was being watched.

She pulled her mug closer. She was staying for a while. She needed a moment to figure out what she needed to say.

"You are angry with me?" he asked.

Syd nodded reluctantly.

"I would be too." He stared into his mug.

"Why would you be angry at you? What do you think I'm so angry about?" She felt a bit of the fire stir up in her chest.

He threw his hands up. "*Everything!* I am here. You must share it all with me or go against your uncle's wishes. You don't know who I am or why I'm here, and I take half of what is yours. And you think that I may have killed your uncle. How could you *not* be angry?" He shook his head emphatically. Syd noticed the outburst was spiced with an accent she hardly heard before.

"I do not think that you killed my uncle."

"The police do."

"You're not in jail, are you?" She used a dismissive tone she sometimes threw at Marcus. "And I'm not even close to processing my inheritance or the will or any of that. I want to know why you didn't tell me he was sick."

"Ah. *That,*" he said with a sigh.

She nodded, growing angrier at his relief, which she felt

trivialized her feelings about something so important. “Yeah, *that!*” she spat.

“I told you. I made a promise to him. Clarence made me promise not to tell you.”

“Well, he's dead now. And you *still* don't tell me?”

“I made a promise,” he said, as if it explained everything. “But I am relieved that you know now.”

“Excellent. Great. I'm happy to make things easier for you.” She knew her sarcasm was childish but she was too frustrated to keep it in. He sat patiently, waiting for her next question.

“Why didn't he want me to know?”

“He wanted to talk to you in person. Here. He wanted to tell you after you had come to the winery and helped with crush. He wanted you to come because you wanted to, not because he was sick. He wanted us to meet. He had a plan to explain it all to you.” He reached over the table and drew her hands together in his. “I am so sorry, Sydney. His plan was romantic and good and noble. He wanted to make amends with you. He wanted to give you your dreams back. It was his sole purpose in the end.”

She pulled her hands away, feeling her anger morph into something more terrible in her chest. A deep dark hole inside her began to draw in her rage. She wanted to be angry; she wanted to lash out at this stranger cooing her most precious and deepest wishes to her when it was too late. She wanted to hit him in his beautiful, empathetic face. Instead, she got up slowly, holding a piercing sharp lump in her throat.

“Well, it was too late,” she said. She retreated from the table and saw the box on the small trailer couch. It was an old Danner shoebox stacked on top of a carved chessboard.

“That’s mine,” she said quietly, pointing at the box as she stepped out of the trailer.

Chapter 22

Syd awoke early the next morning with a hangover. She hadn't remembered drinking so much the night before, but she had very little to eat during the day and she had nearly finished a bottle of her uncle's library reserve, a Rhône style blend. She was unable to get up out of bed, which added to her wretchedness but she decided to deal with her nagging guilt for sleeping in and letting Olivier and Alejandro do all the punchdowns another day. Besides, she was still really pissed at both of them. She imagined them glancing meaningfully behind her back all last week while she continued on ignorantly. And she imagined that they must pity her, which infuriated her even more. Really it would be the only empathetic thing to do. She pitied herself, lying in bed, despising herself for not answering her phone all those times she saw his name on her caller ID. She had ignored him for many weeks, while he was dying. And she had denied him his last wishes in doing so. Because she was mad at him, indulging in her own juvenile vanity. *Because she had been right all along and she wanted to rub his nose in it.*

She lay in bed for hours, falling in and out of a haunting sleep filled with strange images and a mood of despair. She wanted to hide in her dark room forever. She woke up from time to time, alarmed at the heavy presence of shame and guilt, which were so much more consuming than the grief she felt the past week. Grief was a numbing pain; a full body shadow of senses and a hollow hole in her chest. Grief was painful in a steady, weighted way, but this new feeling was excruciating. She had never felt the burden of such shame. She had known loss before. It was like a worn old blanket in a way; a relic of childhood memories with faded details and only wispy emotions coloring the present. But shame was entirely new to her. And she deserved all of it.

Her phone sat on the nightstand and vibrated loudly for the fifth time, dragging her out of a fitful sleep. She wildly flung her arm over to the table to shut it off, but she answered it instead, her guilt over not answering phone calls overtaking her.

"Hello?" she said in a hollow voice.

"Hey, Syd," said Charlie. "Where have you been? I've been trying to call you all morning!" She sounded exasperated and relieved.

Syd's mouth was dry and she couldn't find her voice.

"Syd? You there? Are you okay?" Charlie asked, sounding more alarmed than ever. Syd's reply sounded more like a grunt than words.

"Where are you?" Charlie yelled into the phone.

"Bed." Syd croaked. She wondered if her throat was swollen shut.

"Are you sick?"

Syd reached for the glass of water on her table. It was full, but she didn't remember filling it up. She drained the glass. "I think I'm okay."

"Uh, jesus, Syd. You sound terrible. I can't get down there today. I've got Michelle's magazine launch to go to. I'm so sorry, but they'll have my hide if I bail."

"It's okay. I'm okay, really." She vaguely understood that she was making Charlie more worried than ever.

"Listen, I'm going to be there tomorrow. Thursday morning, right?"

"Okay. He had cancer, Charlie." Her voice sounded thin and lost.

"Who had cancer, baby?"

"Clarence. Clarence had cancer. Clarence had Stage IV pancreatic cancer." Charlie was silent. Syd waited, feeling her throat close up again. "Charlie?" she choked out.

"Yeah, I'm here. Fuck, Syd. Fuck."

"Yeah, and I ignored his calls." Syd squeaked out of a dangerously closing throat. She gasped for air and sat up to catch her breath. Her eyes darted toward the door. The light in the crack beneath the door had darkened. Syd pulled her legs out from beneath the tangled sheets.

"Do me a favor, Charles? Bring me some clothes." She pressed her phone to end the call and shuffled over to the door. Whoever was there before had gone.

~

Syd stayed curled up in bed for the remainder of the afternoon. Her visitor had left some water and a bottle of Advil, which she swallowed down over a sore throat every few hours. Her head throbbed and every joint hurt. She vaguely wondered if she was more than just hungover. She may have manifested a flu in her wretchedness. She slept fitfully, wandering in and out of strange dreams and painful awakenings. She preferred the strange surreal dreams of sleep to the purgatory of waking and the slow remembrance of her current reality.

Later, after a bizarre dream of waves churning in an endless sea, she awoke abruptly in the darkened room and shot up in bed. Her head throbbed, and she saw stars swirling around her head. She braced herself with her arms and lay down gently. She did not want to pass out again, even if it was on her own pillow. As she lay trying to hold on to consciousness, she smelled food and some other soothing aroma. Tea. She turned her head and saw a plate of hot buttered toast and mug of steaming tea next to her. Someone was looking after her. She vaguely remembered her conversation with Charlie on the phone. But it wasn't Charlie taking care of her; she was in Seattle.

She gingerly sat up in bed and propped herself up on her pillows. She reached for the hot mug of tea, held it near her face, sipping it occasionally. She noted that her sinuses were blocked and she had a sore throat. The steam from the tea helped her breathe easier, but she felt her lungs rattle and wheeze with every breath. Her head was another story.

"Great," she said out loud. She had come down with some kind of bug; a cold maybe. It was the bane of every winemaker and sommelier. She was utterly useless without her ability to smell properly, and during Crush it was a detrimental occupational hazard. She was even more useless to Olivier now. She felt herself sink into the sheets a bit, the weight of fresh shame bearing down on her. She savagely bit into some of the toast, and tried to wash it down with hot tea. Chewing the toast strangely amplified in her stuffy head and she hardly heard the voices in the other room above her chewing. Male voices talking softly. She stopped chewing and strained to catch bits of the conversation. Maybe three of them? She swallowed hard, her painful throat protesting. They were at the table in the dining room. Their conversation was intense, but not heated. She caught a trilled high-pitched voice through the walls fading in and out. It was Rosa. She must have been walking in and out of the kitchen. She listened harder for the sound of soft footsteps walking between the rooms. Syd inhaled in rasps, feeling weight in her lungs. She wanted to get up and see what was going on, but she also wanted to hide in bed. *Hide*. She realized she was embarrassed to show her face to whoever was out there. Rosa had known about her uncle's cancer. She stayed and took care of him while he was ill. And she must have known Syd had stubbornly stayed away. Olivier had told her that her uncle was holding on just to see Syd back at home. He was waiting for her to forgive him and move on, and she ignorantly and foolishly held on to her juvenile pride, as if she had all the time in the world. What really shamed her was that she truly had no plans to visit the winery at all that fall. She intended to forgo the drive down to the Gorge until after Crush. The intention was a deliberate punishment, a direct defiance of what she knew Clarence wanted. How could she face Rosa now?

She threw back her mother's quilt and pushed herself to the side of the bed with unexpected effort. She was fueled by guilt and curiosity that couldn't sit still any longer. Her feet found the cool wood floorboards, and she pushed herself up with her hands. She was dizzy and her entire head throbbed, but she held herself steady and found she could stand well enough after a few moments. After finding her bearings she gathered her jeans and a sweatshirt and slowly dressed herself with difficulty. She felt wretched.

She shuffled out into the kitchen only to be greeted by a cast of staring eyes. Jim and Olivier sat at the table, while Alejandro and Rosa stood in the kitchen doorway, their low and somber conversation having ground to a halt. They watched her approach to the table in slow motion with their mouths open.

"*Oh, mi hija!* You look awful!" Rosa said. She floated over to her and gently held the back of her hand to Syd's forehead. "You are burning up!" She turned and hurried off to the kitchen.

Syd shrugged and squinted at the men sitting at the table.

"What's going on?" she asked, sounding hoarse and foreign. Olivier got up and guided her to his chair. He stared at her with alarm.

"You are unwell?" he whispered with furrowed brows.

"I think I'm hungover," she said thickly, straining to smile.

"You have a fever," Rosa interjected. She said the *v* in a softened *b* that made Syd smile. She slid a thermometer into Syd's mouth. Syd sat at the table with the others staring silently at her, feeling foolish and childlike with the thermometer poking painfully under her tongue. A moment later the table bulged strangely in the middle and started to move like boiling mud.

Rosa took the thermometer out of her mouth. "104," she said loudly. She clucked her tongue and padded into of the kitchen. Syd glared at the faces in the room through glazed eyes. The light was harsh and the men looked like caricatures of themselves. Jim sat stoically with his hands folded in front of him. His face was waxy and stern, and yet his emotion was seamlessly buttoned up, only revealing itself in the crease of his eyes and his knit brow. Olivier looked slight and impish next to Jim, his chiseled face contorted with genuine concern and surrounded by a halo of dark curls. Alejandro stood with his hands knitted over his rounded belly, patiently waiting with feigned placidity. All three men were fighting their own battles to hold it together and figure out the next step. Syd observed and noted each man's inner workings like geared clockworks. They watched her for what felt like an hour, but which must have been only enough time for Rosa to return with a bottle of Tylenol.

"I took some Advil already," Syd said, brushing Rosa off with a drunken hand gesture. "Four."

Rosa put a cool washcloth on Syd's head, and leaned Syd back against her torso, cradling her hot head. Syd closed her eyes, knowing that the roomful of men were watching her surrender to Rosa's competent hands.

"Well, that adds to it," a deep voice muttered next to her. Was it Jim?

"Alejandro and me are his alibi, *también*," Rosa said. "So there is no need to take him." Syd could feel Rosa's voice vibrating through her sternum and through the back of her own head.

"I understand the position you are in," Olivier said. "But you need to trust me that I will not be leaving the winery, especially not now with Sydney feeling ill. I know you have your investigation. But I have a winery to run. She cannot do it alone now, most certainly." Syd pried one eye open to watch Olivier gesturing toward her, wincing.

Jim sighed. He splayed his hands out on the table. "In the meantime we will have the car looked into," Jim said. "I don't think I need to tell you how important it is for *you two* to stay put. I have to get over to the hospital and get a statement. He's still in ICU. Rosa, you take care of her, will you? Olivier, it would be best if you leave the house and stay in the trailer."

Olivier nodded and turned sharply on his heels. Syd followed his boot taps as they left the kitchen and pounded a steady bass on the deck outside.

"Rosa, he may have an alibi, but you need to understand that this is a murder investigation. And potentially attempted murder, now." Jim raised his hand in protest before she could speak. "I don't want to jeopardize the winery, understand?" He looked up at Alejandro. "But this could be far more dangerous than we thought." Syd made out a subtle jerk of his head in her direction.

Alejandro nodded. "I'll stay in the house," he said.

Jim got up with a wrenching scrape of the chair and with a groan of his own. He leaned over and kissed Syd's hot head.

"See you later, kiddo. Drink lots of fluids. Charlie will be back tomorrow. Oh, she said to tell you that the Bahamas are lovely this time of year." He shrugged.

The room suddenly felt like a window had opened when Jim Yesler left them huddled around the table. Rosa had been holding her breath and let out a deep sigh, while Alejandro sat down in Jim's empty seat. Syd tried to work out the last five minutes of conversation through her delirium. She realized her entrance had been timely and that her current state of health may have saved Olivier a trip to sheriff's office. She also noted that Alejandro and Rosa were still not exactly on Olivier's side. Although they both genuinely liked Olivier – she was certain they did – she recognized a new degree of mistrust among them.

"Who's in ICU?" she asked.

"Shhhh, *mi hija*," Rosa answered, caressing her forehead.

"No, Rosa! What happened? Who's in ICU?" She shrugged off the cloth on her head.

"Jack Bristol," Alejandro said. "He was in a car accident. His brakes went out on Highway 141 and he went off the edge. His car was fifty feet down. It was held up by trees. He was lucky. It's a 300 foot drop to the river."

"Jesus, is he okay?"

"He's in ICU. Doctors say he'll be alright."

"When did It happen?" she asked.

"Last night, around 8," he said. "Jim came to ask about Olivier's whereabouts last night. Both Rosa and I saw him here. He was here all day. Jim thinks the car was tampered with. The brakes or something. Or maybe the computer."

"So why does Jim think Olivier would want to harm Jack?" she asked.

"No idea. But he seems to have a reason. Jim doesn't trust him, that's for sure."

"Jack doesn't either," Syd muttered. She thought about Jim's gesture toward Alejandro, suggesting that she may not be safe from Olivier. She felt her cheeks growing hotter. "But I do. And so do you two. And Clarence did as well." She swallowed hard, feeling less pain in her throat now.

"But maybe we are wrong?" Rosa whispered.

"Rosa! When we last talked you thought Clarence

committed suicide."

"I talked to Jim," she said, wincing and clearly ashamed.

Syd felt her heart sink at the sight of Rosa's doubt. Rosa had defended Olivier to Jim, but Syd knew Jim had planted a seed of doubt that frightened Rosa to the core. Her maternal protection could allow her to distrust in a way that she would normally never entertain such ideas. Rosa's instincts were golden, and Syd could always count on Rosa to see right through anyone and sum up their true character. Rosa spent her lifetime in flash judgments of people based entirely on micro-assessments inferred from subtle gestures and body language. She could quickly distinguish liars from truthful people. She could find the darkness in a mild-mannered visitor with a polite handshake. Rosa was an excellent judge of character, and yet she had allowed Olivier to enter her inner circle. It bothered Syd to think that even Rosa might have been wrong about Olivier. Had they all been wrong about him?

Syd straightened her back in her seat. "I have to see Jack," she said. She steadied herself on the table.

Alejandro jumped up while Rosa held her shoulders firm. "Not such a good idea, Syd. You have a fever. You need some rest."

"It is after nine and the hospital is closed to visitors," Rosa said. She knew Syd would respond better to the facts than with concern for her well-being.

"Nine at night?" she asked, confounded at the loss of time.

Alejandro nodded.

"Are the punchdowns done?" she asked.

Alejandro looked out the kitchen window with wide eyes. "Being done right now, I think."

Syd shuffled over to the window and stood next to Alejandro. They watched Olivier opening the doors to the winery pacing outside while he waited for the gases to be purged. His silhouette entered the lighted space and disappeared inside. Syd imagined the light as being like a large set of teeth and the red doors as lips devouring Olivier as he stepped inside.

"George fighting the dragon," she said. Alejandro stared at her before helping Rosa get her back into bed.

Chapter 23

Syd awoke to drenched sheets in the wee hours of the morning. She had broken the fever in a sweat and found herself lucid, hungry, and thirsty. She shuffled out of her room in the darkness and made her way to the kitchen. She turned on a nightlight, got a glass of water from the faucet, and opened the fridge door. She grabbed a half-wheel of triple cream cheese and a jar of homemade olives, the kind that Clarence cured in oil and salt. There was no more bread in the house so she rummaged and found some large, flat rosemary crackers.

She sat down at the table in the dark and ate. The old mantle clock downstairs faintly chimed four just as she was finishing up. She contemplated getting another dose of Advil since her throat still hurt when she swallowed. But instead she sat, feeling the food make its way through her esophagus and into her stomach. She imagined the wee microbes of her gut flora working its way over food, rejoicing in its first meal in a few days. She thought maybe she still had a fever. She felt more than a little guilty that the troops had mustered in her defense and she had taken such lousy care of herself. She vaguely remembered the details of the conversation last night, not quite trusting her memory.

She had many delirious dreams that day and she wasn't sure which thoughts were delirium-induced nightmares and which were real. Maybe she had dreamed the entire episode? Maybe Jack Bristol was fine? But then, Rosa would not have put her to bed and Alejandro would not be downstairs asleep on the couch. She couldn't have imagined all that.

She got up carefully and shuffled over to the kitchen sink with her plate. She didn't bother to turn on a light. She turned to grab some ibuprofen from the medicine cupboard when a light outside caught her attention. It was a flash of light, actually. She stared out into the darkness for a while, searching for the light to return. There was no moon and the cloud cover made it unusually dark. She was about to turn away, convinced she had imagined it, when a flash of light shined right beneath the kitchen window. She recoiled instinctively and hid behind the curtain. She could just make out a figure squatting next to the window peering into the downstairs' family room. She watched, holding her breath. She could hardly make out the form but saw that it looked like a man of medium build. He was dressed in black. Oddly, she didn't feel scared. Instead a force bigger than fear rose up from her stomach in a wave of heat. Her heart pounded in her ears and she felt a burning in her cheeks. She clenched her fists tight. It was anger.

Suddenly, she heard a door slam downstairs and a man yell. She ran out onto the deck in a wave of cold air and stopped at the top of the stairs, straining to see what was going on. She could only hear it; a man yelling and the prowler sprinting with surprising speed up the gravel road to the winery. The chase seemed to continue up into the vineyard, from what Syd could tell. She heard crunching strides fade to silence. She made her way off the deck in the pitch black night, gingerly finding the road in her bare feet without making a sound. She headed for the gravel drive. She stopped dead in her tracks when she heard steps approaching her. The sound of wheezing gave him away.

"Alejandro?" she whispered hoarsely.

"*Chinga madre!* What are you doing out here, Sydney?" He grabbed her under her arm and practically lifted her off the ground, dragging her upstairs.

"Who was that?" Syd whispered again, standing on the cold

deck in her bare feet. Her armpit hurt from Alejandro's grip.

"How the fuck would I know?" he answered hotly, abandoning his usual decorum. "Motherfucker can sure run fast. Lucky for him too." He held up something that Syd just noticed. She squinted and made out a baseball bat in the darkness. "Here." He thrust it in her hand, still trying to catch his breath. "Stay here, too. *Don't follow me, Sydney McGrath.*" He snarled and abruptly ran off into the darkness.

Syd stood in her bare feet and black silk nightie on the cold deck, holding the bat by the handle. She searched blindly in the direction Alejandro had headed. She felt her stomach sink when she realized Alejandro had taken off in the direction of the trailer. She couldn't remember it ever being so dark. She couldn't see five feet in front of her. A cold shiver ran up her spine, and the hair on her head stood on end as she waited the longest two minutes of her life.

The violent shivering began to take over her body. She was about to go back to the house to get a better weapon and a coat when she saw a light turned on from inside the trailer. Syd could make out movement and watched the door open and close. A half a minute went by before the door opened and closed again. She heard running footsteps as two men sprinted across the vineyard and up onto the deck.

"Sydney?" Olivier whispered loudly.

"Here."

He slowed down and jogged toward her, stepping on her bare feet when he reached her.

"*Ouch!*" she yelled, shoving him off of her toes.

"So sorry. Where did he go? Which direction?" He squeezed her arm hard with his right hand. He held something long and hard in his left hand. Syd reached out and felt the cold shaft of a shotgun.

"What are you doing?" she asked in her raspy voice. "You can't go after him with *that*."

Alejandro pulled up next to Olivier, breathing hard.

"He was in his trailer," he said, sounding relieved.

"Of course he was, Allie," she said. "And now he wants to go all cowboy on us and chase down that peeping tom." She tried her best to sound flippant through her chattering teeth as she pieced together the last five minutes. Her head throbbed as she worked out the potential disaster these men could ignite if they ran off on a chase into the dark. She grabbed the cold muzzle of the shotgun and ripped it out of Olivier's hand. He was caught off guard and let go of it. She stepped back and glared at him.

"Inside, now!" she said, feeling her way in the dark with her feet. She carried a bat in one hand and a shotgun in the other. They stumbled into the kitchen a moment later. Alejandro reached the light switch first and flipped it on. They looked around at each other, all round-eyed and alert, like animals ready to sprint. Syd stood in her loose black nightie, stiffly holding the shotgun and bat out like ski poles. She was the first to crack a smile and break into a hysterical laughter, stabbing pain in her lungs. The men joined in as they succumbed to the vaudevillian scene they all had played out.

Olivier stood shirtless with pinstriped pajama bottoms and tall muck boots. His curly hair was piled to one side of his head in bedhead fashion. Alejandro was fully dressed in jeans and a T-shirt, but he was still trying to catch his breath. They glanced at each other as their laughter subsided.

"Well, if I'm going to get beat to death, *that's* certainly the way to go," Alejandro said, smirking at Syd. He stole a long look at her nightie. She was still freezing and covered in goosebumps. Her nipples were stinging and hard in her flimsy nightie, a fact not unnoticed by either men. Syd jabbed him in the belly with the bat.

"And you'd be the one to go, slowpoke," She jabbed at him again lightly. Alejandro grabbed the bat from her.

Olivier's smile disappeared and he gingerly took the gun from her, eyes averted. She instinctively covered her breasts with her arms once her hands were free.

"Should we call the police?" Olivier asked.

"Jim would be here in a heartbeat," Syd said, sadly. "I think he's gone, whoever it is." They nodded at each other. "I think I've had enough of Jim today," she added, glancing meaningfully at Olivier. He looked more than a little relieved. "Could you please stay in the house tonight?" she asked, locking eyes with him. She wasn't helpless and he knew it. It was a request for forgiveness and partnership as much as it was a request for help. At least she'd make it clear she trusted him.

He nodded back at her. "It is nearly morning," he said.

~

They got little rest for the remainder of the night. Adrenaline pumped through Alejandro, more as a reminder of his failed chase than out of fear or excitement. Olivier lay awake on a couch upstairs, methodically musing over the events of the evening and his growing entanglement with Clarence's legacy. He kept his ears alert and tried to clear his mind of all thoughts. He froze at the sound of every moan or creak in the old house. But he was pretty certain Syd was correct in assuming that the prowler was gone. He only wished he had been there. He was confident he would have caught up to the man in a foot race. The thought of clearing his name of all suspicion was enough to send a thrill of bitterness through him along with a vein of hope. At least Syd knew that he wasn't a danger to *her*. As much as he would have loved to catch the prowler, he was sure that the thick detective might not make the obvious connection to Clarence's murder or the lawyer's accident. It was another thought made him shudder. He did have to give credence to the Sheriff's notion that Syd was in danger. The prowler may not have been after something, but *someone*. And, of course, he stood to gain the most if something happened to Syd. His heart sunk deep in his chest and his eyes remained wide open until daylight.

Syd returned to her warm bed after taking more Advil and drinking a hot toddy laced with whiskey. She lay awake for a full hour in a state of calm contemplation. The Advil worked its magic and Syd found herself drifting off to sleep and a liquid emotional landscape. She had intended to stay awake and listen for the men stirring, which she knew would come soon enough, but sleep caught her in a web of strange disjointed images. The night sky glowed with a light purple hue, reminding her of her drive along Highway 14 at sunrise a week earlier. Her dreams flashed with images of Clarence in his Austin Healey, smiling at her. The eastern skyline filled with orange and purple clouds churning like the boiling gases of Jupiter. And then it all disappeared and she was somewhere else. She found herself walking in the wet grasses of the vineyard in a luminous green light. She walked toward the trailer, which glowed with the same green light. She climbed onto the step and opened the door. She looked up into the bullet-shaped interior at an odd angle. Olivier sat at the table looking down at the manila envelope in his hand. He looked up at her with sad eyes. She stepped inside and closed the door behind her. She turned and saw that Olivier had come to stand next to her, wearing only his pajamas bottoms. He held his hands out in front of her, with palms up and fingers splayed. He showed her the backs of his hands. She stood mesmerized as he slowly moved his hands to her arms and softly ran his fingers up to her shoulders. She felt an immediate thrill and stepped closer. He kissed her neck softly and muttered words she couldn't make out. His lips moved to her face and she kissed him back with her own lips and tongue. His taste was intoxicating. They floated to a soft couch, where she held him in a tight embrace, still kissing him with restrained urgency. He moved on top of her, and she smelled him with every taste. His body was light, and she sensed him more in the heaviness of his aroma than his physical being. She kissed him with more urgency as her arousal grew, and his scent overwhelmed her. The aroma moved heavily around her neck, like a gaseous rope creeping around her throat, choking her. She moved instinctively and pushed him away from her, gasping for air and arched her back to open up her chest and lungs. Olivier was suddenly gone and she looked down at her own naked, writhing body. She thrust her hands up reflexively, but found no resistance, in spite of the heaviness of the scent surrounding her. She thrust her legs into the cushions of the couch and managed to turn on her side enough to inhale a lungful of air. Her head awkwardly angled and pulled in oxygen as if from an invisible straw. She slowly relaxed and breathed in to gain control of her frantic mind. As her thoughts cleared, she felt her hands tingle and the hair on her arms stand up. She called out to Olivier, who had vanished in the dark. She found she could move her head and look around the room while her body was paralyzed. She called out for Olivier again and the room answered in a hazy green glow. She could make out a figure in the darkness, fading in and out. She called out again, her voice never leaving her throat.

The figure stood over her, menacing. The room had gone

dark, and the figure was silhouetted in pulsing green light. She squinted to make out his face but a light fog rose between them. She reached up to touch his face, but he effortlessly dodged her. She felt him smirking at her gesture. When she tried to get up and reach for him, she found herself pinned at her shoulders to a white-sheeted bed. She looked and saw that she was pinned at the shoulder with large black nails. Red stains of bright red blood oozed from her wounds through a white linen nightshirt she now wore. The pins held her tightly with a force greater than gravity, like a pithed insect. The room grew into a bright white luminescence as she looked back up at her assailant. She could almost make out his familiar features before she saw a large pillow looming over her face. She felt the slow smothering of cool cotton on her cheeks and lips, suffocating her silent screams. She couldn't breathe...

A moment later she sat up in bed, gasping. Her hands and arms were flailing in the air as she struggled out of her dream, pushing away a pillow that wasn't there. She gulped for air and then calmed herself, slowing her breathing. She looked around the room and saw soft morning light filling it with a kind of shocking serenity. She moved her hands along the bumpy surface of her mother's quilt while her eyes searched frantically for traces of her nightmare. She was surprised at the tears that streamed down her face, uncertain if they were from terror or some kind of emotional release. She swallowed hard and felt the sharp familiar pain in her throat. She reached up to touch her throbbing forehead but couldn't tell if she was feverish. She pushed herself up shook and her head, forcing the sinking feeling from her mind.

She was wiping the tears from her face with the quilt when Rosa crept in with a mug of tea. She smiled at Sydney, but then noticed the distraught look on her face.

"Ah, *mi hija*," she cooed. She bent down and kissed her forehead. She reached for Syd's head instinctively. "Still you have a fever?"

"I'm not sure. I just had a delirious nightmare."

"Bad dream?" Rosa asked. "Fevers show us the future." She got up and padded out of the room.

"Great, thanks, Rosa!" She yelled sarcastically out the door.

Leave it to Rosa to imbue a nightmare with ridiculous superstitions. Of course, it was only a dream. Yet she felt her shoulders instinctively. No holes, no blood. But the memory of the dream filled her with concern. She blushed as she recalled her vivid make-out session with Olivier. Rosa came back into the room with a thermometer. She thrust it hard under her tongue and Syd yelped like a wounded puppy. Olivier stuck his head in the doorway a moment later.

"Alright in here?" he asked.

Syd pulled the covers up to her chin and nodded, fervently with the thermometer in her mouth. She felt like an iconic Norman Rockwell painting or a cartoon of female foolishness. Rosa clucked her tongue.

"She's still feverish," Rosa said. She yanked the thermometer out of Syd's mouth. "101. Not bad." She turned and scuttled out of the room.

"But not good for running around outside half-naked in the freezing night," Olivier said under his breath with piercing black eyes.

Syd shrugged and avoided his eyes. He was wearing the same pinstriped pajama bottoms from the night before and a bathrobe she recognized as belonging to Clarence. His scent wafted over to her in a sensuous invisible net. She shivered beneath the quilt. He sat down respectfully at the end of the bed.

"I think we need to tell Detective Yesler today," he said.

"Yeah, I think I'll see him later this morning. Charlie's coming back." She fiddled with the quilt.

"Okay."

"So maybe you could stay in the trailer for a bit longer?" she asked, looking vacantly out the window.

"If that's what you want," he spoke softly through tightened lips. He rose from the bed, sighed and lightly shook his head before he left the room. His gesture wasn't lost on Syd.

Chapter 24

Charlie showed up around noon to find Syd bundled up on the couch in the living room with her laptop balanced on her knees. She was perusing the hordes of condolences posted on social media.

"Man, you're playing up this damsel-in-distress thing," Charlie sneered. She opened an IPA and took a long draw. She had sprawled herself out on a worn leather club chair, long limbs dangling over the arms.

"Yup. Not easy either. You try giving yourself the flu."

"No need. I can do the same thing with alcohol. Hair of the dog." She took another thirsty swig.

"Sooo, how was it?" Syd asked. She slammed her laptop closed and sat up, anxious for Charlie's account of the magazine launch party.

Charlie told her tale of the event with her usual flourish, sparing no ridiculous moment or person. The evening had proven to be excellent fodder for Charlie's voracious appetite for human folly. Her account had the women dressed in stupid clothes and even more ridiculous shoes, decked to the nines in the latest of Seattle's mock New York style. Their desire to stand out was only outdone by a stronger desire to conform. Thus, Charlie said, they all looked the same; "like emaciated stick insects in the same clothes and hairdo," she said. Only a few women stood out as true individuals, and they were the type who drew Charlie like a moth to light: the inked-and-pierced, Fluevog-wearing, steam-punkish outliers. Charlie spared these types the sharp edge of her tongue, although she couldn't refrain from gently mocking the cliché these outliers represented. Of course, their friend Michelle was spared her vitriol since she was tasteful, elegant, and gracious as a host.

"There's nothing new under the sun," Charlie sighed despondently, the high from her salacious soliloquy waning. She drained the rest of her beer. "I just wish you were there."

"Sorry. I've got a murder to deal with," Syd answered glibly, regretting her words immediately. "I would have loved to have been there." At the moment the idea of spending the evening at a soiree like the launch would have been like heaven. It would be such a reprieve from her life here, a romantic return to an innocence she longed for.

"It is so ironic, Charlie. You know we felt so superior? We were so cynical up there in Seattle. We were city girls who knew *everything*. We could watch it all with a sense of superiority and witty running commentary. And we could make fun of our country bumpkin life here. But really, our time up there was the innocent time. Here, in the vineyards and trees, it's the sleepy winery that's the real world tragedy."

"Dad told me about Jack," Charlie said softly. Syd expected a glib comment from Charlie, if only to lighten the mood, but Charlie seemed to agree with her.

"I'm going to go see him today," Syd replied.

"Maybe you should wait until you feel better."

Syd remained silent and chewed on her lip for a few minutes in silence.

"Marcus gives his love," Charlie spoke with trepidation, changing the subject.

Syd looked over at her and sighed. "Yeah, I haven't called him since he left. He's left some messages," she smiled sheepishly.

"Uh, some?" Charlie teased.

"Okay. Lots. And about twenty emails. Facebook and texts.

All of them asking when I'm coming back."

"And when is that, exactly?"

"Not for a while. I have to see out Crush. I promised."

"Dad wants me to talk you into leaving."

"Yeah, he got really pissed off at me the other day. I went to question Jack after he kind of told me to leave it alone. He thinks I'm interfering, but he's wrong. Besides, I gave him information about the insurance fraud. He thinks its Olivier. But after last night he should think differently."

"You mean the break-in? Dad's there now, and I don't think it helps Olivier in any way whatsoever." Charlie said incredulously.

"There was no break-in. Just a prowler. He was *looking in* but he never *got in*."

"What are you talking about, Syd? He got in and made a huge mess! The entire office is trashed." Charlie frowned at her.

"Where? What office?"

"Jack's office. I was just there. I met up with Dad before I came here. The place is a mess. Whoever did that was obviously looking for something."

"When did *that* happen?" Syd asked, jumping up off the couch.

"Not sure. I heard a White Salmon cop say it was early this morning. A cruiser went by the building at 5 am and everything was normal. But the window was broken, and it would be hard to miss. So it must have been after 5 am." Charlie narrowed her eyes at Syd as she paced the floor. "What were you talking about, Sydney?"

"Here. We had a prowler here last night. A Peeping Tom, sometime around four." Syd paced in front of the couch, picking at her lip.

"Fuck, Sydney. Does Dad know?" Charlie was growing angry with Syd as she spoke. She wore a formidable scowl that held an uncanny resemblance to Jim's.

"No, we decided not to call him," Syd spoke hesitantly. It seemed like such a rational decision last night, but she could see how Charlie might disagree. "He was gone and he wasn't coming back. Alejandro chased him off with a bat."

"Right, because a murderer twice over is going to be put off by a farmer with a bat." Charlie hissed back at her in a flat voice.

"Anyway, Olivier was here the entire time. And he was in his trailer when the prowler came, so that certainly was *not* him. And he was here in the house when Jack's office got broken in to, if it happened this morning." Syd spoke rapidly, ignoring Charlie's angry glare. She took a deep breath and processed what Charlie said.

"Twice over?" she asked.

"Dad's convinced that Jack's car was tampered with. Something to do with the ABS. There was a recall on the car for brake failure related to the ABS, but Jack had it fixed a few months back. And after this morning there's no question."

Syd sat back down on the couch, picking at her lip. Jack had a meeting with Paul about insurance fraud the afternoon before his accident. She had seen him that morning. It felt like a lifetime ago, but it was really only two days earlier. She couldn't believe she had missed the connection herself. She had been preoccupied with her own grief over Clarence's illness, and then her own feverish virus had been a big distraction. Still, she felt like an idiot. She took a deep, raspy breath and fought off the feeling of losing the air in the room.

"I have to talk to your dad. Did he talk to Paul? Did Jack talk to Paul? Jesus, Charlie. I think I could have prevented Jack's accident. I told your Dad, but I didn't realize what it meant." She got up again and paced the room. Charlie sat still and watched Syd cover the same stretch of floor for a few minutes.

Explain it to me, Syd," Charlie said in a forced calm voice.

Syd talked through the details of her conversation with Jack; about the will and the key man insurance policies. She explained Jack's suspicions that the medical examination required by the policy would easily have revealed the cancer in Clarence's body in the full body scan. The exam was only six months before Clarence's plane crash and the hospital stay that revealed a blood test replete with Stage IV pancreatic cancer diagnoses. The exam had been a forgery, or at the very least it had to have been tampered with.

"But the cancer could have not shown up in the first exam, right? I mean, it didn't really show up on the autopsy report. But

Dad says that's just because they determined cause of death from laryngeal spasm, or something like that." Charlie's voice trailed off at Syd's expression.

"Maybe. Seems unlikely. But that doesn't explain Hans's behavior after the deal went sour. He continued to pay a hefty premium on a policy, even when he had no vested interest in Clarence as a business partner. It doesn't explain why he lined up a buyer so quickly for the winery. Or why he lined up a winemaker. Or how he planned to cut Clarence out of ownership for the corporate buyout. The point is that if Jack blew open the policy as fraudulent, Hans Feldman had a good deal to lose. Again."

"So why would he kill Clarence then? I mean, if he knew he had pancreatic cancer, he could have just waited it out, right? Pancreatic cancer moves fast." Her voice faded again as she sensed her friend's discomfort. Syd sighed despondently.

"Maybe he grew impatient. It would have been an expensive premium. Clarence was 64, after all."

"But Jack had a policy too?" Charlie asked.

"We can pretty much rule him out now, I think." Syd frowned while her fingers worked over the skin on her lips. "But he had the medical report in his office, you know." She explained that he had mentioned that he had found something in the report that might be incriminating. "And then...and then he gets in a near-fatal car accident and his office gets broken into."

They were interrupted by a polite "uh-hem", the sound of Olivier clearing his throat. He stood stiffly near the kitchen table at the end of the room, holding a beaker of red wine. "Sorry to interrupt."

"Hey, Ollie!" Charlie said, she turned in her chair and greeted him with more warmth than Syd expected. At least she had convinced Charlie of Olivier's innocence for the moment. Syd could just kiss Charlie sometimes.

"Hello, Charles," he replied, flashing a genuine smile. He had lovely ivory teeth in a wide mouth. Syd felt a jolt in her stomach. The room was quiet for a moment, and Syd looked down at her fidgeting hands. Olivier remained on the other side of the room, as far away as possible. Charlie glanced at each of them quizzically.

"You might want to check this," he offered the beaker to Syd, striding over to the sitting area with natural feline grace.

Syd took it and sniffed. She swirled it and sniffed again. She tasted it and handed it to Charlie, who did the same thing. Charlie grunted.

"Is it stuck then?" Syd asked.

"Yeah, I think so. The temp has dropped to 17 degrees Celsius, and the Brix stopped moving at 8. It's been the same for two days."

"It's got some hydrogen sulfide on it. When was the last time it was fed?"

"At 12 Brix. It was 26 degrees, so I didn't want to bump it too much. Clarence always wanted the ferments on the cool side."

"Yeah. Whole berry?"

He nodded.

"I'd expect it to stay the same at different levels of temperature and alcohol when the berries break down. But the skins should all be broken at 8 Brix. Hmm. And it has had a vigorous punchdown? Is this Tempranillo?"

"Yes and yes." He smiled at her, not unimpressed. It wasn't easy discerning a varietal during fermentations.

"So maybe we should bring in a coil and heat it up? I wouldn't worry too much about the hydrogen sulfide. Tempranillo can throw a lot of it, and this vineyard is prone to reduction anyway. We have another tank of this, right? Same yeast? So we can grab some juice from the other tank too."

"I agree," he said, nodding at everything. He turned to leave, but just before he reached the door he turned back. "It's good to have you back, Charlie." He smiled another heartbreaker grin at her and left through the kitchen door.

Charlie feigned a gunshot wound to the heart, keeling over. "Fuck, if that ain't one of the most gorgeous villains I've ever known," she said in her best Scarlett O'Hara accent.

"Yeah," Syd muttered, faking disinterest.

"So what's up there?" Charlie prodded, wearing a shit-eating grin.

"Nothing. What are you talking about?" Syd skirted her look as she got up and made her way to the kitchen. Charlie followed her in hot pursuit.

"Oh, now I *know* there's something there. Don't tell me you slept with him. Fuck, Syd, did you sleep with him?" She squared Syd's shoulders in the middle of the kitchen, looking down into her face.

"*No*," she said grumpily at her friend, and wrestled out of her grip. Charlie had only been back for ten minutes and she was already annoying her. She fumbled around in the cabinet for the Advil. Her head hurt.

"Okay, okay. But you like him, Syd. There's something there. I know it. You could cut the tension with a knife."

"There was tension because I asked him to stay in the house last night after the prowler, and then I asked him to leave this morning." she snarled at Charlie in exasperation.

"Why'd you do *that*? Seems kind of like it would be handy to have a guy around when there's a murderer on the loose." She meant to be funny, but it came out too close to the truth for comfort.

"I wanted the room for *you*, actually. I was going to ask you to stay here with me. Think of it like a Bahamas vacay, but on a budget." Syd tried to remain calm, but knew she looked scared.

"Okay, consider me moved in." Charlie turned her friend around and gave her a long hug. "But really. There is something there, right?" She smiled slyly at Syd as she moved out of the hug.

"Okay. I had a sex dream about him last night. Really, it was only a make-out dream. But it was the hottest thing that has happened to me in years." She blushed through a shy smile.

"Oh my, oh my. What would the honorable and smitten Mr. Marcus think about that?" She smiled maliciously.

"Fuck, Charlie. Don't tease me. I've got to work with this guy. He's a stranger, and for all I know he could be my brother." The thought came out before she could stop it. The shock hit Charlie like a slap in the face. They stared at each other for a moment.

"Wow. But it's not incest for me, right? Cause if you aren't going for that, then I am!"

Syd punched her square in the shoulder, harder than she ought to have. Charlie yelped and swung back with a wild haymaker in slow motion, replete with sound effects. Syd's frustration gave way to a violent snort of laughter, while Charlie continued with her vaudevillian slapstick. Syd buckled over, gasping for breath as Rosa padded into the kitchen.

"You should have been Lucy," she sneered as she passed through to the living room, parting with a hard slap on Charlie's butt.

Charlie stood upright and yelped in pain, holding her ass as she stared at Rosa. "*Ouch!* What is it, beat on Charles day?" She bellowed at Rosa and stole a glance at her audience. Syd was still wiping tears from her eyes, bracing herself up with one hand on the counter. She wheezed with laughter.

"Best medicine, babe," Charlie said, looking rather proud of herself.

"What? Kitchen shadowboxing?" Syd choked out between giggles. Charlie leaned against the counter with her lanky legs crossed at the ankles and her arms crossed around her chest. She watched Syd thoughtfully while she recovered in slow gasps.

"So we need to talk to dad, Syd," She said quietly.

"Yeah." Sydney nodded. "Is it logical to think that *our* prowler was the same person who broke into Jack's office? Am I just connecting the dots in a weird fever-induced conspiracy thing, or does this make sense to you?"

"For once, Syd, I think your conspiracy theory's right on. Have you ever talked to this guy Hans Feldman?"

"No. I shook his hand at the memorial. He was smug. Actually, it was more like contempt." She frowned.

"What do you mean?"

"More like he was being dismissive. You know the type. I'm a girl and I'm not worth his time or energy. And he's annoyed that he has to perform the whole "I'm sorry-for-your-loss" thing. Like he was bored too."

"All that in a handshake?"

"Yeah." She answered defensively. "He certainly wasn't sorry for my loss."

They looked up at once, up at the sound of a car pulling into the gravel driveway. Charlie stepped over to the window and peered out.

"Speak of the devil," she muttered.

"Hans Feldman?" Syd asked, alarmed.

"Dad, dummy," Charlie said. "We better make him some lunch before we tell him about your prowler. He's much nicer with a full belly. He'll be barking mad at you, Syd."

Chapter 25

Jim Yesler was less mad than he was concerned. His face revealed a paternal panic that instantly melted Syd's defensiveness as she told him about the night before. She began to feel that she may have been foolish to think that she could handle it by herself. Still, she hated the feeling of helplessness that came with admitting that she shouldn't be making judgment calls on her own safety. It railed against her very being to think she should acquiesce to the notion that she was frail or helpless, or in need of male authority. She felt that inviting Alejandro and Olivier into the house to provide protection was tolerant enough. She was frustrated by Jim's patronizing tone, in spite of his obvious concern. It was a characteristic of men like Jim to seem charming and well-intentioned while still emitting a gentle brand of sexism. The Grand Protector. Charlie had issues with her father's paternal coddling all of her adult life, and it was often a topic of conversation between them. Her father was her only parent for a while, and he cherished his daughter above anything else in the world. Instead of showing his love by assuming she could do anything, be anything, or even take care of herself, he preferred the role of knight in shining armor. The magnanimous hero. And wherever there was a male hero there had to be a damsel in distress.

Charlie put up with it well enough. Syd secretly felt that Charlie liked it in a way, although she complained about it. But Syd grew up with a different kind of male parent. Clarence always felt that Syd was the champion. Syd was the strong one; the hero of her own story. Clarence had no such delusions about male strength and female fragility. Syd was an equal to her uncle in times of tranquility and in times of duress. She was suddenly quite grateful for her uncle's firm grasp of reality, in spite of the prevailing sexism that surrounded them now.

Syd pondered her own capabilities while she listened quietly to Jim's admonitions. She instantly forgave him for his poor assessment of her judgment. But she also knew that she was right. She would have to figure out a way to help Jim feel the way she needed him to feel while continuing to piece together the events of the past week. Jim was the investigating Sheriff on the case of her uncle's murder. He had the legal authority to investigate her uncle's death and follow all of the leads in the case as he saw fit. But she also knew that she had the moral authority to find out who killed her uncle, and that Jim's declaration that she had no business in the case was just plain wrong. And she couldn't help but feel it was sexist as well.

Jim sighed. “And why are you smiling?”

“Oh, just something Clarence used to say to me. “When a man is born in a soup he can't help but smell like the broth'. Something like that.” Her voice trailed off. Charlie raised her eyebrows at Syd. She had heard Syd say the same thing to her during their conversations about Jim's patronizing ways. Syd had encouraged her to forgive her father for his sexism since he was a product of his culture, in spite of his best intentions.

“Well, I'm just saying that you two girls should come stay with me for a while,” Jim said, frowning at them. He looked a little hurt at the inside joke they shared.

Charlie stepped forward and patted her father's hand. “Sorry, Pop. We've got a slumber party planned. Pillow fight and all.”

“But we’ll call you if another Peeping Tom shows up,” Syd said.

“Immediately. Call me immediately.” His voice rang with

authority. Charlie rolled her eyes at Syd.

"Was there any way to tell if something had been taken from Jack's office? Uncle's papers were in the safe, I think. I remember Jack getting the files from the safe." Syd changed the subject, trying to appear only casually interested.

"The safe was unopened, if that's what you mean. Too heavy to lift. Papers were everywhere. The file cabinet was dumped out on the floor. The place was a mess. Becky said it would take weeks to figure out if anything was missing. And she said she hardly knew what Jack had in his files anyway." Both women followed his eyes to his large hands. Jim drummed his fingers on the table.

"Jack's awake, by the way," Jim said. "I'll see him later."

"How is he?" Syd asked.

"Doctors say he's good. He's somewhat alert now. Still having trouble remembering things. The head injury was about all the damage. He has a broken rib or two from the airbag but nothing life threatening. He got lucky." He paused. "Is Mr. Ruiz around?" Jim finally asked. Sydney grew instantly alarmed at the formal use of Olivier's last name.

"Olivier? Yeah. He's in the winery fixing a stuck fermentation. Why? You know he was here last night. *In the house*. And he was here the entire day of Jack's accident. I should think it was obvious."

Jim held up his hand to stop her. "I've just got some questions about his airplane. And why he said he arrived a full month after he had. In *June*. Two days before Clarence's accident."

Syd's jaw dropped reflexively, in spite of herself. Jim took out his notebook and read from it.

"He flew in on June 23rd at 4 pm on a flight plan from Northern California. He flew out June 25th, plotted to British Columbia. His extended flight plan follows all the way from Argentina. He had been making his way up north for two weeks. But he stopped here and went for a joyride in Clarence's plane on the 24th."

Syd and Charlie were silent.

"The point is that he lied. He said he arrived in July. Syd, he lied about when he came and he was *in the plane* the day before your uncle's accident."

"Uncle's will wasn't changed until after the accident," Syd said. "Olivier had nothing to gain at the time. This does nothing but explain to me why Uncle left him the plane."

"Or the accident was how he bullied Clarence into changing the will," Jim offered.

"Really? Have you actually spoken to this man? He's utterly heartbroken."

"Sydney, he has a point," Charlie interrupted. Syd glared at her.

"Pretty risky way to get someone to change a will," Syd said. "His plane was in a full stall for Christ's sake. He only recovered it at the last second. You've got to be kidding?" She put her hands on her head in exasperation. Charlie caught her eye with a meaningful look, urging Syd's complicity. She was up to something. Syd frowned, a bit confused. Charlie raised her eyebrows at her and Syd relented. "Okay, fine. Olivier's up in the winery. Go question him again."

"He's far more of a flight risk, literally, now that we know he has a plane here," Jim said. He shoved his chair back, gathered the dishes from the sandwiches the girls had made for lunch, and walked over to the sink. He paused while he held open the kitchen door. "You girls stay out of trouble." He glared at Charlie. He turned and walked outside, his boots scuffing against the deck.

"That old fart's too smart for his own good," Charlie half-whispered.

"What's going on, Charlie?" Syd asked.

"Buying time," Charlie said. "We both know that Olivier's in the clear. Dad mostly knows it too. He's just eliminating him, I think. He doesn't like the idea of him, actually."

"So why are we buying time?" Syd asked.

"I wanna know what's in Jack's safe. Don't you?"

Chapter 26

Syd scrambled out of the shower and brushed her teeth before she could digest what Jim had said about Olivier. She considered if he could have had something to do with the plane accident. He was here in the Gorge right before the accident and he had been in Clarence's plane. The fact that he knew how to fly added to his potential guilt. Syd looked out the bathroom window up to the winery. The doors stood open, and Jim had not emerged yet. Olivier might be sweating it out under Jim's pointed questions. Jim could be overbearing, and Olivier had let on that he really didn't enjoy his interrogations.

Charlie waited in the living room while Syd was in the shower. She was pacing when Syd entered a moment later, her hair still wet.

"About time! Sheesh, let's go." Charlie grabbed her jacket, keys, and a bottle of Uncle's private reserve. Syd was wearing some fresh clothes that Charlie had brought down for her.

"What are those?" Charlie asked, looking over Syd in her favorite pair of jeans.

"My jeans. Why are you looking at me like that?"

Charlie reached down and pulled the waist band of her

pants. They gapped a full four inches from her stomach.

"What can I say? Grief is a good diet."

"And you hardly ate your lunch. Great. Now I have to add nursemaid to an anorexic to my list of Sydney nanny tasks."

"I've got the flu, for fucksake." Syd said in her defense, but she secretly noted the concern in Charlie's voice and made a vow to pay more attention to her appetite. Charlie strode out the door in her long strides, with Syd trotting to keep up. They looked in the direction of the winery for signs of Jim as they climbed into Charlie's Jetta. In spite of everything, Sydney felt a thrill of excitement, just like she used to when she and Charlie were out on a naughty adventure.

"Okay, so what makes you think you can get into that safe, Charlie?" Syd asked.

Charlie coasted stealthily down part of the driveway, trying to not make too much sound in the gravel.

"I talked to Becky this morning," Charlie said.

"Yeah? I'm pretty sure Jim did too."

"Mmhmm. He did. Only Becky doesn't like him much. She thinks Dad looks down his nose at Jack. She's right, of course. Anyway, she didn't say much to Dad. And she was pretty shook up. I'm thinking that after hours of cleaning up she may have recovered a bit and she might have more to say to us girls. Especially for a bottle of that reserve. It's her fav. She had four glasses of it at the memorial." She turned and winked at Syd.

~

They discovered Becky on the floor behind Jack's desk ten minutes later, muttering to herself. As usual, Charlie's instincts were dead on. Becky had been stacking loose papers all morning, dealing with insurance agents and police while trying to field the calls for Jack from concerned clients. She looked completely frazzled.

Charlie poked her head in the door. "Hey, Becky. Need a hand?" She had her hands in her pockets and sauntered in the room with her stiff-legged nonchalance that made Syd nearly burst into a fit of giggles. Her lack of subtlety was lost on Becky.

"Oh, hi," Becky stammered. "Uh, I guess I could use a hand." She brushed a stray strand of hair behind her ear. She was nearly the same age as Syd and Charlie and had gone to school with them. But she adopted the dress and mannerisms of local females that made her appear a decade older. She wore a nondescript office wardrobe heavy with gray gabardine and polyester, Dansko clogs, and wild-printed socks. Her hair was done in a new style; long layers with a few colors of a fresh weave striping her flat-ironed tresses. Her nails were fake acrylics with a french polish and rhinestones. She wore heavy makeup and her eyes were streaked with tear-stained mascara.

Charlie plopped down on the ground next to her like a long-limbed six-year-old and began sorting papers. Syd slid inconspicuously into the room, feeling uncomfortable about pumping Becky for information while she was in the middle of a crisis.

"Hey," Syd said shyly.

Becky sat up on her heels. She squinted with suspicion, glancing at them one at a time. "Okay, you two. I didn't just fall off the turnip truck. What's up?"

'So...we were wondering," Charlie began. Syd stood by the doorway, feeling disgusted. She felt bad for Becky.

"I had a prowler last night too, Becky," Syd said, speaking before Charlie could continue. "Some guy peeping into my house. I think it happened before he got here. The same guy, I think. Alejandro, our foreman, ran after him with a bat and scared him off. I'm not sure he would have stopped at burglary if he had gotten in either, by the way. He wanted something that your boss had, and something that I have too. So it must be something to do with Clarence's will. Or his papers. Either way, we need to know what's missing here."

Becky listened blankly. She sat still, digesting the thought for a full minute in silence. "And what about Jim Yesler?"

"The Sheriff is on another trail right now," Charlie said. And then she whistled a cliché version of non-complicity, rolling her eyes.

"Right," Becky said, smiling. She crawled over to the safe a few feet away and worked the dial. "Jack put all of Clarence's stuff back in here the day before yesterday. I shouldn't do this, by the way. Client privileges and all that. But I'm guessing you're the client now." She opened it and pulled out a stack of papers and files, including the red file of Clarence's will. "So I don't think the guy got what he was looking for. The safe wasn't opened."

"Cool, thanks," Charlie said, sounding more than a little surprised that the plan was working.

Syd rifled through the stack carefully. "Well, don't just stand there, help me," she said with mock exasperation. Both women jumped to it, grabbing files and poring through them.

"What are we looking for?" Charlie asked.

"A medical report for insurance," Syd said. "It would be separate from the policy, I think. In a fax? Somewhere in this stack, maybe?" The women searched the entire stack of files, looking through the papers page by page after a cursory look didn't pan out.

"He said it was here," Syd said more to herself than to the women in the room. She jumped at a knock on the open door.

"Sorry if I'm interrupting anything, Becky," said Paul Renquest, appearing suddenly at the door. "Hello, Sydney. I've got the glass guys on for the insurance claim. We'll get this window fixed up by close today. Geez! What a mess."

"Hey, Paul," Syd said. Just then she had a sudden epiphany. "Hey, Paul. Did Jack have a chance to meet up with you on Tuesday?"

"Yup. As a matter of fact, he did." His expression changed at her question and he looked tight-lipped and reluctant to talk to her.

"Something about a falsified medical report?" she asked.

He threw up his hands in defense. "Now, Sydney. I'm not really at liberty to discuss–"

"Come off it, Paul. I met with Jack on Tuesday morning. I know all about it. Do you have it?"

"Yup," he said, giving up.

"Have you contacted Feldman?" Syd demanded.

Paul shook his head.

"Oh, God!" Becky interjected. She covered her mouth with her hand.

"Oh God what?" Charlie asked, alarmed and having trouble keeping up.

"Hans Feldman. He came by right after you left, Sydney.

He was really pissed off. He left the office screaming at Jack."

"Did you tell the Sheriff this?" Charlie asked.

"I've been a little preoccupied," Becky answered cagily.

"Preoccupied?" Charlie raised her voice.

"And," Becky took a deep breath, "and Jack told me not to tell anyone about it."

"Why on earth would he tell you *that*?" Charlie demanded.

"Because Jack was a benefactor in the same life insurance policy," Syd said. "That could potentially incriminate him too." Paul nodded silently.

"But if he didn't know about it–" Charlie asked.

"Doesn't matter," Paul said. "He'd stand to gain from it and it would look really bad for him. We were trying to find a legal way to clear Jack before investigating it. The signing doctor is conveniently on sabbatical and I haven't heard back from the medical director."

"Okay, so Hans Feldman came and threatened Jack," Charlie said, hands on her heels and sitting back. "Any other nefarious plots unfold that you aren't telling us about?" She glared at Becky, who was sinking into the mauve carpet.

"A phone call," Becky said. "A man asking Jack if he had all the files for Clarence's will, I think."

"Jack told you this?" Charlie asked.

Becky looked guilty again. "I listened in from my desk. I don't usually do that, but after Hans threw something at Jack and stormed out...he threatened him. I was concerned." She pleaded.

"Who was on the phone?" Syd asked.

"I didn't get on the line soon enough to hear. But he asked if Jack still had something. Jack said it was none of his business. The guy laughed and said it was entirely his business. Jack told him to go fuck himself. Called him a weasel. I've never heard Jack say anything like that before. Then he just hung up." Becky shook her head in shock, looking unglued. Charlie crawled over and put her arm around her.

"God, I'm glad you're a nosy bitch, Becky Sanford." Charlie kissed her on her forehead. Becky managed a meek smile.

Sydney sat on the ground, perplexed. "What did Feldman throw at Jack, Becky?"

Becky shrugged her shoulders. “This, I think.” She picked something up from the desk that Syd hadn’t seen earlier. Syd held out her hand. Becky gave her a small ivory figurine roughly carved into a female sitting in a chair. It was the white queen chess piece from an Isle of Lewis chess set.

“Feldman had opened a box that Jack had for him. It was from Clarence's will.”

Syd worked the piece in her hand, remembering the feel of the ivory in her fingers. The weight of it. A queen's sacrifice. She held it up to Charlie to see.

“Well, first I think Dad needs to pay Hans Feldman a visit,” Charlie said, looking pleased with herself.

Chapter 27

The women rolled back into the driveway, only to find a massive 18-wheeler blocking the road. Olivier and Jim were loading barrels from the semi into the back of the ancient winery flatbed truck, working together in silence. The 18-wheeler couldn't make it up the steep gravel road to the winery, and the forklift could not be driven on gravel. The ritual of unloading barrels and large pallets of bottles in the middle of the driveway had become a common event at the winery. The two women got out of the car and watched the men for a moment before Syd swung her leg up and climbed up into the container of the delivery truck. She started to roll out barrels wrapped in plastic wrap with the driver. She counted a dozen more with *Blackwell* written in blue marker on the plastic.

She rolled the barrels expertly, end over end. She stopped each barrel when it reached the lip of the truck, where she eased it down to the two men standing ready. Olivier grabbed the barrel end by the head, and Jim caught the other end as they took the weight off the trailer. They hoisted the barrel onto the flatbed behind them while Charlie righted it on the barrel heads in the flatbed. They managed to unload over a dozen barrels in less than ten minutes. Syd dropped down from the container onto the gravel, feeling dizzy. She steadied herself on the bumper. She looked up to see Olivier watching her with a frown. Charlie and Jim were glaring openly at each other, the silent hostility with which they worked for the last few minutes now in danger of breaking into a screaming match.

"I'll sign it," Syd said in an overly cheerful voice when the driver presented the invoice to the Sheriff. Apparently, the driver was as unnerved by the Sheriff unloading barrels as they were. Syd felt sorry for Jim for a moment, always intimidating people before he got a chance to show his sweet side. But at the moment, he wasn't exactly making friends.

She walked back over to the flatbed after chatting with the driver. There she found Charlie and Jim snarling at each other through clenched teeth. They were equally matched, as far as she could see. All three stood on the flatbed, working the barrels close together for the short ride up the gravel drive to the winery.

"I said to *stay out* of trouble, young lady," Jim growled as he butted the barrels closer together with demonstrative violence. Syd jumped up into the bed with them and timidly helped Olivier with the ratcheting straps.

"Face it, Dad. Becky wasn't going to tell you all this stuff. We *helped* you. Besides, you were too busy looking in the wrong place." Charlie stood with her hands on her hips. Olivier adjusted the barrels that Jim moved into place gently and in silence, keeping his head down.

"I would have taken her in for questioning if she wouldn't talk to me," he growled.

"Nice, because she deserves that. Her boss tells her to stay quiet and he nearly gets himself killed. And then her office gets trashed by some maniac. And what do the cops do? They take her away in a cruiser. And you wonder why the general populace loves ya', Dad." Charlie stared her father down, almost eye to eye.

"I would have asked her nicely," he sneered back at her, but he was losing steam.

"Right. Interrogating the victim is a nice thing to do." Charlie smiled, aware she was gaining the upper hand.

"Yeah, well I'm trying to keep you girls from being victims

too."

"Are there any girls here, Dad? Because as far as I can see, Syd and I are two grown women. We're in our thirties for fuck sake." Charlie smiled to soften the blow, but Jim looked truly beaten.

Syd finished tying off the loose end of the strap and patted Jim on the back. She suspected that Charlie had gained them enough ground to warrant their participation in the investigation for a few hours at least. Jim was crestfallen that his girls had accused him of being patronizing or over-protective. Syd guessed that Charlie would play it out as long as she could, but their time was limited. In the meantime, she would have to play along with Charlie and let Jim brood a bit. She stepped toward Olivier to help with the last strap.

"Why are the barrels so late?" she asked.

"The cooperage in Napa was behind. And then I postponed the delivery last week. I forgot the truck was coming today." He avoided her eyes and looked toward Jim.

"It's blocking the cruiser, at least," she smiled back at him. "And the way to the airport, in case you were planning on flying out of here."

Olivier closed his eyes and shook his head. "So the fact that I flew here and stopped for a day before I flew up north makes me a murderer?" He looked tired and weary. She regretted saying anything.

"I have no idea what to think, Olivier. I don't know anything about you. All that I know is that you're busting your ass to hold this harvest together in all of this chaos. And I'm grateful for that. I'm going to try to help more, I promise."

"You might have to. He asked me down to the station. I don't know what that means." he said, looking a bit lost.

"Well, Charlie just bought you some time. And I need help unloading these barrels."

"Okay. So who buys a forklift that can't go in gravel?" he teased, looking relieved.

"A man who's too cheap to trade in for a better model." she answered.

"Or one who's too sentimental to get rid of the one his

daughter painted."

"Niece," she said, correcting him. But she knew that he made the mistake on purpose.

~

After they unloaded the barrels up on the crushpad, they all stood around leaning on the barrels. Jim listened to Charlie and Syd recount the details of their conversation with Becky and Paul with surprising patience and interest. He entertained their theories with equal patience. However, he drew the line when it came to his visit to Hans Feldman later that afternoon. He was going alone. He made the girls promise to stay put. They had no intention of interfering with the questioning at any rate, so it wasn't difficult to comply, although Charlie made a show of it anyway. Syd was beginning to understand the complexity of the dance that Charlie could play with her father when she needed to. Charlie handled the man with deft manipulation, without compromising his feelings or best intentions. She managed to turn him around by the time he had left them, unconsciously bolstering his fragile paternalism with genuine affection. Syd marveled at their relationship.

After Jim steered his cruiser down the driveway, the women strolled down back to the house and rummaged through the refrigerator for beers.

"Do you think your dad will take him in?" Syd asked.

"Take who where?" Charlie asked, opening a beer and shuffling into the living room.

"Feldman to the Sheriff's station," Syd said impatiently.

"Oh. Maybe, yeah." She frowned again and plopped down onto the couch.

"At least Olivier's safe to do punchdowns tonight," Syd joked. "I'm so weak I might faint."

"Mmhmm," Charlie mumbled, sipping her beer.

"Okay, where are you, Charlie?" Syd asked.

"Something Marcus said to me last night," she said, pausing in thought as she sipped her beer. Syd waited patiently for Charlie to finish. "It's probably nothing. You should call him though. Maybe share your dreams with him?" she teased.

Syd blushed in spite of herself.

Chapter 28

Jim returned to the house frustrated. He and Charlie were discussing his visit with Hans Feldman at the table when Syd came looking for the voices that had awakened her from a nap. She had gone to bed that afternoon with a throbbing headache and a painful throat. She may have napped for a few hours. She woke up with a large pool of saliva on her pillow and a dry mouth. Her sinuses were as stuffed up as ever, and she had to breathe with her mouth open in her sleep. Jim and Charlie sat with plates, beers, and a few paper bags of food. Syd's mouth watered as she sat down with them. She was grateful for the burritos and spicy hot sauce from her favorite taco stand, compliments of the contrite man in uniform. Syd listened as she took a seat and loaded her plate. She popped the top off a sour beer.

"But can Han's wife give a real alibi?" Charlie asked between bites of a juicy taco.

"Yeah."

"But what if she's lying?" Charlie asked.

"Yeah," he answered, taking a large bite of his burrito.

They all sat chewing and swigging beers in silence.

"Does he know Paul's looking into the medical report

now?" Syd asked.

"I didn't say anything about Paul, but I can imagine Feldman has a clue. I kept our conversation to his visit to Jack. The threats he made. I didn't let on that I knew anything about the medical report."

"Did he tell you about the meeting in Ted's vineyard last Sunday?" Syd asked. "What was that about?"

"Yup. Another investment opportunity. And Jack's in on it too, you know. Same cast of characters as your uncle's takeover. Another buyout of a vineyard, plus the building of a winery this time. Feldman lined up the same buyer for a different opportunity up here. He seems pretty business savvy." Jim didn't mean it as a compliment.

"Another corporate buyout in a small AVA. They're going to own it all soon enough." Charlie spat out bitterly.

"Well, it certainly explains Feldman's need to keep that insurance policy," Syd said. "And maybe the urgency to collect. Maybe he needed the cash to fund the investment?"

"I haven't checked into his bank records yet. I've got phone records to check up on too. Airport records from Canada are slow coming." He shoved back his chair and gathered up the mess of wrappers and hot sauce cups. He left to throw away the trash and came back to collect the plates.

"Airport records?" Jim nodded at her through a scowl. Syd winced. "Thanks for dinner, Jim."

"Yup," he answered with a nod and disappeared back into the kitchen. The silence was heavy when he walked back in, his boots scraping the floor.

"You ladies take care tonight. Lock up." He let out a resigned breath. "I don't think it's a good idea to have Olivier in the house tonight, Syd. I agree that he's most likely not a threat to you, but I've been wrong before." He walked toward the kitchen door, clearly reluctant to leave. "Lock this behind me!" He jabbed his thumb at the deadbolt with a dark frown and closed the door behind him, his jaw set in a hard line.

Chapter 29

Her phone buzzed on the table. The vibration moved it into the beer bottle sweat collected on the surface throughout the evening. Syd glanced at the caller ID while Charlie and Alejandro snickered and exchanged knowing looks over their poker hands.

"Maybe you should answer that," Alejandro said for the fifth time that night. All of them knew it was Marcus. Alejandro's empathy obviously lay with the jilted lover, Syd thought to herself. But was she really jilting Marcus? She told herself that she was merely waiting until she had a better answer for the question that he asked in nearly every text and email and phone message. She didn't really know when she was coming home or even if she was coming back.

"I replied to his text earlier," she said defensively. But it wasn't much of a text; she had only written that she had been ill and she was feverish. She knew it was a lame excuse for her silence over the past three days. She wrapped the quilt tighter around herself.

"Go to bed if you're cold," Charlie scolded. She was annoyed at Syd's nose blowing and general sobriety. Syd hadn't felt much like drinking with them, and Charlie was well into her fifth beer. Charlie hated being in a room with sober people when she was tipsy.

"I'm not tired. I took too long of a nap," Syd answered, lying to them. Really, in spite of her big talk, she was too frightened to go to sleep. It was after midnight and she jumped at nearly every sound outside. She was questioning whether Charlie and Alejandro could offer much protection so far into their cups. She regretted the ban on Olivier, alone in his trailer out there.

"So how does a big white dummy like this Marcus guy get to hang out with our Syd anyway?" Alejandro asked.

"Tsk, tsk, Alejandro," Charlie said. "Marcus is a very important person. He teaches young people about wine distribution and marketing and stuff. And I've got a straight." She lay out her cards and reached for the small cluster of quarters and nickels.

"Sounds like an ordinary schoolteacher to me," Alejandro said, He shuffled again and pitched out the cards.

"Oh, no," said Charlie. "He rubs shoulders with all the biggies in the industry. He's the golden boy of Seattle. Friends with editors, critics, and somms all over. He was looking mighty fancy last night in his tuxedo. All the cheerleaders were fawning. He looked a little lost without Syd though," she added, thoughtfully. "None of his cronies were there really. The old guard was all sitting in the other room, and Marcus usually has a way in with Joe Donner. But he wasn't there either."

"Why no Joe Donner?" Syd asked from under her quilt.

"Oh, I wouldn't let him go until he finished his homework, Syd," she answered in a Mom voice. "How the fuck should I know?" The hyperbole was enough to fool Alejandro into a chuckle, but Syd knew Charlie was holding back.

"Joe would *never* miss a chance to hold court," Syd said. "That's interesting." Syd left the bait dangling and she watched Charlie squirm in her semi-drunk state.

"Marcus thought so too," Charlie broke.

"Why would Marcus think so?" Syd asked.

"Because Marcus said Joe Donner had called him the day before to see if you and he were going, that's why. He told Marcus he might do a piece on females inheriting wineries."

"Good timing. Three days after the memorial," Alejandro

said. "Wait a minute. Is that the Joe Donner I took a video of last winter? The one taking bribes from Francois for reviews?" He faked ignorance. "What a fucking weasel. Your boyfriend hangs out with *that guy,* Syd? Never mind. Don't answer your phone." Alejandro clucked his tongue in total disgust.

"Oh, that's right. I forgot you took that video," Charlie said approvingly, "right on, *ese*!" She gave Alejandro a high five, which he reciprocated in an elaborate secret handshake that ended with a fist bump and Charlie's wet fake explosion sound effects, which sprayed all over the table. Alejandro giggled like a girl.

"Great," Syd said, shoving herself from the table and shuffling into the kitchen. She was going to have to face her dark room alone, but not without one more dose of flu syrup. She looked warily out the window into the darkness.

"Yup," Charlie said loudly from the other room, her voice echoing throughout the house. "Do you know how Joe and Marcus got to be friends? Joe's dad is a mechanic. Joe grew up in a mechanic's shop. A few years back he helped Marcus in the school parking lot. Marcus drives a classic Jag, some old '60s model, but he's retarded with machines. Kind of useless all around, actually." She stole a look at Syd. "But Joe can fix anything. Anyway, Marcus and Joe have been buds ever since. Marcus helped Joe get his introductions a while ago. He helped him in his first level somm tests too. For a while they were inseparable. Total bromance. They hung out at ball games, shooting ranges, pool halls, and killing small animals. You know, guy things. Only they got cooler when Marcus started dating Syd. *Joe hates Syd.*" Charlie fake-whispered loudly.

"Yeah, well, Marcus has shitty taste in friends," Alejandro said.

"But if you ask me Joe couldn't have found a better friend himself. Marcus is obtuse and enjoys being flattered, and if Joe's anything he is a sycophant to the right set of guys. The frat boy types all hang out and stroke each other's egos, a circle jerk of male congratulation. And there's no better set than a bunch of male winemakers and somms. Joe wanted in on that. He went from a nobody to an honorary frat boy on Marcus's coattails. Marcus is the natural prince of the wine world, all easy and entitled. But Joe had to scratch his way into it all. And now he writes a syndicated column on wine. *Syndicated.* Someone recently told me he's one of the most read critics in the country. He's really risen to the top. I have to give him that." Charlie pitched her hand in and pushed the small pot of coins to Alejandro.

"By taking bribes for his scores," Alejandro muttered under his breath. Charlie sniggered and collected the cards.

"So why would he miss the launch then?" Syd asked, popping her head out of the kitchen. "He *is* the most ambitious man in the industry. Why would he miss that launch?" She pulled at the skin on her lip as she leaned against the door.

"And why was he at that meeting with Feldman and Bertrand the day Clarence was killed?" Charlie muttered under her breath to Alejandro. He shrugged, took a swig from his nearly empty beer, and frowned into his cards.

~

Syd slept for five hours without interruption in spite of her fears. She woke up early and realized instantly that she felt much better. Her head wasn't throbbing and her throat was only a bit sore. She was fully stuffed up though. She got up to make a Neti Pot to clear her sinuses.

The house was gray in the predawn glow when she crept into the kitchen to boil water for coffee. She passed Charlie, who lay wrapped up in a Hudson Bay wool blanket on the couch, her long limbs painfully tucked into her body, curled up like a frozen spider. She didn't want to wake Charlie after last night's attempt at guarding the homestead. Charlie needed as much guarding as she did, and she was looking worse for the wear after so many nights of drinking and worrying.

She made the coffee as quietly as possible, finding grinds in a Weck jar. She was grateful to make coffee without starting the noisy grinder and waking up Charlie. Clarence would often grind up coffee and put it in a jar to bring up to the winery for the espresso maker in the lab. He would drink small espressos in demitasse while working on lab samples, puttering mostly. He was always happy in the lab.

Syd ventured back into her room, yanked the quilt off of her bed, and wrapped it around herself. She shuffled out onto the deck with her steaming mug. She let her mind wander to images of Clarence sipping his coffee and managing titrations with one hand. He wore prescription safety glasses in the lab, which made his eyes look huge and buggy. When she was little she would sit on a random plastic crate marked with blue painter's tape as *tartaric acid* or *Potassium Metabisulfite* and watch him with awe.

Syd smiled unconsciously while her mind drifted into memories of Clarence. She hadn't thought about Clarence in the lab for a decade. Or Clarence's little rituals of making bread, or his habit of humming to himself while he worked in the garden with his tomatoes. She had spent so much time remembering those things that annoyed her. She had allowed herself to be consumed with resentment that tore a hole in their relationship. Now, she felt a dark hole in her chest while she wondered how a person could forgive herself for such a tragic mistake.

She wandered along the deck this way, lost in her memories and feeling safer with the dawning light than she felt the night before. The air was crisp and smelled of slightly rotting wet leaves. It was too cold to be outside in pajamas and a blanket, but Syd sat down on one of the Adirondack chairs and watched the morning come anyway. She could see her breath and she warmed herself by keeping her face under the blanket. She curled her legs up under herself, sitting like a ball in the Adirondack. She felt oddly like she was floating in a tiny dingy in the damp fog, an insignificant ball of fluff with a head cold. She was sitting perfectly still when she heard the shuffle of feet on gravel a short distance from the house, straining to discern friend or foe. She relaxed after a moment, and let herself breathe again.

She heard Olivier's approach and listened for him opening the kitchen door. She kept her head under the blanket. He went inside for a moment, presumably to get some coffee, and then came out again. He walked over to her and pulled a chair next to her. The creaking of the chair subsided as he got comfortable. He sat silently next to her.

She took several sips of the coffee she nursed under the blanket, warming her face on the steam. He sat silent and still next to her, waiting for her to say something. But she hardly knew what to say or think. She found herself in the rare position of being completely unsure of her instincts. She was usually confident in her judgments, but with Olivier she was constantly lost in a fog. She would rather follow her head and logically deduce her thoughts and behaviors accordingly. And if she did, she knew she'd likely agree with Jim. However, her instincts told her that his footsteps were not a threat to her. Her instincts told her he was here to help her. Her instincts told her he was perhaps her greatest ally. Still, the more she attempted to extricate him from her suspicions, the more he seemed to get tangled up in them. And he remained silent amid all of it. He worked in the winery and held her world together while she crumpled into a million pieces on a daily bases.

"Good morning," she said. Her muffled greeting emerged from beneath the quilt. He didn't reply. She waited for a response and poked her head out from under the quilt.

"Good morning," he replied, looking her in the eyes. He gave a succinct nod and turned to look out at the fog on the river.

"You're up early," she said, filling the uncomfortable silence. She felt rude and unaccommodating. She could just make out his faint scent, which mingled with the autumn air and the coffee. Her stomach grew nervous. He nodded again and sipped his coffee.

"It looks like it will clear up today," she said. *Oh, god! I'm talking about the weather!* She tucked her head back under the quilt, confounded at her awkwardness.

"It will be colder. We will need to heat up the winery," he said. His chair groaned with his shifting weight. She found it oddly comforting that he moved in his seat. She peeked from beneath the quilt.

"Are we pressing soon?" she asked. "How many ferments do we have left?"

"We will press today. The Zinfandel. We have thirteen tanks left to press off."

"How's the Tempranillo?" She knew not much could have changed in less than 24 hours.

"Too early to tell. Heat is on it now. I haven't been up yet this morning." He sounded weary.

"How long has it been since you had a day off, Olivier?" She grew more embarrassed at her self-centeredness. She searched her memory over the last two weeks and realized he hadn't stopped working the long hours of Crush since Clarence died.

Olivier remained silent.

"How long?"

"I prefer to work," he said quietly. He looked over at her. "I wake to find the distraction. And the work needs to be done."

"I should be helping," Syd answered, feeling the guilt hit her chest, and a sinking feeling in her lower lumbar.

"No," he said firmly. His voice startled her and he shook his head. "No, you have lost your parent. You need time to grieve. There is nothing more terrible than losing a loved one and not grieving. Or finding resolution."

"Grieving is one thing," she said in her raspy voice. "Resolution? I'm not sure I'll ever find that." She heard the words escape her mouth, but they were foreign and sadly bitter; a surrender to a reality she didn't want to admit to herself.

"You will have to forgive yourself, eventually. Clarence would have wanted you to forgive yourself. He certainly forgave you. He was optimistic that you would come around."

"But not in time," she whispered under her quilt. If Olivier heard her, he didn't let on. He cleared his throat.

"I have made a mistake. With you. I think I should tell you about my relationship with Clarence so that you understand. Clarence made me promise not to talk to you. He wanted to do it himself. I think he wanted to choose the story he would tell you. But my story is different, anyway. Besides I feel that you might trust me more if you knew why I am here."

Syd peeled the quilt down from her face and looked at him. He was tired but determined. He reminded her of Clarence when she was a teenager and they fought so much. Or more recently of Jim Yesler, trying to make his intentions clear to her and Charlie. She felt badly for these men who worked so hard to communicate their emotions to women they obviously cared for, but who ultimately misunderstood them. Deliberately misunderstood, in some cases. She felt another pang of empathy for Olivier.

"I trust you already, I think," she said. She would rather he remained silent for the moment. The morning was quiet and gentle, and the fog was more welcome than any clarifying sunshine might be.

He ignored her attempts to dissuade him. “I flew here in June, in my own plane. Well, it's my father's plane.”

“I know all this. Jim told me.” She tried again to silence his confessions. The peaceful reprieve of the morning started to slip away.

“But I wanted you to know it from me.”

“I explained to Jim that your joyride on Clarence's plane was coincidence, and that the will hadn’t been changed yet.” Olivier's eyebrows rose. He clearly had a plan of what to tell her, but he couldn't help his curiosity. “What did he say to that?” he asked.

“He said you could have used the accident as leverage to change the will,” she jeered back at him, making it clear how ridiculous she thought the theory was.

“Risky,” he muttered.

“That's what I said.” They stared out at the river, which was covered in an inversion layer of churning fog.

“I came here because I needed to leave my family for a while,” he began again, choosing his words carefully. “My father, to be exact. I left our winery right after Crush, last March. In South America our season is opposite yours here. I flew around the North region for a while before making it to Panama. I stayed in Panama for a few weeks. Then I made my way up to Mexico. I had to wait a while for clearance to the States. I spent a long time in Oaxaca City and then flew over to the Yucatan. In mid-June I flew into Texas and then flew up here for a short visit. My plan was to make it to Alaska and then come here for a longer visit. But then Clarence had his accident while I was in Canada and I came back here as soon as I heard, albeit two weeks late.”

“So you came back here then?” she asked, interested in spite of her plans to stop the confession.

“I flew back here. I stayed across the river for a while, never intending to intrude on the house here. I spent the days with him while he recovered. I helped with some of the winery tasks; some bottling and blending trials, and getting ready for Crush. But mostly we played chess and talked about wine and the past.” He ran his fingers through his hair, smoothing away the emotion that thickened his voice.

"And then he rewrote the will?" she asked. She knew he would be offended by the implication of her question. At least it would bring him out of his fragile emotional state and back into anger, she thought. She found his anger less jarring on her nerves.

He looked sideways at her, his mouth tight. "I did not ask for anything Clarence gave me. I did not encourage it. He begged me."

She nodded without making eye contact. They sat in silence for a few moments again. She found herself much more comfortable with a wall of tension between them than the intimacy of shared grief.

He cleared his throat again a minute later. "When Clarence found out that he was ill, he had a change of heart about the winery. Before, he was weary and tired of the politics and the business end of it, especially over the last few years. I think he was beginning to feel the futility of it all. He had worked so hard to build a winery, but for no plausible end. He had worked so hard . . . for a dream. So he decided to sell it. But then he found out about the investor selling it behind his back, and then he had his accident and then the cancer..."

"What do you mean he worked for a dream?" She sounded more defensive than she wanted. She was feeling bruised again over Olivier's knowledge of Clarence's intimate life, while she remained confused and in the dark.

"My mother," he answered, defiantly.

"Your mother?"

He nodded and kept his eyes on the river of fog. Syd's mind whipped around the details Olivier laid out before her. Clarence's mysterious entanglement in the Argentine winery that she had known about since childhood was always a source of intrigue for her. Her uncle was gone for many long visits to Argentina during her childhood, under the pretense of helping out at Crush during the winter months. He did this while their own barrels of wine silently struggled through winter malolactic fermentation in a cold barrel room. She and Rosa would enjoy long movie binges by the wood stove and eat Mexican food every night for dinner. Rosa became her sole guardian during those stretches of his absence.

The trips often seemed interminable, and Syd resented his time away from her. One of these longer visits was the impetus for a particularly ugly fight they had when she was sixteen. It was a fight Syd replayed in her mind so often that it morphed into a kind of dreamlike memory that she grew to distrust. But Clarence said one thing in that fight that stayed with her. He pleaded with her through her slammed bedroom door, "Aren't I entitled to some kind of hope?" She knew at the time that it wasn't a statement meant for her alone. Instead it was some kind of desperate query made to the universe at large. She was furious at him for presenting his fragile adult male wounds to her self-righteous teenage mind, however convoluted and mysterious they might be.

Now she sat picking the skin off of her lip. Olivier patiently allowed her to remain adrift in her memories, piecing it all together while he collected his thoughts.

"Are you Clarence's son?" she asked timidly.

"No," he answered after a moment of hesitation.

"But he loved her? Your mother?"

"Yes, he loved her. They were lovers. But I am not his son. I would have liked to have been. He was a good man. To her and to me." He sighed deeply and she sensed his raw sadness, "My father hated him, of course. Hated everything about him. His love for my mother. His love for me. His skill as a winemaker and his grief over your mother's death. All of it. My father thought he was weak and called him the–"

"What? What did he call him?"

"Something rude about his manhood. It doesn't matter. He is Argentine. Only, it is ironic."

"Were they openly involved? I mean, how could Clarence keep going back if your father knew about them?"

"Well, he didn't know, exactly. He only vaguely knew. And he denied it all anyway. No man of his upbringing and culture could be a cuckold. So he joked about Clarence being gay, and then he started to believe it. My mother was in love with Clarence. There is no doubt that she married the wrong man. She was young when she married and then very shortly after fell in love with another man, your uncle. They were discreet. But not so much that I didn't question it when I was young. My father is an obtuse chauvinist, mostly unaware of my mother as a human being. But I was very close to her when I was small, and I was aware of her emotions. I could feel her cringe at my father's loud voice at the dinner table or go to a distant place when he began a tirade on every trivial thing. I saw her light up when your uncle came to help at harvest. She woke up completely then. She would laugh and sing and blossom. Her art flourished." His face contorted with unabashed bitterness. "She should have come here years ago. He asked her often enough."

"So why didn't she leave?"

"Me. When I was little she stayed for me, not wanting me to be raised in a broken home. And, of course, divorce was not made legal in Argentina until the late-'80s. There is still a stigma in my country for divorced women."

"But they must have been lovers for decades."

"Yes. Thirty or so years, I think. Clarence would stay away, but only because she asked him to. And then he would come back because she asked him to. She had him on hold for his entire life, all because of me."

"Or because it wasn't even legal to get a divorce. Jesus." she muttered under her breath.

"Yes, we are backwards in some ways. Culturally more so than politically. We have a woman president, you know." He sounded peevish when he was defensive.

"Yeah, and my country has eradicated racism by electing a black president. We're all so progressive. And isn't your political system a ruse for corruption and misspent IMF loans? Don't your elected leaders fleece the public?" She knew her criticism of his country was ridiculous, but her desire to appropriate blame for her uncle's heartache grasped at the first culpable source.

"Don't yours? Our systems are the same, only your politicians are more sly about it. Argentine still remembers the dictatorship. We move through life with a veneer of political compliance and the heart of deep mistrust. At least that is what Clarence would say." Olivier smirked at her.

Syd searched his face. His features were sharp and smooth. Only his full lips offered a softness to his face. His eyes could be dark and clouded or sharp and bright, depending on his thoughts.

He didn't look like Clarence in the least. But he did look like someone familiar. He was familiar to her in a way she couldn't name. She tried to puzzle her way through the pieces of her memory – what she knew of her childhood – but it was an impenetrable fog to her.

"But women are still treated badly in your country, right? Is your mother treated badly by your father?"

"No, no. Well, he is not violent with her. I have never seen him hit her. He only bullies and abuses with words and meanness. He humiliates her. She is an intelligent woman with talents and aspirations. She paints. But she remained with him for too long, and she is worn down. She is a gentle, passionate person with a natural buoyancy. But news of Clarence's death put her in a terrible place. She is staying with her brother's family now."

"Do you need to go see her? Do you need to go home?" She felt more like a burden than ever. A streak of guilt settled deep in her stomach.

"I have a duty here."

"You have a duty to your mother."

"She wants me to stay here and see this through," he said slowly. "And I made a promise to Clarence. Why? Do you want me to leave?"

"No. Well, not unless you're still the number one suspect. In that case, you might want to get in your plane and hightail it south."

"I thought you would be upset by all of this."

She sighed. "I don't know what to think of anything anymore."

He nodded, "Can I ask you to do something for me, Sydney?"

"Yes, I think."

"Would you please accompany me to the hangar? I would like to check out the plane I am suspected of tampering with."

"Absolutely." She paused, feeling relieved to be offered a task other than waiting. "Jim won't like it though."

Chapter 30

Syd and Olivier had to wait several hours for the museum to open. Olivier had morning winery duties to finish, and Syd found herself rummaging through the two suitcases of clothes and accessories that Charlie brought down for her from her apartment. Her clothes were fitting her quite loosely now. She would have welcomed the idea a few weeks ago, but now she felt light and willowy, unsubstantial. For the first time ever she wished for her size-10 jeans to fill out better in the thighs and not require a cinched belt. She spent too long dressing, which was completely foreign to her usual routine. Memories of Clarence crowded her head, and she found herself lost in a haze for long periods of time. Then she would get up and search for some reassurance in the mirror, reaching for a tube of mascara or to fiddle with her hair. She was only thankful that Charlie was still passed out on the couch, allowing her to escape the endless teasing she would attract with her girlish primping. But this was less a departure into vanity than an exercise to keep her preoccupied mind from floundering. So much of what Olivier told her was something she suspected in the recesses of her mind. But the story unfolded into more tragedy than she could have imagined.

Syd's body felt airy as she walked across the gravel to the winery truck. The truck itself was enough of an antique to be featured in the museum they were headed for. Olivier sat in the idling vintage Ford for a few minutes, quietly waiting for her to come out of the house. She emerged a moment later, slammed the door, and settled herself in without a word. He drove off into the cloudy cool autumn morning along a road lined with red and yellow trees that glowed like fire.

~

The 1929 Waco Taperwing was on permanent loan to the Western Antique Airplane & Automobile Museum across the Columbia River in Hood River, Oregon. The museum was adjacent to the small municipal airfield, and all of the machines in the museum were in working order. The airstrip allowed pilots to fly their antique planes during fly-ins or demonstrations without requiring a hangar rental. Almost all of the airplanes were in excellent condition or in the process of being restored. Syd had not been to the museum since it opened a decade earlier. Before the museum opened, Clarence kept his plane in a hangar in Vancouver, covered in a tarp, alone in the dark. She remembered how excited he was to have his plane on display in the museum for the rest of the aviation world to salivate over. For a man who put little stock in material possession, Clarence was prodigiously proud of his biplane.

The plane was in a hangar for restoration, still being patched up after the bumpy landing Clarence made last June when he deftly pulled out of a perilous stall. It took Sydney a good deal of time to explain their circumstances to the tiny, ancient docent at the museum. He was perplexed that they were so interested in the restoration hangar while they had so many lovely examples of biplanes of a similar make in front of them.

"We'd like to look at that particular plane," she said, wondering if she was giving too much away. "It belonged to my uncle." She knew the nature of their mission needed to stay secret. But the doddering old man was either feeble-minded or he was determined to deflect their questions. After five minutes she realized they were getting nowhere and she would have to divulge more information.

“Clarence's Waco?” he asked, his sharp eyes looking her over with renewed interest. Syd was instantly aware that this crooked body standing before her, bent over in what had to have been at least 8 decades of life, housed a youthful and sharp brain. His eyes sparkled and he winked at her.

“A Skamania County Sheriff was asking questions about that plane yesterday. He spoke with Frank, our primary mechanic, for a long time.” He smiled a toothy grin, revealing an astonishing set of perfect dentures. He winked at her again. “But he left disappointed.”

“Can you take us to the plane, sir?” Syd asked, smiling sweetly.

“Albert, sweetie. Call me Albert.” He winked at her again and turned sharply on his heels. She would have wondered if it was a tick but for the mischievous twinkle in his eyes.

He set off at an astonishing clip for his bent body. Olivier, who remained completely silent during their short interview of the docent raised his eyebrows at Syd as they followed Albert’s echoing footsteps through the vast and airy hangar. Syd grew instantly fond of the little man; at his sense of humor and apparent glee at the Sheriff's expense. This suggested an independence of mind that she welcomed in the elderly. He reminded her of a feisty leprechaun.

They wended their way through two hangars that housed hundreds of planes and antique automobiles. Now and then, Albert pointed out a subject of particular interest as they passed without slowing down. He paused for a moment in front of a gorgeous black 1959 Austin Healey 3000 without a word. Syd smiled sadly, longing to climb back inside the machine and wait for the purr of the engine and the comfort of her uncle driving. But Albert kept moving and Syd jerked out of nostalgia to follow his trot from one hangar to the next. They entered a side door large enough to run an airplane through and were hit by the odors of oil and machines carried on an inexplicable draft that whirled through the massive hangar. The giant space was overwhelmed with the carcasses of dead machines in various states of dilapidation, waiting for the attention of a loving mechanic or the scrapyard. Shells of Model T’s took up a large portion of the space, while the airplanes sat in the far corner. Only a few specimens were in the center of the hangar, each in some form of repair or restoration. On the far side she saw a gorgeous 1929 Waco Taperwing that stood out in the cavernous room full of machine expiration. It was bright red with black features and nine black engines circling the propeller. It was truly a bastion of bygone days. The prop shone bright with deep wood grain, highly polished and elegantly curved. It was the belle of the room, poised and ready, its nose pointed toward the ceiling in unabashed pride.

As they walked across the concrete floor of the hangar, Syd squinted to make out the elegant writing on her uncle's beloved plane. It was a lovely script in black with tiny traces of white trim that let the lettering stand out on the deep red fuselage. It read *Belle Donna*. Syd always found her uncle's flashy red plane to be far too much of a plebeian cliché for such a modest emblem. It needed a motif of a larger than life blond bombshell, breasts popping out of a yellow polka dot dress. Or some kind of humanoid animal, like a bulldog or a shark, bearing its teeth with threatening bravado. Instead, it bore a simple and discreet inscription, like a wedding invitation. Syd traced her hand over the lettering, feeling the groove of the paint through the polish.

"My mother," Olivier said, speaking for the first time since they left the house.

"Hmm?" Syd looked at him confused, still mesmerized by the beauty of the machine.

"My mother is Donna," he said. He walked around the plane and stopped at the nose.

Albert clicked his way across the hangar to a set of rows of high metal shelves that apparently housed every imaginable spare part for the contents of the hangar. He disappeared, but they could hear the faint murmuring of voices, peppered with the sharp echoing percussion of tools hitting metal in a random clattering. Syd continued to walk slowly around the Belle Donna without lifting her hand from the cool surface. Held in the spell of the machine, she surrendered herself to so many memories of her uncle in this plane, and his constant cajoling to get her to fly with him. She always preferred to watch him fly from the safety of the tarmac. The haunting memory of her parents' untimely end in a fast moving machine had always made her leery of her uncle's sports car and antique plane. But standing here she could finally understand his passion for such a lovely machine. As a child she feared the plane would be the death of her uncle, and the irony of its namesake wasn't lost on her. But she never knew it was named after his beloved. She always assumed he named it after the deadly herb as a joke. He had cared for this plane with painstaking affection, and he was not a man to obsess over possessions. He could have left for Donna at any time, she thought to herself. She was suddenly struck by the futility of the hope he suffered.

Olivier had found a stepladder and expertly removed the engine cover off the nose of the plane. He pulled a small Maglite out of his pocket and stood on the top step, meticulously inspecting every engine housing. She watched him from the tail of the plane as she stroked the smooth red paint and the contours of the rivets. Olivier's dark head bobbed in concentration. She knew he must have stood by quietly watching the tragedy of his mother and Clarence for decades.

"Why did you come here?" she asked him thoughtfully, alarmed at how her voice echoed in the hanger.

He swung his head around the nose to look at her incredulously. "To look at the plane." His furrowed eyebrows were pinched tightly. "To figure out how it was tampered with."

"No. I mean, why did you fly up here in the first place?" she tried to speak quieter to avoid the acoustics.

"Oh," he said, scowling in thought. He clamored down from the ladder and walked over to her, the workings of his brain clearly displayed on his face. His eyes squinted and relaxed. He sighed and smiled sheepishly. "I'm not so sure now." His face was open and readable for the first time. Sydney's heart lurched in her chest.

"Would she have followed you if you had decided to stay?"

"I think that might have been my plan," he answered, looking perplexed over the discovery of his own behavior. "But I came because my father and I had fought, and I was finished with him." He raised his hands in supplication. "It's a long story."

"You fought about *her*?"

"Yes. In the end I think it was about her. At the time I

thought it was something different." He returned to the stepladder and the task of inspecting the engine. Syd pondered the intensity of a love for a child that could outbid the love of a man. She may have known such a love when she was small. It was the kind of love that offered no choices or wins, and always trumped personal happiness. But Olivier saw that kind of love to fruition, and felt the terrible burden of it in his own life. He fled to her uncle to free himself. She let out a deep resolute sigh.

She waited a few more minutes before patting the side of the plane and trotting off to find Albert. His muffled voice could be heard coming from the innards of a library of oily steel and iron parts on the other side of the hangar.

"Albert?" she called out.

Albert called back to her. He was hidden behind bookshelves holding an array of manuals. She walked over to him, standing next to another old-timer in classic blue work overalls smattered with oil stains and white chalky stuff. *Frank* was embroidered on a patch over his right breast, mended several times with yellow and red thread. He was an unkempt man with wispy white hair combed over the top of his head, floating like feathers in the ambient breeze. He had the same white powdery stuff on his whiskered face, and Syd smiled as she suspected a penchant for powdered sugar donuts. His eyes were heavy and bloodshot, sad and unfathomably blue.

"I'm so sorry for your loss, dear," he said gently, taking her hand and patting it. His huge hands were rough and stained black in the creases, and his thick fingers were sprinkled with sugar. The kindness in his eyes instantly cut through Syd in the worst way, and she withdrew her hand and cleared her throat reflexively. She could see his forgiveness for her in his empathetic smile and warm eyes.

"I've known your uncle for years now," he said, nodding toward a door in the far corner of the hangar. "Me and him played checkers sometimes." Syd smiled at the thought of Clarence playing checkers in the greasy side room of a machine shop. She wondered if he ate powdered donuts with Frank. "Clarence asked me questions about airplane mechanics too," he said, nodding and winking. It was clear both men viewed winking as a common means of communicating with women.

"Are you working on the plane now?" she asked.

"Not really. Nothing wrong with her, I suspect."

"Not after the accident?"

"Nope. Just some dings from a hard landing. Her landing gear shocks was bent up a bit, but I'm pretty much done restoring her from that. She was built for rough landings on sod fields. I'm just trying to match the paint and get the woodwork in the cockpit refinished." He looked thoughtfully up at the top of the hangar. "Nothing wrong with her before the accident neither. We inspected her together, Clarence and me. Before every flight."

"So what happened then?"

He squished his mouth in an upside down C. "A clamp in the wrong place, I reckon." He lowered his voice a little.

"What do you mean?" She whispered back.

"A clamp on the elevator cable preventing the correction of pitch fully. Also one on the rudder cables. The ailerons are stable on that craft, so he was able to rudder into a slow barrel roll in spite of the cable range and pull the gimbal hard to level her out when he got the chance."

"Are the clamps still on the cable?"

"Nope. I took em off. And I gave em to Clarence." He sucked his teeth and shuffled his worn boots.

"How did they get there? Didn't you see them before he took off? You said you checked the plane before every flight." She sounded accusatory and the old man looked hurt.

"I did check it. Not an hour before he left the tarmac." Syd wondered for a moment if Frank could be trusted.

"Don't you have to file reports for those kinds of accidents?" She pressed. He grimaced at her suggestion and only screwed tight his mouth.

She tried a different tack. "Do you have security cameras?" The old man shrugged and shuffled his feet again. She had put him on his guard, and it appeared he finished talking to her.

She would have to play on his sympathy and what she suspected might be a knack for subterfuge and collusion. She sighed and moved closer to him, touching him on his sleeve.

"Okay, I'm going to come clean with you. My Uncle's

friend, Olivier Ruiz is the guy who flew with my uncle that day before the plane had troubles."

"Yup. That boy can fly, for sure. The Taperwing takes a daring pilot," he said, delivering his highest standard of approval.

"And the police think Olivier may have been responsible for my uncle's death. And they think that the plane accident in June was another attempt on his life."

"It was. Someone tampered with his plane, if my name isn't Frank." He whispered back into her face, so close that Syd could smell the coffee and powdered donuts on his sour breath. Syd sighed. He might not be any help at all, she thought.

"You removed the clamps and gave them to my uncle?" she asked.

"Yup. And then he put it back on and ran some tests on the ground." Frank stared at her, eyebrows raised in conspiracy.

"And...?"

"Like I said, someone tampered with the cables to prevent a recovery from a flip or a deep stall."

"My uncle knew this," she said flatly.

"Yup. And he knew it weren't that Argentine boy neither."

"Jesus," she said, realizing what Frank meant. Clarence had survived an attempted murder and had known about it just as he received his diagnosis of pancreatic cancer. Syd's gut wrenched with guilt and empathy.

"So he asked me to keep an eye out on her. And to keep my mouth shut about the shenanigans."

"Why? Why would he ask you to do that?"

"His way, I guess. He said something about a mess to clean up. Said they would get theirs anyhow. Said he didn't want to worry the ladies. Think he might have meant you." He winked again.

"And you kept this secret? Even if it was attempted murder?" She was more than a little peeved that so much secrecy could allay the fact that a crime was committed. He nodded sheepishly, holding his hands up in surrender.

"Now understand, I wasn't too excited about keeping it a secret," he said. "But he said the cancer would do the job anyhow and he assured me that the culprit would get their just desserts.

Now understand that the man had got himself in a pickle with some bad sorts who were going after his life's work. He wanted time to rectify it all. And he wanted to spare himself and his loved ones the pain of a protracted investigation and trial." He was talking faster than he had before, clearly venting some long pent-up anxiety over his concession to Clarence's demands. He grabbed Syd's hands and held them in his own firmly. "Now understand that your uncle was a man of integrity. But he did things his own way. He held no truck with laying out his business with the police or the newspapers." Frank's obvious respect for Clarence spread out over his wrinkled face. His eyes welled up with tears. "I ain't a man to tell anyone how to live. Especially a man who's honest and lives with honor. And any man who lives his life loving a woman he can't have, raising a kid who ain't his own, and asking for nothing for himself in return is a man worth keeping secrets for."

Syd lowered her eyes, but she let him keep her hands. She could feel the rough skin of Frank's strong fingers against hers. She stood frozen in this hand grip before hearing the shuffle of Albert's boots and the light clip of another set of footsteps moving closer.

"Ah, hullo there, Olivier," Frank said. He let go of her hands.

Olivier strode gracefully past the shelves of greasy parts, and shook Frank's hand.

"Hello, Frank," Olivier said. Syd watched Olivier's eyes soften when they met the old man's, which were still misty from their conversation. They shook hands longer than normal. Then Olivier moved in for an embrace. They patted each other's backs as hard as they hugged.

Frank pulled away first, leaving Olivier looking vulnerable and young. He stepped back from Frank, who patted him hard on the shoulder one last time.

"One hell of a pilot, son," he said, nearly yelling at Olivier.

Olivier nodded, seeming too emotional to speak. Syd watched, flabbergasted. She had no idea who this man Frank was, but he apparently had an emotional connection with her uncle and Olivier.

"You two known each other long?" Syd asked.

"Uh, no, actually. We just met once. Last June, when I flew

up with Clarence."

"And then we had some beers," Frank said.

Beer. It was the male version of oxytocin. Syd was struck by what she could never understand in men. Somehow sharing mediocre beer between men made them a close-knit tribe unto themselves.

"But Clarence loved this boy like a son, you know," Frank continued. "Talked 'bout him all the time. Proud of him as a pilot and a winemaker. I know this boy never could have harmed Clarence. Told that Sheriff so too."

"You told the Sheriff about the clamp though, right?" Syd asked again.

Frank looked at Syd as though she had lost her mind. "Nope. Like I told you, I promised to keep it a secret."

"But you lied to a Sheriff," Syd said.

"I might have to take that up with my maker in the end. But I sleep fine at night anyhow." He screwed his face up philosophically, " 'sides, sometimes the law ain't worth abiding if it gives more grief than if things are just let be. Clarence fixed it up so the culprit would get theirs. He had his own style of poetry, I won't deny it."

Olivier nodded firmly and turned on his heels. He put his arm around Syd and pushed her out of the rows of shelves without a word. Syd looked back at Frank, who nodded and winked.

Chapter 31

Syd sat next to Olivier in the old flatbed Ford in complete silence. She wasn't sure if her throat was hurting from her recent illness or from a lump of tragedy taking residence after her morning of revelations about Clarence. Her mind was spinning. It appeared that her uncle was closer and more candid to an old mechanic than his lifelong best friend. But then again, Jack had been involved in some nasty business at the time when Clarence may have felt compelled to bear his soul to someone. And now, Jack was as deeply involved and lucky to be alive. Syd made a mental note to visit Jack later in the evening while Olivier steered the old truck up to the winery. "I've got to get the Zin in the press now. Alejandro has set it up." He squinted at his hands on the steering wheel. "You should maybe rest. You've had a rough day."

"I'll just go down to the house for a bit," she answered, feeling defeated and a bit helpless. She slid off the seat of the truck and floated back to the house in a fog. She entered through the kitchen to find the house empty. She called out, to no avail, wandering the rooms upstairs. She found a note on the kitchen table from Charlie.

Siddy,

Where the hell are you! I've gone to meet Dad at the station. Jack is out of ICU.

Leave a fucking note!

Charles

Syd read the note a few times before folding it up and discarding it in the waste basket under the sink. She felt guilty for leaving without telling Charlie, but she remembered how disgusted her best friend was at Becky for not informing the police about the mysterious phone call when the office was torn apart. Charlie was willing to break the rules and follow a hunch when it came to amateur sleuthing, but Sydney instinctively knew that she would not approve of going off with Olivier, her father's primary suspect, to investigate. Pensively, she puttered around the house for a while after she made a quick meal of toast and peanut butter. Her feet absently toured the empty house, leaving her to feel lonelier than she could remember. She realized that she was exhausted and dizzy, and soon she took heed to Olivier's advice and laid down for a nap. She stirred restlessly in bed for a half hour before giving up. Five minutes later she pulled on her muck boots and rain gear and found herself standing next to Alejandro at the press, with a new understanding of Olivier's strategy to stay busy.

They worked for a few hours outside in the cold, crisp day. The sunlight faded around four in the afternoon, giving way to a freezing autumn breeze. They siphoned off the free run wine into a tank until the pomace was dry. Then they raised the fermentation tank over the press opening and tilted it to dump the skins into the press. Olivier stood on a scaffolding over the press, raking the pomace out of the tank. They could only fill the press with three fermentation tanks, which meant they had to do two cycles. Syd worked hard shoveling the dry cake of the pomace out of the press after the press cycles ran dry. They filled a harvest bin with the dry grape skins and Alejandro used the old tractor to empty the bins in the compost pile near the upper vineyard. Syd cleaned the press and the equipment between cycles.

The day grew colder as the sun disappeared. Syd shivered in her damp quilted Carhartts, dipping her hands in a bucket of warm water to keep them agile. Alejandro had kept his distance from her, which she dismissed as reticence to regale her with the previous night's exploits. She spent the day in a cloud of memories and contemplation. Her body and hands moved automatically while her head worked through the details of the morning. The men left her alone, speaking to themselves quietly. At dusk, she silently prepped herself to climb into the press for the final cleaning. She tightened her rain gear around her face like a slick wimple and gathered her brushes and cleaner. Only as she was ready to climb under the stainless steel bullet-shaped press to get inside did she catch part of their conversation.

"He hit him? Or did he have a weapon?" Olivier asked, looking shocked and amused all at once.

"He only had his deadly hands," Alejandro answered, waving his hands in mock kung-fu motion.

"But he attacked him?" Olivier asked.

"Yeah, man. He jumped him in a bar. Like some kind of gangsta." Alejandro was obviously excited and amused. He fell into sniggering that reminded Syd of their trysts so long ago.

"Who? Who attacked who?" Syd butted in.

They turned to look at her in surprise, and she remembered that she wore a slicker tightened around her face. It was very unflattering. She felt she might look terrible. She preferred it when they treated her as if she was invisible.

"Francois Bertrand. His majesty, the winemaker," Alejandro said, smirking while be began squirting Syd with the hose.

"He was attacked?" Syd asked, glaring at him.

"Nope. He did the attacking. He's cooling his heels in jail now." Alejandro smiled, enjoying hosing her down.

"This is really old rain gear, *pendejo*!" she said, more than a little peeved at the soaking he was giving her.

"Oh, sorry," he said mischievously, turning his hose off. "Yeah… So, that asshole who was buying the winery got his ass kicked by a winemaker. And Francois's now in jail and all those wineries he makes wine for are shit out of luck." He took a swig from a flask that he retrieved from the breast pocket of his flannel shirt. He offered it to Syd and she took a long pull.Syd choked a bit on the rough whiskey. It stung her still raw throat.

"So Monsieur Bertrand is in jail," she said, wiping her

mouth on her sleeve. “He attacked Hans Feldman.”

“Yup.” Alejandro nodded.

“When? How’d you find out?”

“Last night. It was at that fancy bar downtown that you made me take you to when you turned 21, remember? My uncle texted me. Francois was supposed to get the late harvest grapes this morning and the pickers had to work the vines instead of apples, so they were pissed off anyway. It was fucking cold this morning. And then the bins just sat there in the vineyard and never got picked up.” He raised his eyebrows and whistled through his teeth. “Man those wineries are going to be pissed.”

“Why would Francois attack Feldman?” She interjected, looking between the men. Olivier frowned.

“Because he's a sleezebag, *m’hija* wouldn't be surprised if Francois is our Peeping Tom.” Alejandro offered, sagely.

“A 60-year-old Peeping Tom who can out run you?” she teased.

Alejandro's face grew serious. “Maybe. And he had reason to kill Clarence.”

“Why? Jealousy? Revenge? I don't see it, Alejandro.”

“Never underestimate the compelling power of envy,” Olivier piped in for the first time. He reached for the flask. “Your uncle said that to me once,” he explained.

“But does Francois envy Feldman? There is something else between those two. I saw them arguing at the memorial service. Francois looked desperate while Feldman was cool as a cuke.” She chewed on the inside of her lip while she climbed under the press to hose out the loose grape skins, hoisting half her body inside the huge stainless steel tube. Both men watched her enter the tight space with puzzled looks on their faces. She started to rinse out the echoing chamber with very hot water, while her mind mulled over Alejandro’s gossip. Although her mind was bursting with the events of the day the hot steam and closed space cleared up her stuffy head, leaving her completely soaked and completely lost in thought.

~

Syd got back down to the house a little before seven. She was instantly struck by the delicious smells of dinner as she made her way down the drive, but she found Charlie cooking when she stepped inside instead of Rosa. She stood in front of the large AGA stove-top frying taco shells. Small colorful Fiestaware bowls were spread out in the center of the table, holding taco fixings. There were at least a dozen of them. Syd loved Charlie's tacos almost as much as Rosa's.

Charlie wielded her long chef's tongs like a cattle prod. "*Where were you this morning?*" She jabbed her tongs at Syd's wet clothes. Syd thought she looked more like a 1950s-era snapshot of the-good-housewife with her apron and her hair held in a bandanna than she could have ever imagined. Syd dodged her and escaped into the other room.

"I'm talking to you, young lady!" she bellowed through the doorway in a shrill falsetto.

Syd shrugged and grabbed a handful of shredded cheese out of one of the bowls as she passed the kitchen table on her way to the spare room. She kicked off her rubber boots and peeled off her wet clothes, leaving them in a sopping pile on the floor. Her skin was freezing and goose-pimpled, and she was shivering. She clamored into a pair of yoga pants and pulled on her favorite oversized sweatshirt. She finished dressing by pulling on a pair of Clarence's old wool socks. They were far too large for her, with the heel high up on her ankle. Feeling unbearably cold, she grabbed the old quilt that she uncharacteristically folded up that morning and draped it around her like a shawl. Charlie stood guarding the table when Syd shuffled her thick wool clad feet across the wood floorboards. "Ah, eh, eh," she yelled into Syd's ear and slapped back her hand as Syd reached for more shredded cheese. "Not until I get answers." Charlie stood with crossed arms, tapping her foot.

"You've watched way too many sitcoms in your life," Syd said, flashing a grin. Charlie's hyperbole was never lost on her. At the moment, Syd felt like everything about Charlie was fabulous, especially the tacos. Charlie hammed up the role. She put her hands on her hips, still holding onto the tongs.

"So, I wake up..."

"…after *noon*…""and the damsel in distress I am supposed to protect…""…whilst in a drunken stupor…""Is missing! M.I.A.! Vanished without a note!"

"Sorry about that. I really planned on writing a note and then I just left. I forgot."

"Sure." Charlie feigned a lovely pout.

"You looked so peaceful. Reminded me of a dead spider, limbs all curled up on the couch. Shelob in repose. You could have gone downstairs to bed." Syd moved into the kitchen for some decongestant. Charlie followed her.

"Yeah, well, Alejandro took the bed downstairs."

"The way you two were last night I expected to find you both in the same bed," Syd said. She swigged the terrible purple syrup from a bottle she pulled from the cupboard.

"*Gross!* Now no one else can use that medicine. You're a pig, Sydney McGrath." She returned to her taco shells at the stove. "Besides," she muttered low, "Alejandro has a *girlfriend*." She spoke the last in her best snotty five year old voice.

"*What?*" Syd wheedled, shuffling close to Charlie.

"Turned me down flat," Charlie answered, all joking aside. "Tell me, Syd. Have I lost my mojo?"

"He has a girlfriend. And I think he's happy. Pretty serious, too, from the looks of it. But he always had a thing for you, Charlie." Syd consoled her with real affection. Charlie was a goddess and she wasn't used to being turned down. Especially not by someone who has had an obvious crush on her for decades. Syd put her arm around Charlie and squeezed her shoulder.

"Seriously. Where did you go with Olivier, Syd? Dad and I were worried." Charlie changed the subject.

"We went to look at the plane. It was Olivier's idea. He's pretty hell-bent to avoid jail time. I think he thinks that I can't handle the winery alone." Syd half joked.

"Dad already talked to the mechanic yesterday. There was no evidence of the plane being sabotaged."

"Frank lied. He checked the plane after the accident and there was a stop on the cables for pulling up out of a stall. Clarence could have maneuvered the plane fine until he tried to pull up hard out of a stall."

"Frank's the mechanic?" Charlie asked slowly. "Did Clarence know someone had sabotaged his plane?"

"Yup," Syd answered. Charlie looked at Syd thoughtfully.

"So Clarence was aware that someone was trying to kill him and he didn't tell the police."

"Yup."

"Why?" Charlie's face fell into sad confusion.

"I don't know. But maybe he discovered that he had cancer at the same time he discovered that someone tried to kill him and he didn't feel such a terrible threat. But he did change everything about the winery takeover. He changed his will and he changed his attitude about me making wine."

"But maybe the same person who tried to kill him in June ended up doing it right the second time," Charlie nearly shouted in exasperation.

"Yeah, but we're talking about my uncle here, Charlie. Besides, Frank told me that Clarence told him to keep it all quiet because the culprit would get theirs in the end."

"Like putting a stop to the buyout? Hardly seems like punishment for attempted murder."

"Or losing a lucrative position as a winemaker in a prestigious winery. Someone who has the ambition to bribe a wine critic might be unscrupulous enough to try to kill someone." Syd wrapped the quilt around her tighter, still shivering.

"Francois Bertrand killed your uncle? Hmm. A possibility. Dad went to see him at the Hood River Jail today. He attacked Hans Feldman at a restaurant last night." Charlie raised her eyebrows as she delivered her juicy news. Her voice had a certain tone when she had important information, and Syd could hear the controlled excitement in the pace of her words.

"I know," Syd said, feigning boredom.

"What? How could you know? Damn it!" Charlie whined.

"Alejandro told me. His uncle told him. He's a foreman on a harvest crew in Hood River. The workers always know what's going on. They picked some grapes for him this morning and he never showed. I'm not sure if the grapes were for him or another winery he does custom crush for, but his no-show caused a ruckus. Anyway, word spread fast, and the pickers don't like Bertrand so the gossip isn't pretty." Syd explained.

"Do you think it could have been him?" Charlie asked.

"I don't know. Maybe. He certainly was weird at the

memorial service. Jumpy. And he had an argument with Feldman at the memorial. Your dad and I watched it. So maybe the two of them worked together? He was at the meeting up at Ted's the day my uncle was killed, you know." Syd stood in the middle of the kitchen wrapped tight in the quilt. She felt numb and emotionally detached talking about her uncle's murder in blasé hypotheticals. The buoyancy she had felt when she came into the house faded and she felt adrift again.

"Dad's coming for dinner," Charlie said, changing the subject. She sensed Syd growing distant. "He'll be here at eight."

"Did you make enough for Alejandro and Olivier? We should ask them. Have you seen Rosa today?"

"Nope. She didn't come at all today. Day off? Maybe she's spending a little of that money, huh? Yeah, let's ask the guys. I want to see Alejandro squirm anyhow. I might run my hand up his thigh under the table." Charlie meant to put Syd at ease about her failed tryst from the night before. She was a genius at self-deprecation to assuage tension. Good old Charlie, Syd thought. She wrapped her blanket around her and held her in a long embrace.

They set the table for five, busily placing plates and flatware. Syd was hunting for the variety of hot sauces in the fridge and pantry when Charlie suddenly left without a word, slamming the kitchen door and setting off into the dark. Syd was seized by a sudden panic. She rushed to the window to watch Charlie's ascent to the winery. The darkness swallowed her twenty feet up the drive. Syd knew she had gone up to talk to the men about dinner, but she was seized by terror nonetheless. Syd stood alone at the window, wrapped tightly in the quilt but shivering. Her heart beat hard in her chest and she felt her breathing constrict. Her knees turned to jelly and she nearly collapsed. She grabbed the counter to steady herself, staring transfixed on the blackness outside. Her hands were slippery and wet with sweat. She searched for meaning in the surprisingly visceral response of her body to an unseen threat. *It's all in my head*, she reassured herself. *She had just walked the same path herself not fifteen minutes before. Her fear was irrational.*

She had not yet come to terms with the danger she faced; not until this very moment. Her best friend walked stoically into the dark night, while she stood trembling and frozen in place. Her ears filled with the swooshing of her own blood, in a pulsing dread. She hardly heard the car drive up or the distant voices of her friends outside. She wasn't sure if she was terrified more for herself or for Charlie.

Jim strode into the house first. If he was alarmed to find Syd alone he didn't show it. But Syd was so grateful to see him that she bounded across the room from her post at kitchen window and gave him a desperate hug, dropping the quilt on the floor. She battled to keep her legs steady.

"Hey, Siddy-biddy," he said, squeezing her back and lifting her off the floor. She felt extraordinarily safe in his embrace and didn't want to let go, but she didn't want him to know how frightened she was either. She recoiled slowly and walked across the kitchen, feeling her shivering subside. She took a deep breath and feigned a level of strength she could only imagine.

"So no bogey man last night," Syd said, forcing herself to walk to the fridge to find a beer for Jim. She opened it on a mounted bottle opener on the side of the cupboard and handed it to him. Jim's face was implacable, but his eyes narrowed.

"This isn't a joke, Syd. This man is dangerous." He tipped the bottle back and downed the beer in a few gulps. He placed the empty bottle back on the counter. The strain of the last week was wearing on him. Everything about him seemed to sag a little. Syd felt a stab of guilt in her chest.

"I know, Jim. I'm just a little scared."

"Well, that's the first sensible thing I've heard in this house for days." He smiled and walked toward her. He tussled her hair before reaching into the fridge for another beer.

"Smells so good in here," he said, nosing his way around the foil-covered dishes warming on the stove. "Charlie make tacos? She promised me tacos."

The door opened a moment later and Alejandro appeared in a gust of cool air, carrying with him the scent of fall. Charlie and Olivier followed closely. They huffed and blustered their way into the crowded kitchen, rubbing their hands together.

"Cold.. *Soo cooold*," Charlie crooned, holding up her long fingers like the stiff hands of an old crone.

"Well, you shouldn't have left without a jacket," Syd chided her. She was irrationally hurt that she took off without a word, leaving her alone to battle her inner terror.

"You were outside for ten minutes," said Alejandro, teasing Charlie. "We've been out there for the whole day." He obviously didn't feel awkward about the previous night.

"Do you want a beer or something warm?" Syd asked, feeling the paralysis creep out of her stiff body.

"Beer...tea," the men chimed in at the same time.

"Tea with whiskey?" Syd asked, turning to face Olivier. He nodded silently. Syd noted that he had a flush in his olive skined cheeks that bordered on a feminine shade but for his dark stubble. Charlie looked between them and grabbed a beer for Alejandro.

Syd busied herself with preparing tea, while the rest of them carried pots and plates to the table in the other room. Their breezy banter steadied her, and the cold dark fear slowly loosened its grip. Still, she stood for several minutes in the kitchen, breathing deeply with her eyes closed to gather her thoughts. She opened her eyes to find Olivier standing in the doorway, watching her.

"You okay?" he asked. He took the tea from her hands. Her nerves melted and she averted her eyes.

"Mmm-hmm," she said, nodding. But she was struggling to keep tears from surfacing. As the numbness of her fear subsided she felt a flood of emotion and fought it with everything in her.

"I'm going to lie down for a minute," she said thickly. She turned and bounded for the safety of her bedroom.

Syd hardly made it to the door of her room before she burst into tears. She ran to her bed and buried her face in her pillow, sobbing. Somewhere in her mind she thought her body was expelling the pent-up fear in some kind of emotional emetic. She needed to cry out the stress of it all. Her sobbing continued violently for nearly five minutes and then stopped as suddenly as it had started. She felt loose and exhausted, but much better, like she had just gone for a long run or enjoyed a night of unbridled dancing.

She sat up and pensively worked her way through the last half hour. She was frightened; perhaps more frightened than she had ever been. She kept thinking that there was no eminent threat. It was just the thought of a threat that brought on irrational fear. *Oh my god!* she thought to herself, shuddering at the memory that just that morning she had sat outside at dawn alone. She made a promise to herself to heed Jim's warnings and take precautions.

She emerged from the bathroom after splashing cold water on her face. She found the group engaged in a raucous conversation and realized she hadn't been missed. Charlie was doing her usual shtick, depicting a drunken Francois Bertrand in a bar fight, challenging Hans Feldman to a duel. Her slurred French accent was remarkable, Syd noted. Jim was clearly struggling to keep the brevity of his investigation in tact, while he succumbed to his daughter's antics. Syd moved over to rub his shoulders fondly. He patted her hand absently while engaging the debate.

"*Yes!* He admits to attacking Feldman, and he admits to bribing a writer to give scores he didn't deserve," Jim bellowed over the noisy group.

"He said that?" Charlie asked loudly. She had two empty beer bottles in front of her.

"Well, not the *didn't-deserve* part," Jim said. "He went on about the unfairness and arbitrary nature of scores. He seems to be fine with bribing the writer. He said it's no worse than the countless dinners and long visits to wineries that these critics partake in. He seems to think that wine scores are chockfull of nepotism."

"Well he's right," Charlie said.

"Not entirely," Syd piped in, taking her seat next to Olivier. She loaded her plate with four taco shells and filled them with fixings. "Most critics have decent palates and give scores that indicate some kind of quality." She stopped to take a bite of a delicious greasy taco.

"But they are not consistent and are biased to varietal wines and a particular style of wine," Olivier said. "Your uncle said this to me not a few weeks ago even *after* he got some excellent scores. They are biased to regions too. In the Uco Valley we had to struggle to get noticed, and after a few good reviews, and the incessant pursuit of friendship with a few critics we are now the premiere region in Mendoza. But, of course, the wine hasn't changed at all."

"Mmm," Syd said, nodding, but squinting her eyes incredulously. She went in for another bite.

"And Clarence said that old and tired palates of the all-male critic inner circle were driving the industry to make hot, jammy high pH wines," Charlie said, "which are totally imbalanced and terrible with food." Charlie was clearly enjoying herself. She reached for another beer in the center of the table. Alejandro grabbed it from her, opened it with his keys and slid it back across the table to her waiting hand.

"Not *all* male," Syd muttered with food in her mouth, stating the facts with grease sliding down her chin.

"And hardly any of them are trained somms," Charlie said.

"Snob!" said Syd.

"Or winemakers, or trained at all in sensory evaluation," said Charlie. "And Clarence had me read some articles on the arbitrary nature of critics a few years back. In one blind study a group of critics were tricked and rated the same wine differently. The same wine! With scores as different as five points. A five-point variance!" Charlie was on a roll.

Syd polished off her first taco and licked her fingers unabashedly, letting Charlie finish her rant unchecked. Olivier, stoney faced, offered her a napkin.

"*And* scores can vary up to five points in a tasting in front of the winemaker at the winery compared to samples sent in or blind tasted," Charlie said, tapering off. She searched her mind for more facts on the deeds of plotting critics.

"In Argentina, the system's far more openly understood as a network of influence instead of an objective review," said Olivier. "Americans somehow expect critics to hold some kind of scientific level of objectivity and analysis. These are just people. Men, mostly," Olivier nodded to Charlie, "who feel important enough to write about wine. The critics get to know the big players in the business and they pander to them. Yes, it is nepotism. Yes, it is highly unfair to small producers who don't buy ads in a magazine. And everyone hates a critic. But imagine making wine without them?"

Syd swallowed her first swig of cold beer. "Look, no one says the system is perfect," she said. "It's a tool, that's all. We send in wine for review to assure the public that the wine is good. But a loyal public knows and trusts you if your wine is consistently good. Score or no score."

"Then why would Francois bribe a critic?" Jim asked.

"Credibility, maybe?" Syd said. "He hasn't garnered excellent scores ever. Good scores, yes. The high 80's for almost everything that he made. You know, he started out making wines like my uncle. European-style, less extraction, low oak, lower alcohol. And blends. But then he gave way to prevailing ideas in the industry and started making only varietal wines. He played to the Robert Parker-style palate and then he made over ripe monsters better found down south. Elegance and balance were gone in favor of pursuing scores. He's not a bad wine maker. He's just pandering to critics."

"The scores matter for cash, Dad," Charlie touted.

"How so?" he asked.

"Wines that score big can raise the price," said Charlie. "It's simple; A 95 score equals double in price."

"Did Clarence ever do that?" Jim asked.

"Nope. He never got a 95 either," said Alejandro, clearly proud of Clarence. "American blends don't get really high scores. Industry bias. And he used cost-based pricing anyway. He wanted people – *real* people – to drink his wine. He didn't want them to collect it."

"But I don't think Francois was trying to garner scores for the profit margin," Syd said. "I think he was trying to gain credibility as a winemaker. Didn't he have a contract with Feldman to be the winemaker of Blackwell's once my uncle was out of the picture?"

"Yup. He said something about that in our interview this afternoon."

"If the big guys were going to buy out Blackwell's they would want a heavy-hitter winemaker on the ticket," said Charlie, bouncing in her chair with excitement. "To take Clarence's place."

Jim glared at his daughter across the table.

"But wouldn't that mean that Feldman knew about the bribe?" Syd asked, keeping her own excitement buttoned down.

Jim narrowed his eyes at her. Syd was unsure if he was

going to answer her or tell her to butt out of his investigation.

"Not necessarily," he answered thoughtfully.

"But isn't it plausible that he knew about the bribe?" Syd asked. "Couldn't he have stipulated that Francois get better scores to add him to the deal? I'm not sure Francois would have taken the initiative to do that kind of thing alone. Not in his character."

"No *cajones*." Alejandro added.

"And couldn't Feldman have reason to sabotage Clarence's plane after he had assurances that he had a wine maker for the buyout?" Charlie said. "Knocks out the problem of eliminating the partial owner. And he gets a hefty insurance claim." Charlie bounced in her seat again and Syd glared at her.

"The plane was not sabotaged," Jim avowed, his voice full of authority. "I talked to the mechanic yesterday. Clarence was simply in a long stall during a trick of some kind and he pulled up too late." Jim's sonorous tones expounded confidence and finality. Charlie and Syd exchanged glances. Olivier kept his eyes averted, staring at the grease on his empty plate.

"And that nearly eliminates your suspicion too," Jim said across the table to Olivier. "But don't take off just yet."

Olivier merely nodded. Silence surrounded the table for a moment. Syd was mystified. Once again, the world of men defied all logic. Here was a resolution to a problem that had weighed heavily for a solid week, threatening Olivier's freedom and credibility, threatening the very existence of the winery. And all of it disappeared with a single subject/verb sentence and a nod.

"Well, I have to get going," Alejandro said. He slammed both palms down on the table. "Sylvia made me dinner." He winked at Charlie.

"Another dinner?" Charlie asked. "You ate five tacos."

"Yeah, I was saving my appetite. She made *rellenos*. She's a really good cook." He winked at Syd this time. Charlie socked him hard in the arm.

"I'm a good cook," she pouted.

"Yeah, for a *gringa*," he muttered under his breath, and got up with a swagger. He was clearly having fun with Charlie.

"I'll meet you in the vineyard at seven tomorrow morning?" Olivier asked Alejandro while he pulled on his jacket.

"So late? Yeah, I guess it won't be light until then anyway," he said, answering his own question.

"What are you doing in the vineyard?" Syd asked. She felt annoyed that she wasn't included in their plans.

"Red blotch," said Olivier. "We need samples for testing."

"But can't you just tell by the color of the leaves?" she asked.

"No. The red leaf is a final symptom. The vine can have the virus for several years before the leaves turn red. We need to pull up the vines that are infected now." Something about Olivier's commitment to keeping the vines healthy for future vintages comforted Syd.

"Well, I'm in," she said.

"Fine," Olivier said. He flashed a disarming white-toothed smile, which made Syd's stomach sink. His dark eyes crinkled and lit up. Charlie looked at them one at a time. "Not me. I'm sleeping in," she said with a shrug. She got up and walked into the kitchen with a stack of plates, wearing an enigmatic smile.

Chapter 32

Syd found herself underdressed and huffing as she walked uphill to the winery in the early dawn chill. She clung to a steaming coffee mug, wishing she had filled a thermos instead. The morning was clear and frosty; the purple haze of the early light woven in and out of the familiar treeline. The huge doors of the winery were open, and she could hear the muffled voices of men working inside. She knew Olivier would have to do punchdowns before they worked the vineyard. She felt a tinge of guilt for not anticipating this. How was she ever going to run the winery herself when she couldn't remember the basics? She was certainly grateful for Olivier, but his efficiency was an occasional reminder of her own incompetence. She wondered if the men only humored her in letting her tag along today. She thought about how she asked herself along, wondering if they were patronizing her. Or worse, dreading her intrusion.

She was filled with self-doubt when she entered the large red doors, feeling like she didn't belong. The winery was an artifact of her childhood, an iconic symbol of her uncle and all things family. The smells, sounds, and energy of the place drifted down into her deepest feelings of comfort and familiarity. But she doubted she could rightfully claim it as her own.

Olivier stood in a far corner on the edge of a fermentation tank, driving the long punchdown tool into the pomace. He looked like he belonged here. Syd watched silently for a minute, staring at his cat-like grace as he walked along the thin strip of plastic of the tank walls, wielding the punchdown tool for balance. He reminded her of her uncle, absorbed in some kind of zen flow and using every sense at full capacity to understand the wine.

Alejandro sidled up next to her. He silently looked in the direction of her eyes and poured her some steaming coffee from his own thermos.

"Thanks. Morning," she muttered, lowering her eyes.

"He's a good guy, Syd," Alejandro said.

"Not a murderer then, huh?"

"Nah," he growled into his own mug and shuffled out the huge doors. He disappeared up the path to the upper vineyard.

Syd watched Olivier move to another tank and work the skins down in smooth circular motion. She walked over to the tank he was perched on and peered over the top. The long stainless steel tool never stopped moving. It circled into the dry cap of seeds and skins, pushing the deep purple mass down deep into pink bubbles like sea foam. The tool pierced the cap with relentless grace, slowly and carefully breaking into the mass in a perfect arc. It followed the invisible line of a sphere into the juice below the cap. Olivier did not move like her uncle. His punchdowns were a dance of fluid grace in perfect time. Clarence had jammed and jarred the cap, pulling and pushing with rigid motion and dominating the tank in linear, syncopated jabs. But Olivier rolled the pomace in undulating, churning waves that were inextricable from the next plunge.

"You do that so differently," she said, staring into the pink foam and feeling the sting of carbon dioxide in her nose. The gorgeous earthy aroma of fermenting Cabernet lingered deep in her nasal passage and made her light-headed.

"Clarence said the same thing," Olivier said, his head cocked to one side. "He said that I do punchdowns like your mother." He frowned at her from his perch above her. Syd looked away, unwilling to get swallowed up in emotion so early.

"It was a compliment," he said. "One of few. Your uncle

worshipped your mother as a wine maker. He said she made wine in a sacred dance. A feminine ritual." He smiled sardonically, amused at her uncle's sentimental theories on women and wine making. He teased her with an intoxicating twinkle in his eye.

Syd raised her eyebrows, taking the bait. She stared up at him. "Wine is innately female," she touted defiantly. "It was invented by women and for a long time only women were permitted to make wine." She put her hands on her hips in a mock gesture worthy of Charlie. Olivier laughed.

"It's true!"

"Where did you hear such a thing?" Olivier asked, using a tone reserved for incredulous claims. He squatted on the balls of his feet to get nearer to her, still balancing on the one-inch edge of the tank wall.

"*The Epic of Gilgamesh*," she said, inching closer. She jutted her jaw near his bent knee. His eyebrows arched. "*The Epic of Gilgamesh* tells of women making wine and beer. It goes back at least 5000 years." She faked an imperious glare, but knew he was worthy of the education.

Olivier shrugged and straightened his legs again like a spring while balancing gracefully. He plunged the tool in the pomace again, breaking up the cap in his borrowed style. Syd watched him for a few minutes, hoping for more conversation. But Olivier had immersed himself back into his simple task and he ignored her. Syd turned to leave but stopped when he cleared his throat.

"Truth is, I learned this technique from my uncle," he said, "who learned it from your mother. It prevents bruising the skins and it's easier on the shoulders." He spoke softly, mesmerized by his own movements. Syd nodded and kept her thoughts to herself for fear of losing her composure. She watched him for a minute before venturing outside into the upper vineyard. Her mind worked to untangle the mess of her mother, her uncle, and the Ruiz family.

Alejandro drove down to her on the steep road between the blocks of vines in an ATV. He had a crate mounted to the front of it that held a box of Ziploc bags, Sharpies, and clippers. He handed her a small crate that held a pair of new gloves and clippers. His own gloves were worn and stained.

"We'll start at the bottom here," he said, pointing to the starting row on a southern block.

"How do we know which ones to take?"

"All of the vines with red leaves, then the vines next to 'em. Then every other one or so. Mark the grid in rows and count the vines from the start. Like one dash two for this one." He pointed to a vine, cut a cane with one leaf, and stuffed it into a baggie. He wrote on the bag with his pen.

Syd nodded and set off to work on the vines. The air was still cold and dry, and she was thankful for the leather gloves. The work required her to remove the gloves to open the plastic bag for the samples and the writing, so her fingers grew stiff with cold. After a few moments she noticed that Alejandro was three times as fast as she was, moving through the adjacent block with astonishing expertise. She forced herself to work more efficiently. The sun glared into her eyes as she worked, and she noticed that Alejandro faced west. But she wanted to see Olivier approach when he strode up hill.

After several rows and a few embarrassing but essential breaks to warm up her fingers for fear of cutting one off with the razor sharp clippers, she felt her heart skip a beat at the sound of crunching gravel under boots. Olivier turned into the soft ground cover of the vineyard and silently walked through the grid of vines toward Syd. He stood next to her and inhaled deeply.

"*Qué bonita,*" he whispered, his gaze fixed eastward toward the sun rising over the river. Syd froze and nodded.

"All of this hell we are going through and the world is still beautiful like this," he said. "Nature is cruel and indifferent, but beautiful." He was quoting something that Clarence said often. Syd nodded again, remembering the first time she understood the reverence Clarence held for the natural world. He taught her to marvel at the greatness of nature, to illicit the ultimate lesson of human insignificance. Clarence saw the world through the humble, sad eyes of a poet who believed in no god or master plan. Instead he believed in the profundity of beauty and love. He worshipped the loneliness of insignificance. He drowned dutifully in a sea of nihilism with a passion for human frailty as his lone buoy. She realized now that Clarence understood everything. Tears filled her eyes at the thought.

They stood together for several minutes, staring at the view, each lost in memory of Clarence. Suddenly, a sound from uphill jolted them.

"*Órale!*" Alejandro shouted from the neighboring block, at least twenty rows above them. He stood with his hands up in the air. Syd copied his gesture and turned to Olivier, who chuckled.

"What are we doing, bosslady?" he asked Syd, teasing her lightly.

Syd explained the task, showing him how to label the bags and count the vines out. He smiled while she explained it, and she realized that he must know exactly how to do everything she was explaining. He did not demonstrate his usual forbearance.

"What is it?" she asked as he continued to smile.

"Nothing," he said, grinning.

"No, what?" She looked hurt.

"You remind me of Clarence, that's all."

"Oh," she said, returning to her task. She wondered what he must have meant. She trudged off two rows up from Olivier to give him space. He would have to leap frog her rows, which wasn't the best system. But she was reluctant to move too far into a block by herself, thinking of her vow to be more careful.

They worked in silence for a half hour. The sun was well above the horizon but their fingers were still frozen. Syd remembered a day in the vineyard with Clarence when she was ten, on a morning very much like this one. There had been a deep frost the night before, and Clarence wanted to check on damage from a freeze so early in the season. Clarence explained what he was doing in a slow, methodical manner. Syd rolled her eyes as he spoke, to which he responded with silence. Of course, he suspected that she didn't care about the vines or what he was teaching her. But her real objection was his condescending tone, and his assumption of her ignorance. With Clarence, the elementary lesson rarely evolved into more depth and complexity while gauging his student's intelligence or understanding. He simply taught lessons according to his own plan. When she was a teenager and she had shouted at him that he treated her like a small child, he was perplexed and sullen for days. Now she realized that his methods for explaining or teaching were a simple means of conveying information. There were no assumptions or room for mistakes. He spoke in the lowest common denominator to ensure accuracy. Just as she had with Olivier.

Syd smiled at her own self-discovery. Her hands moved efficiently over the vines, clipping leaves and canes, and marking the bags. Olivier said she was like Clarence. Just two months before she would have been offended, but today she was proud.

She smiled to herself and took comfort in her thoughts. She bent down to pick up the crate of supplies and heard a buzz of wind rush past her left ear, carrying with it the sharp report of a rifle. She stood up again, confused. Olivier shot straight up and turned to Syd, twenty yards above him on the hill. Another two raps echoed through the vineyard.

"*Sydney!*" he yelled. He ducked to run bent over, taking shelter in the vines.

Syd stood paralyzed. Confused. She searched for Alejandro, who had disappeared. More gun shots. Her legs started to run, and she ducked low in the vines. Another bullet whizzed by her, this time above her head. She sprinted with her back bent and sudden excruciating pain in her left elbow. She stumbled and landed on the crate she was shocked to discover she still had in her hands. The corner pierced her side. She recovered her feet and ducked low. Another bullet whizzed by her right side, blowing her sweatshirt backward.

Olivier met up with her at the edge of the block and tackled her face down. He lay on top of her, his body taut and ready, listening hard. Syd's head rung with echoing shots. Adrenaline rushed through her in massive waves. She tried to focus on the sounds around her, between the swishing in her ears. They lay together on the ground for thirty seconds, holding their breath. It felt like an eternity. He poked his head up slightly when they heard no more gun shots. His shifting weight pressed heavy on Syd and she couldn't breathe.

An engine fired up a few seconds after Olivier had tackled Syd to the ground. Olivier got to his knees, straddling Syd's legs, and popped his head up. He saw the ATV racing uphill to the neighboring vineyard and Alejandro's flannel shirt flapping in the wind like a cape. Olivier watched him disappear into the vines uphill.

"Alejandro took off after him," Olivier said in a hollow voice.

"How do you know?" Syd whispered hoarsely. Her face was still buried in cold clumps of dirt near the base of a vine.

"He must have seen where the shots were fired from up there," he said. He moved off of her and straightened slowly to get a better look. They strained to hear the sound of the ATV whining at top speed.

After a moment, Syd rolled off of her aching arm, which was wrenched when she hit the ground. It ached deep in the bone, and she wondered if she had broken it in the fall. She cradled her left elbow in her right hand as she turned over on her back, looking down in horror.

"Olivier?" she gasped.

He looked down at her lying on the ground, the front of her shirt covered in blood. She was pale as a sheet.

Olivier fell to the ground next to her with terrible shock on his face, which sent Syd into a panic. Her eyes opened wide as he gently lifted her arm away from her body. She yelped in pain and whimpered. His face filled with despair.

"Is it your belly?" he asked in a husky voice.

"I don't think so," she whispered, feeling faint. She concentrated on the pain and tried to navigate through the echoes in her head, the whirling intensity of her throbbing pulse. She looked down at her torso. *So. Much. Blood.*

"Is it your arm?" he asked tenderly.

"My elbow, I think," she whispered. Olivier took her right hand away and gingerly raised her left arm. He unbuttoned her flannel sleeve and pulled it up over her bicep. The bullet wound was just above the elbow. The entry and exit wounds ran through her arm below her bicep, with the entry wound on the outside of her arm. The holes were tight and oozing dark blood. The exit wound on the inside of her arm was bleeding profusely. Olivier pulled out a pressed, white linen handkerchief and folded it into a long strip. He tied it to her arm tightly across the bullet wounds. Syd winced before smiling faintly.

"It really doesn't hurt so much," she said softly. She swallowed hard in a dry mouth.

"That's the shock," he said gruffly through a clenched jaw. He tucked the ends of the handkerchief into the tight band. He bent her arm tenderly and placed it across her chest. His hands moved thoroughly over her stomach, sides and breasts, searching. He held his breath.

"I feel like an idiot. How did I get shot?"

"What?" Olivier exhaled. His cheeks turned red and he yelled very near her face. Her ears rang at the sharp tone of his voice and she winced. He grabbed her thighs and shook her legs, and she saw the fissure in his composure behind his black eyes. "You have been shot, Sydney. Someone tried to kill you."

"Not me," she said stupidly.

Olivier muttered something in Spanish through clenched teeth and stood up. He began to pace in the gravel access road. Syd saw his nervous anger tethered to her like a short leash tied to her prone body. She suddenly understood the scene with acute awareness. He could not leave her, though he desperately wanted to chase after whoever it was shooting the rifle. Not at birds, she began to understand. Whoever was shooting at them was actually shooting at *her*. He was staying to protect her, although his anger seethed out of every pore in him.

"You can go," she said, trying to regain her composure.

"*No, I cannot*," he snarled. He stopped, transfixed, searching for an invisible foe and abruptly resumed pacing furiously.

"I'm sure he's gone," she said. "Alejandro scared him off." She moved to get up. Her dignity began to hurt as badly as her arm.

"Keep down!" he bellowed at her ferociously.

She winced reflexively. His eyes moved over her wound. Blood pooled rapidly through the handkerchief, which had turned entirely bright red.

He moved quickly over to her with a mix of concern and terrifying anger congealed on his face in a bizarre grimace. Syd felt terrible for him. He was helpless.

"Don't yell at me," she whined in a half whisper. It was the only defense she could offer amid the confusion of emotion and fear.

He snorted through his maniacal grimace and tended to her wound. He pinned her down with his knee painfully pressed against her chest. She couldn't have gotten up if she wanted to. His hands moved over her arm with trembling fingers and Syd lay transfixed. *Breathe*, she shouted at him in her head. *Breathe, dammit!* His face was purple. Suddenly he sat straight up on his heels. The whine of the ATV filled the air around them.

Olivier ran uphill to meet Alejandro in the ATV, which skidded into a spray of gravel on the steep access road.

"He got away, *pendejo*!" Alejandro shouted over the idling engine. His eyes were almost as wild as Olivier's.

"On foot?" Olivier shouted back.

"Yeah, he got a good head start!" Alejandro looked winded and flush. He dismounted from the ATV and walked over to Syd lying on the ground. He fell to his knees when he saw her.

"*Syd!*" he shouted, gawking at the blood, "I saw you running. I thought you were okay." He squatted near her with his hands hovering over her. The blood rushed from his face.

"I'm fine," she said loudly. "Really."

"You're shot?" he asked. His eyes searched her body as she lay in the mud.

"Yes. In my arm. Olivier won't let me get up." She shot Olivier a nasty look. Olivier still paced the road and Alejandro followed him with his eyes.

"He's gone. I almost caught up to him but he dodged me in the woods. Too thick for the ATV."

Olivier stared at him furiously.

"It was a man? Shooting at birds?" Syd asked. But she knew the answer.

"Yes," said Alejandro. "A man with a 30-aught-six, I think. Something long range. He was way up in the trees. And he just disappeared. We have to get you to the hospital." He began to lift Syd up to a sitting position.

"And call the Sheriff," Olivier said through flared nostrils.

"I'll get the ATV. You stay here." Alejandro instructed gently. He leapt up to retrieve the idling machine.

Olivier paced the gravel road, shooting looks up to the

copse of woods a quarter-mile off. Syd managed to stand upright and glared at Olivier when he moved to help her. She stood upright, even though her instincts screamed for her to remain as close to the ground as possible.

She cradled her left arm close to her body as she staggered to the four-wheeler. Her head spun, but the pulsing echo in her ears subsided as she struggled to remain conscious. The back of her throat burned and saliva swished in her mouth violently. Suddenly, she bent over and vomited on the front ATV tire, bracing herself on the wheel well.

Olivier froze and stared dumbly at her fifteen feet away, while Alejandro ran to her and held her up gently. He wiped her mouth when she finished. He lifted her up on the four-wheeler seat and sat down behind her, cradling her in his arms. Syd stared back at Olivier as he watched them descend the hill, pale-faced and wide-eyed. She felt small and cold as she leaned against Alejandro. She wondered vaguely how she must look to him covered in blood and vomit. She felt wretched and succumbed to the sinking temptation of self-pity.

She had been shot.

A moment later she was sitting on the idling four-wheeler alone while Alejandro ran to get his truck. He pulled up to her, carried her into the front seat, and pulled out in a rain of gravel. Syd watched Olivier jog downhill as they pulled away. It was the last thing she saw before she passed out.

Chapter 33

Charlie walked silently into the hospital room. She sidestepped around the bulky bed and sat down to hold Syd's hand. She blinked hard at the throng of bodies standing at the foot of the bed and asking questions. On the other hand, Syd laughed and chatted with them. She dismissed the pain in her arm, which was wrapped up in a huge white bandage. Charlie marveled at her friend's resilience.

"I'm okay," Syd answered Charlie for the third time. Charlie insisted that Syd tell the police and visitors to leave her alone. "It's only my elbow, Charlie," she bellowed. Olivier raised his eyebrows at her declaration as he entered the room.

"She was shot," Charlie explained helplessly.

"Yeah, he knows," Syd muttered, staring at Charlie's pale face. "He was there, for Christ's sake."

Olivier frowned at her and moved over to Charlie. He took Charlie's arm after whispering something in her ear and escorted her out of the room. He returned a minute later and sat in the chair Charlie had vacated.

"Be easy on her," Olivier said. "Her best friend was almost murdered."

Syd burst out laughing. She was trying her best to hold it together, and the pain meds were suddenly making it difficult. She felt numb all over, especially in her arm. But she found her emotions too spiky to grapple with before they escaped into the room in volatile gusts.

"I know, I know," she whined. She fidgeted her shoulders and kicked her feet in the bed. She wanted to get up and go home. The doctor told her that was a product of the adrenaline still coursing through her. But she had seen too many movies featuring a victim in a hospital bed like a sitting duck, waiting helplessly for another attack.

"Where did Jim go? I want to go home now. When can I be released?" She tried to work her voice in a calm adult manner but knew she sounded petulant. She had answered everyone else's questions for hours, while hers were still being ignored.

"Jim left a while ago, Syd," Olivier said. "Jack is outside."

"Oh, geez. I really meant to see him at the hospital." Syd winced at a sudden knot that gripped her chest. She had neglected her uncle's best friend. Why hadn't she visited him? The past two weeks began to unravel in a vague series of events.

"Do you want me to have him come in?" he asked her. His tenor was restrained and patient, like that of an adult talking to a child. Olivier was solicitous toward her since she was admitted to the hospital. Syd hadn't forgotten how angry he was at her in the vineyard. She wasn't going to forget that easily.

"Of course. Jack," she screeched toward the door.

An old, balding, broken man stepped into the doorframe. He wore sweatpants, a sweatshirt, and Birkenstocks. His shuffle revealed the pain of a slow-healing injury. He didn't look anything like the Jack Bristol of her childhood; polished, dapper and cheerful.

"Hey, Jack," Syd whispered, as if he were the one in the bed.

"Hey, Sydney," he said, smiling back. His face was still swollen with ugly yellow and purple bruises that disappeared under a bandage on his right cheek.

"I meant to come see you, Jack," Syd said.

"No, Syd. I understand." He sat down gingerly on the foot

of her bed. Syd was unsure if it was for her comfort or his.

"Hey, if I got here earlier we could have shared a room!" Syd joked. She grabbed his dry papery hand. Jack smiled weakly until the worst thing she could imagine happened. His face crumpled into a grotesque grimace and he sucked up air in a strangled gasp.

"I am so sorry, Siddy!" he cried. "My fault! This is all my fault."

Syd pulled him into her, ignoring the excruciating pain of his weight on her left arm. His poor broken body shook silently for several minutes. Syd held him and cooed sounds of reassurances every now and then to his cradled head. Charlie stepped into the doorway, alarmed by the sound of him. But Syd silently shooed her off. She could sense Charlie and Olivier hovering near the door.

Syd's left arm soon grew alarmingly numb. She gently asked him to shift his weight. Jack's violent emotional surrender left as quickly as it had arrived. He sat upright and apologized. Self-awareness overtook his face and he hung his head, looking more wretched than before.

"God, Syd. Did I crush your arm?"

"No," she lied. Circulation returned to her arm in painful stabs. She had to focus hard to not wince. "And it's not your fault, Jack. This is all the work of some crazy person. Some sociopath. A murderer."

"Who we have arrested," Jim announced to the room suddenly. He had burst in and stopped at the end of her bed. He wore the expression of a deeply determined man, with a furrowed brow and authoritative glare. At the same time it was clear he was wholeheartedly distraught by the reality of a very close call. Syd looked from one man to the other, each feeling the pain of her attack as if he had inflicted it himself. Each was equally delusional in his patriarchal sense of duty. One was racked with guilt while the other was bold with triumph. Syd felt a surge of restlessness streak through her. She felt like she was trapped in some bad cop film, riddled with stereotypes of damsels in distress as hero's traipsed into hospital rooms shouting victory.

"Who?" Syd demanded.

Jim swallowed hard. Syd watched in growing horror that he

misunderstood her demand as righteousness. He was going to patronize her and explain the arrest to her like she was child. She wanted to throw something at him.

"Hans Feldman. His Lexus was parked up in the easement between the neighboring vineyard. He purchased an ought-six at an antique gun show last October. We found the bullet that went clean through your elbow. He has no alibi, Syd. And he's not Hans Feldman. His name is Walter Solomon. He's wanted for fraud in New York."

"Oh," Syd answered. She had expected him to say it was either Bertrand or Feldman. She looked down at her huge white arm held in a sling from her right shoulder and pondered the facts. Of course, Hans Feldman – or Walter Solomon, or whomever he was – stood to gain from Clarence's death. And he lied about the winery buy out and about selling it out from under Clarence. And he had potentially forged a medical examination. And he kept Clarence from knowing about his cancer early on; maybe early enough to get treatment. But she had gone over it in her mind again and again and it didn't ring true.

"Did he have the rifle?"

"We haven't found it yet. We picked him up in the vineyard talking to Ted. Pretty brazen, if you ask me. He was just standing there having a conversation. Claimed he didn't even hear the gun shots."

"How do you know it was his rifle then?" she asked, still frowning.

"Bertrand told us. Claims to have seen it in Feldman's study right after he purchased it last fall. It still had the tags on it."

She wondered if Bertrand was believable. "So he owns a sniper rifle. Why didn't he run?"

"Best place to hide is in plain sight," Jim answered.

"But wasn't Ted his alibi?"

"Nope. They had only just met up. It was after 8 am when the deputy showed up at the vineyard. You were shot at 7:45." Jim appeared to be growing impatient. "Listen, Sydney. We've apprehended the perp and we feel confident we have the right man. You should too." He raised his eyebrows to signal that the discussion was over. Dismissed. Syd frowned as her mind worked over the details.

Charlie was creeping into the room while her dad explained the arrest. She stood next to him when he delivered his speech and turned to leave. Charlie stepped out of his way. Olivier stood in the doorway and nodded to Jim as he passed into the hall, apparently on his way out of the building.

"I guess that means it's over," Charlie said timidly once the room filled with silence in the vacuum that Jim Yesler had left behind.

"I can't believe I didn't run a check on him before I drew up the contract," Jack said. He buried his face in his hands again.

"*It's not your fault!*" Syd shouted suddenly at the distraught man sitting on her bed. He jolted up and stared at her, startled into confusion. Olivier stepped over to him and led him out of the room, speaking in low tones to Jack. They both looked back at her from the door way, Jack grimacing compassionately. He shuffled off down the hallway while Syd avoided Charlie's glare.

"*Fuck!*" Syd yelled at the top of her lungs. Olivier quickly shut the door, while Charlie waved her hands at her and pounced next to her on the bed, looking ready to cover Syd's face with a pillow.

"You can't yell *fuck* in a hospital. Syd," she said, chastising her through giggles.

Olivier stood and leaned his forehead against the door. He had blood on his shirt and dirt all over his left cheek. He was having a terrible day.

"I am so *fucking* tired of being treated like a *fucking* child!" Syd yelled at Charlie, only a little quieter than before.

"Uh, yeah. You've made that clear enough," Charlie said, grinning. "But at least no one will be taking pot shots at you in the vineyard or lurking around your house at night anymore."

"And what makes you so sure of that, Charlie?" Syd demanded.

"Excuse me? Because my dad said so, that's why. And he's a pretty fucking good detective, you know. And he's the one doing all of investigating, and putting together the facts and trying to protect you while you defy every instruction he gives you. Jesus, Syd." Charlie bounded up off of the bed. She paced the room once and moved to the door. Olivier got out of her way. "And, after you're finished being a drama queen and realize that closure is a good thing, you might want to call dad to say thanks." She turned and walked out the door.

Olivier closed the door behind her. A nurse in pink scrubs opened it a second later and popped her head in.

"Ah-em. There's no screaming of profanities in the hospital please," she said, stepping forward to check the morphine drip. "You can push this button if you need more pain medication, dear." Syd noticed a delicate gold cross around the nurse's chubby neck.

"Or maybe I could just pray for less pain," she feigned a saccharine sweetness, surrendering to a gnawing meanness seeded by the bullet wound. The nurse was not amused. "You have been warned," she said to Olivier before scuttling out of the room. Olivier stood staring at her for a full minute after the nurse left. Syd squirmed under his stare.

"Good. At least if I'm kicked out of here I can go home," she muttered to herself, trying to fill the unbearable silence.

"Is it the pain?" he asked. "Why you are so angry?"

"The pain? Really?" She shook her head. "I'm pissed off for so many reasons, Olivier. So. Many. Reasons."

Olivier slid the chair next to the bed and sat down. He held his fingertips together to listen and stared implacably.

"First, I'm really sick of the men in my life acting like I need constant protection and pandering. And I'm sick of them being almost right. I fucking hate that you slammed me down into the dirt face first."

"Instinct. Sorry."

"Whatever. *And* I'm really sick of having someone hunt me down and being really fucking scared." She choked back the tears welling up in her throat and lowered her voice. Olivier sat and listened quietly. She spoke softer, "And I'm sick of thinking you'll go to jail. Or leave. And I'm sick of being such a fucking useless person in the winery. And I'm sick of Clarence being gone."

Olivier waited for her to wipe her nose on the hospital sheets and find her composure.

"None of it makes any sense, Olivier. None of it! Why would Feldman want to shoot *me*? He had nothing to gain by shooting me. So many other people knew about the insurance policy and the medical report." She took a deep breath. "And where's Rosa? I'm in the fucking hospital, for Christ's sake!" Her voice sank into a childish whimper that she surrendered to without concern that Olivier might find her petulance as ugly as she did. The cat was most certainly out of the bag. By now he had seen her at her absolute worst.

"Good question," he said, raising his fingertips to his lips.

Chapter 34

Syd was released late that afternoon and Charlie drove her home in silence. Olivier had disappeared from her room when the nurse came in to check her IV and had not been seen since. Syd was ashamed of her outburst in the hospital room, but she still felt a surge of rebellion moving through her in waves of righteousness more native to a teenager than a grown woman. She could not discern her emotions from reason at the moment, drowning as she was in a tsunami of feelings. She was uncertain if the doubts she felt were the residual effects of having her world turned upside down or the logic of her deepest instincts. She knew that her frustration with the helplessness of her situation was real. She also knew that the people surrounding her were not doing their best to support her. She felt like she had been treated like a child. And she wasn't so certain the morphine hadn't elicited her paranoia and uncertainty. She stared out the window on the ride home.

The lights of the car reflected off of a passing car, and Syd caught a glimpse of a startled face in an oncoming Jeep. It was a face she vaguely recognized staring back at her. Something about it jarred her into contrition. She turned to Charlie when they were nearly home.

"I'm sorry I yelled at you, Charles," she said flatly.

"Yeah? I can tell."

"Well, fuck Charlie. I got shot today. My uncle was murdered last week and half my inheritance was given away. I got the flu and I started my period. I'd say you could cut me some slack." Charlie pulled the car over.

"Everyone's trying to help you, Syd. But you're such an ungrateful bitch sometimes." Charlie yelled at the steering wheel.

"I'm not ungrateful, Charlie. I know everyone's trying to help me. I know they're doing their best. But I hate being treated like a child. My uncle was murdered and I have a right to know what's going on. I have a right to ask questions, to talk about it. And I'm not so sure your dad has the right man." She paused to wipe the tears from her cheeks and take a deep breath, "I know I've been a wreck and I'm so embarrassed..."

"That's just plain stupid, Syd. Just stupid. Do you hear yourself? Your uncle died, you lost half of your inheritance, you got the flu and you got shot today! Geezus. Mother Theresa herself would be having a nervous breakdown. There's nothing to be embarrassed about.."

"But I feel like I'm drowning..."

"Yeah, I know. You've got a lot of healing to do, Siddy. I know you like to think everything through for yourself, but you might want to let this one go..."

"But Feldman's driven by greed, Charles. *Greed*."

"Yeah, and he killed someone for it."

"But he had more irons in the fire. Better paying irons. He had a lot to lose."

"Isn't that the point, Syd? He had too much to lose. He needed that insurance payout to cover his part of the new scheme."

"Do we know that? He had money for the initial scheme with my uncle, so he must already have some cash to invest. And why shoot me?"

Charlie threw up her hands. "Hell, I have no idea Syd. Maybe because you knew about the insurance fraud."

"So why didn't he go after Paul the insurance guy? Jack met with Paul."

"They're all questions my dad has worked out, I'm sure." She restarted the engine, "I think you need a long bath, a good meal, and a few hundred hours of sleep. Maybe some nice dreams about a dark Argentine man." Charlie pulled the car back onto the road and Syd stared out the window silently.

"Are you still mad at me?" Syd asked.

"Yeah, but I'll get over it. It's nearly Christmas and you just inherited a lot of dough. Guilt makes great gift-giving." She smiled slyly and punched Syd's knee.

"*Ouch!* Fuck, Charles. I just got shot, you know." Syd feigned a pout that felt much more like a grin. It was always better to have Charlie in her corner. She was looking forward to a night of popcorn and snuggles with her friend. Lying next to her felt as much like home as the quilt on the spare bed.

~

Charlie busied herself in the kitchen that night making Syd her famous mac and cheese. Charlie used four cheeses and the last of the home-cured bacon from Clarence's larder. Clarence cured excellent pork belly in a spare refrigerator that he used for cheese wheels, home-cured prosciutto, and his pickled vegetables. She clambered around in the kitchen looking for the right pot and utensils while Syd fell in and out of sleep on the couch. Her waking moments were filled with regret over her behavior that day. She began to feel the immediate need to wean herself from her meds, deciding that the drugs removed her ability to filter her thoughts and control her emotions.

Her arm began to throb around 7 pm while Charlie puttered in the kitchen. Syd shuffled her way into the kitchen to find some ibuprofen. After swallowing 800 mg with a swig of tap water she searched out the kitchen window for the winery truck or any sign of Olivier. She hadn't seen him since he left the hospital. The winery remained dark and unopened. She contemplated the need to do evening punchdowns, and what seemed like Olivier's uncharacteristic neglect of the winery duties.

"Not him too," she said, her voice sounding hollow and distant.

"Who? What?" Charlie asked. She turned away from the mortar and pestle she was using to pulverize stale bread for the crust on the mac and cheese.

Syd collected herself. "I guess I mean Olivier," she said.

“What’d he do? And who else did it?”

Syd stood and shook her head.

“Syd? What are you talking about?” Charlie walked quietly forward and hugged her gingerly, avoiding her bandaged arm in a sling.

“Well, Rosa’s gone, right?” she asked Charlie, still hugging her.

“Hmm. She’s had a few days off, Syd. That's all.” Charlie released her and stepped back to look her in the eye.

“But she didn't say anything to me. She normally would have said something.” Her voice trailed off.

“Maybe it was her day off and she forgot to tell you. Or maybe she said something to someone else and it didn't get passed on.” Charlie searched for a plausible answer.

“And now Olivier’s gone.”

“Uh, we just saw him at the hospital, Syd.” She felt Syd's head and realized she was hot. “Maybe you should lie down again.”

Charlie led Syd back into the living room and onto the couch. Syd lay down obediently. Her arm was throbbing and she wondered if maybe she should reconsider taking the pain meds, heavy narcotics haze and mood swing or not. Charlie retrieved the quilt and gently tucked it under her arm. She stood over her for a moment, looking worried. Syd closed her eyes and ignored Charlie's furrowed brow.

She dozed off for a while, feeling the hot throbbing of her arm subside enough to make sleep inviting. She heard clattering in the kitchen and the worried hum of whispering voices in between strange dreams. She awoke to whispering at the table in the same room, permeated with the delicious aromas of baked food. She struggled to push herself off the couch with her right arm and sat up.

Charlie and Jim were seated at the table, their heads drawn together in furrowed brows and furtive whispers. Charlie watched for Syd's movements and jumped up over to her when she sat up.

“How you feeling, sweetie?” she asked, supporting Syd's right arm and helping her stand up.

“It really hurts. I think I may have to take those pain meds after all," Syd said, admitting defeat. Her arm was excruciating and the throbbing was getting worse. She had been warned that the wound could get an infection, and she was already on powerful antibiotics. Still, she wondered now if her insistence on going home was a bit premature. Nausea swept over her and she had to sit back down to avoid vomiting.

Charlie left her to find the pain meds and some water. When she returned, Syd had recovered a bit and took the pills obediently. She sat upright on the couch for a few minutes, waiting for the pulsing in her arm and the waves of nausea to subside. A few minutes later she braced herself and got up again. She shuffled over to the table and joined Jim and Charlie. A hot cup of tea was waiting for her.

"Hey, Sydney," Jim said with evident trepidation and worry, his voice full of gravel.

"Hi, Jim. Hey, listen, I'm sorry that I gave you such a hard time at the hospital. You're right. You are a good detective and I was wrong to second-guess you." She reached over awkwardly to squeeze his plate-sized hand with hers.

Jim and Charlie exchanged looks. Even under the fogginess of pain, Syd could see their expressions.

"What's up?" she asked in a small voice, feeling very young. The hair on the back of her neck rose and a chill swept through her.

"Our case isn't water tight," Jim said. "But we're working on it, Syd."

"You still believe it was Feldman, right?" she heard herself plead. She wanted to believe it wholeheartedly. She needed to know it was over.

"Yes. He's just really clever. Listen, Siddy-biddy, I just need you to rest and heal that arm. Let me worry about the case." He shoved back his chair and cleared the stack of plates. Syd sipped her tea while Jim rinsed off the dishes. Charlie sat and tried to avoid staring at Syd with a face wrought with worry.

"I'm gonna head out now, ladies," Jim said. He shuffled into the great room. "You two take care and look after one another. A cruiser will be here all night, just outside. I'll be back in the morning, okay?" Syd heard his voice as if through a large pair of ear muffs.

"What time is it?" she asked, more as a statement to herself than a question.

"About 8:30," Jim answered. He bent over to kiss her cheek. "Good night," he said to Charlie, who bit her lip. "Lock the doors, babe."

They sat silently together at the table. Charlie stared at her clasped hands while Syd pondered the possible whereabouts of Olivier. She was beginning to feel the incessant nagging of a task undone in the winery, and her mind worked out the risks of leaving them undone. A Tempranillo ferment was awry and unchecked today. Punchdowns had not been done since early in the morning. Two had been missed so far and there was no sign of Olivier.

"I need to get up to the winery, Charlie," she said, her voice echoing strangely in her head.

"What?" Charlie turned to look at her in slow motion, her voice muffled and deep.

"Punchdowns haven't been done all day."

"I think the wine can survive a day without punchdowns." Charlie wasn't about to let Syd go up to the winery and attempt punchdowns one-handed. Or negotiate the stepladder on opiates.

"But the Tempranillo is..."

"I'll call Alejandro," she said and jumped up out of her chair. She returned with her phone to her ear a moment later. There was no answer. She left a voicemail and texted him. She found another number and called it. Still no answer. She texted again.

"Who's that?"

"Olivier," Charlie said. "I've been trying to call him all afternoon."

"He's got a cell phone?" Syd asked, incredulously. Charlie smiled and nodded, still texting.

"So why doesn't Rosa have a god damn cell phone?" Syd asked. The pain meds were beginning to chisel away her filters. Charlie set her phone down and reached for Syd's shoulders. They sat in a half embrace for a long time. Syd began to feel unbearably sleepy, and shuffled off to bed with Charlie behind her, ready to help Syd into her pajamas. She lay down on the bed on her back, the beloved quilt tucked under her arm along with a pillow to prop it into the most comfortable position.

"Night, Syd. Rosa will be here in the morning, don't you worry." Charlie kissed her on her forehead and tip-toed out of the room.

Syd lay in the dark for a while, making out strange shapes in the shadow of the dim light on the table across the room. The light was yellow but tinged with gray by the darkness. It reminded Syd of the bruises on Jack's face. Then she thought of Jack. She mused over his friendship with her uncle and the memories of his presence in her childhood. Jack was like a gift-bearing happy uncle to her, replete with trips for ice cream. He was always a guest at Thanksgiving dinner and had a special ticket at graduations. But even though he was beaten and bruised, and nearly killed, she still wondered what possessed him to take part in conversations with Feldman about his most recent scheme. Maybe he was just Feldman's lawyer? She tried to recall what Alejandro had told her about the meeting in the vineyard that Sunday less than two weeks ago. It felt like a lifetime ago.

She squirmed in bed, regretting it as soon as she moved. Her arm throbbed. The overwhelming fatigue she felt earlier vanished into fitfulness and she lay poring over random thoughts and worries. The pain in her arm brought her mind to sharp acuity in jolts. She listened for the sounds of a truck on gravel for a long time, but it never came.

Soon she drifted off into a disturbed dream. In it she heard laughter from Rosa and Olivier through the open door of the winery. The door was unusually heavy when she pushed on it, feeling it push back the more she shoved. She lifted her left arm, which felt heavy and stiff, and pushed higher up on the door. The bandage was gone but the gunshot wound was still there. Only now there were no stitches; only an open blackish hole. The door still wouldn't budge. Syd called out to the voices inside, but they couldn't hear her. Rosa's cackle rolled out beneath the crack of the door. She turned to see her uncle standing next to her, studying her troubles with a look of concentration. His glorious scent of cedar and exotic spices overtook her. His hair was tinged with purple and his skin was ashen, but his eyes were alive and smiling.

He stepped over to the door and said, "like this, Sydney,"

without moving his lips. He pushed on the door slowly, effortlessly with some kind of miraculous expertise that left her exasperated and awestruck. They entered the winery and were greeted by the noxious burn of CO2 gas. It repelled Syd back and out of the winery gasping for air. But Clarence entered freely and walked over to Olivier and Rosa, each of whom smiled at him. They stood together in a cluster around a tank. Olivier handed Clarence a sample in a beaker. Clarence frowned and nodded, sipping and spitting the wine into the drain in the floor. Syd called out, but they couldn't hear her. She paced outside the door and looked up at the sky. A heavy purple gossamer veil hid the moon, leaving the clouds in a giant ripple like raindrops in a pond. The sky was oppressive and ominous. She attempted to enter the winery again, but the gases were too heavy to breathe. She watched Clarence and Olivier argue over the sample. Rosa puckered up her face in disgust and clucked her tongue. Suddenly, both men turned to look at her as she hovered in the doorway, shaking their heads in disappointment. She had ruined everything. She stared at them, her mouth working like a fish, pleading. She begged for them to understand that she couldn't do it. She was injured and in bed and she was forced to stay away by the gases. But they didn't listen to her or they couldn't hear her. Olivier walked into the recesses of the darkened winery and out of sight. Clarence followed him and Rosa vanished altogether. Syd stood just inside the door, shivering with terror and indignation.

She waited in the thin strip of the open door for a long time, trying to make out the shadowy shapes coming from inside the winery. The sky made terrifying moaning sounds, and the vines shuddered in a portentous wind. When she turned to look toward the vineyard, the rustling stopped abruptly. Suddenly the full moon shone brightly between the drawn curtains of the purple clouds and the doors of the winery gleaned a bright red. Syd tried to push open the doors again. They were a little easier to move this time, so she continued to push her way inside. The gas was present but not suffocating. She pushed the doors for what seemed like hours and stopped for a breath when the door was nearly all the way open. She bent her head while she gasped for air and noticed something directly behind the door. A shoe, attached to a leg. She peered around the corner, suddenly terrified again. A figure of a man lay against the door, blocking it. She realized she had been pushing his dead weight. But he wasn't dead at all; his eyes looked up at her as she crept nearer for a better look. It was a face too familiar to be forgotten.

Syd awoke with a jolt, jarring her arm out of position. A bolt of searing pain radiated through her and she realized that she may have torn one of her stitches. Her mouth was dry and she reached for the glass of water at her bedside. She gulped greedily, looking to fill up the hole in her chest burrowed by the nightmare. Her right hand pressed hard on the wound to squeeze out the pain, stanching any bleeding that may have occurred. She forced herself to breathe steadily. She contemplated waking up Charlie out of desperation to be held. Marcus would be nice, she thought to herself. *Marcus*. His huge body, his strange marmalade smells and incessant scratching in his sleep. She would endure his worst habits for the comfort of his embrace right now. She wondered if Charlie had called him when she was in the hospital. She had no idea where her phone was and she hadn't checked any messages for days. Guilt settled into the hole left by the nightmare. She had been unkind and unfair to Marcus. He deserved an answer. She knew she had to cut him free soon. She knew he'd wait patiently for her to do it. And he'd argue with her and tell her that he loved her, all the while putting up the effort to delude himself into thinking he had tried to stand by her during her time of need, a *Boy Scout*.

She lay struck by the sudden clarity of her relationship with Marcus, grateful for the distraction from her pulsing arm. He was the perpetual Boy Scout, predictable and comfortable. Marcus held no mysteries, no secrets in his past to uncover. He was a good-looking place filler, a known variable. A warm body to break against when she wanted one. He was outgoing and eternally faithful. He was less concerned with her own introversion than she was. He was a natural mask for her, the sleight-of-hand that deflected any real interest in herself. Besides, he mastered the trends and fads of the social elite like a natural. They looked good together, and he wore a lovely tuxedo. A hot surge of shame ran through her at her thoughts, and she swallowed hard.

She realized she had chosen a shallow life. Deliberately.

One replete with labels; wine labels, clothing labels, and self-branding as a floor working sommelier. And the perfect boyfriend was the perfect accessory to her self-abasing life. She had compromised everything that mattered with several casualties along the way. There was no truth, no beauty, no love. There was only a caricature of a life built in her own ironic cynicism. A life unauthentic, the kind she most despised. Even worse, she had squandered the love of the man most important to her in an attempt to find her own way; a way machete'd through a false jungle of first world problems mired in the swampy recesses of a selfish princess's mind. Her sense of entitlement sickened her. And now she had to break Marcus's heart too. She was a wrecking ball. But perhaps thinking she was a wrecking ball was part of her self-importance. Her self-pity sickened her more; narcissism was the worst epitaph imaginable.

Syd leapt out of bed, not caring if she tore open all of her stitches. She wandered aimlessly through the house, searching blindly in the dark. She was a succubus, an energy vampire sucking life out of everyone around her. Clarence lived for love, passion, and art, and she had learned nothing from him. He faced his own truths with a lifetime of dignity and authenticity, while she sneered at his genuine life floating like a ghost through a life full of every imaginable gift, only to squander them.

"I am so sorry. *So sorry*," she whispered to the dark kitchen, choking on the ball of shame lodged in her throat. She wanted Clarence to hear her. She wanted it more than she had ever wanted anything in her life. She loathed herself for wanting forgiveness so badly, feeling that she really deserved was a lifetime spent in purgatory. Yet she would have given over to any religion in order to speak to him once more and beg forgiveness. The loneliness of the dark, cold kitchen engulfed her, and she fell in a heap on the floor, sobbing. She tried to pray, but the hypocrisy of it stuck in her throat. Instead she worried her hands in knots while she spoke out loud to Clarence. She babbled through her tears, gesticulating at her phantom listener with passion. Eventually, she finished with dry coughing sobs. Her legs grew stiff and her arm ached with the weight of the blood entering her wounds. Over time the hole in her chest felt smaller; exactly the size of a bullet hole. She used the counter to pull herself up gingerly, using her awkward right arm.

She felt no sense of absolution, but she did feel a little lighter. Besides, there was one thing she could do for Clarence. She struggled with the medication bottle for a few minutes with her right hand, but she eventually managed to open it and took one of the Oxycontin with water. She stared out the window. It was too dark to see if the truck was back. She couldn't make out the Sheriff's cruiser either. But Jim had said it was there, and she imagined it parked out in front of the house. The road to the winery was dark and ominous, but she knew it well. She would have no trouble in the dark without a flashlight. The way was branded in her. She took another pill, as an after-thought.

Punchdowns would not be easy.

After a few minutes of struggling with a pair of yoga pants under a black silk slip and her uncle's oil-slicker, she tiptoed her way onto the deck, closing the door silently behind her. She didn't want to wake up Charlie.

Chapter 35

Syd was grateful for the security lights that beamed on when she got near enough to trip them. She usually would have waved her arms around for the motion detector, but her right arm was cradling her left arm in the sling and she had forgotten about the motion detector anyway. She reached the door and struggled to unlock it with the hidden key. The doors opened freely to the outside. She remembered her dream with a shudder, the red doors opening inside and giving such resistance. She flung both doors open and waited outside, letting the gas escape. She sat waiting in the lighted area on an Adirondack chair until the light went off. She nearly panicked while she leapt up to set off the motion light again. She took a big breath outside and stepped inside to reach the panel of lights just inside the door. She didn't want to face the sudden darkness again while she waited.

The night was crisp and gorgeous. The cold made the night air crystal clear, and she could make out the tendrils of the Milky Way in the midnight sky. The lights from the bridge on the river below shone bright, and the whistle of the train going by two miles away sounded much closer. She held up her left elbow in an embrace and began to feel a little better about herself. Maybe it was the painkiller kicking in, but she felt a warm surge coursing through her. She didn't mind being alone for the moment. The stars and the view were enough.

After she waited a long while outside – certainly long enough to purge the carbon dioxide from the room – she entered the winery with trepidation and an alert nose. Once she was a few steps in, she realized it was safe to enter and she focused on her plan. First she would remove the covers of the tanks and find which wines absolutely needed punchdowns and which ones could stand to wait until she had help in the morning. There were still ten tanks left in active ferments; all of them placed in the middle of the winery. She would take their temperatures too. She wasn't sure how she was going to do the work with her right arm. She was always dominantly left-handed. She plotted how she might get the tool through the drying caps after sitting all day without submersion into the juice. They would be under a great deal of pressure and she would need strength. But she could devise a way to dig through the skins and make a hole to get it started. She had done it before, albeit using her stronger arm.

In fifteen minutes she had managed to take the temperature of all of the tanks. She found three that needed immediate attention to release the heat and CO2 built up under the cap. She prepped a five-gallon bucket with steaming water and metabisulfite to dip the punchdown tool in. It slopped on the floor when she carried it with her clumsy right arm.

She dug a hole in the skins of the first tank and tried to use the heavy punchdown tool. She experimented with every possible angle, but her right arm was not nearly as useful as she would have liked. She cursed her dominant left-handedness, feeling the burn of defeat when she realized that she could not maneuver the tool. Her right arm simply wasn't coordinated or strong enough. She carefully placed the punchdown tool back into the bucket of water, removed the overcoat, and sanitized her arm in the sulfur water. She stood on the stool and plunged her arm in the pomace up to her armpit, using her arm as a stir rod or a mixer. The ferments were warmer than the outside air, and she enjoyed the work on a visceral level. There was a sensual weaving of smells and sensations. It took her three times as long as it would have taken with a good arm and the tool, but she felt satisfied as she finished one tank.

The next tank took longer than the first. She was growing tired, and worse, she felt loopy from the pain meds. She worked the skins with her right arm as she stood on the step ladder. The outside motion light had long gone out and the cold air of the autumn night crept into the open doors, making her shiver violently. The front of her nightie was wet from slopped wine. She knew she should have been miserable, but she had not felt so determined in a long time. She was taking care of the wine when there was no one else to do it.

The last tank was the Tempranillo that had given Olivier such trouble two days before. It still had a slight off odor of hydrogen sulfide; a red flag for unhappy yeast. She took a Brix reading with the hydrometer and found that it was at 7 Brix. It had moved a little since Olivier brought it to her attention. Or had it moved? She couldn't remember. She considered just throwing in some diamonium phosphate, unnatural chemical nutrients that acted like candy for yeast. But adding nutrients now would be tricky. Adding too much would make the wine a lovely nutritious medium for future unwelcome spoilage yeasts, but too little would not stimulate the ferment. She would have to do further tests. She grabbed a sample of the juice after bathing her arm in the sulfur water. Her arm was now purple, even after all of the wine had been washed away. Stained. She pulled on the overcoat with her right arm in the sleeve and stood shivering, working to keep her mind from remembering the details of Clarence's purple stained hands. She padded back into the barrel room.

The barrel room was a dark, familiar labyrinth of oak barrels stacked to the top of the twelve-foot ceilings. It smelled like vanilla, tobacco, and wood, a mixture of aromas that Syd loved with her entire being. She made her way through the first stack to find the bank of lights and switched them all on. She was not used to the way the barrels were lined up. They were usually stacked in a different direction, but she could see that the current system used less space. She made her way to the lab door off of the barrel room, somewhere near the middle of the maze.

The fluorescent lab lights buzzed and flickered when she turned them on, which was a terrible nuisance for long stints in the lab. Syd found the small cylinders necessary to do a test in the spectrophotometer. An unfamiliar cell phone sat silently near the spectrophotometer, on top of a legal pad with cryptic notes in a familiar slanted masculine handwriting. She recognized it as Olivier's. She found comfort in knowing that he left his phone behind, sitting like a beacon or tether to this place. She opened the old-school flip phone and scrolled through the menu. He had five missed calls; four of them from Charlie and one from Alejandro. She scrolled down through his history and saw many recent calls from *Madre*. Some were from unknown numbers, but most were from Alejandro. She was surprised to see a few from Marcus. She scrolled down a few weeks back and stopped on a name. Clarence. Then another from Clarence, and then several more. Then a few from Antonia. She put the phone down and felt guilty for having pried. She looked around for the test tubes she needed.

Syd filled the vials with wine to test the yeast assimilable nitrogen-YAN- content in the spectrophotometer. The test would help her determine how much nutrients to add to the stuck fermentation. She prepped the vial and calibrated the machine, remembering vaguely how to run the test. It had been several years. She used to do all of Clarence's lab work, but tonight in her OxyContin fuzz she couldn't remember the test procedure. She botched the sample on her first try. She thought about leaving it for the morning, but obviously Olivier thought it was important to run a YAN test too, and she didn't want to let him down. He could have done the additions already, but what if he hadn’t? Determined, she grabbed another beaker to get a sample of the Tempranillo, turning the light out as she left.

The silence and darkness caught Syd off guard and she gasped. The barrel room was pitch black. She turned to find the lab door and turn on the lights, but she was disoriented by the new barrel arrangements and had to feel blindly along the wall. She put the beaker in her pocket to free her hand. She was nearly inside the lab door and reached for the lights, but she was shocked motionless at the sound of shuffling feet in the darkness.

They were near her; very near her. Maybe a few feet away on the other side of the barrel stack.

She stood petrified, holding her breath. Her ears strained to listen. A soft swish, maybe a hand on a barrel, barely audible. A slight moan of leather, possibly from shoes. She stood staring wide-eyed into the darkness. The winery and the barrel room were dark. But she could make out the faint glow of light from the motion lights outside. The gentle green glow terrified her more than the darkness. She realized the reality in front of her. Someone had entered the winery and turned off the lights. And he was now standing feet from her. Panic choked her, collapsing her throat. She gasped again reflexively. She knew immediately that the sound gave her away. She bolted toward the door, feeling her way along the barrels. There was only one way out of the lab, down one aisle of barrels. And once he stepped into the aisle with her she knew she was trapped. She struggled to quiet her breathing to listen. He was still far from her, possibly at the end of the aisle. She heard by the sound of his footsteps that he was moving quickly. She scrambled forward, acting before she could think.

Her right hand darted into her pocket and she grabbed the beaker. She threw it on the ground on the other side of the barrel stack closest to her. The glass shattered everywhere. She stood motionless, listening. The sound of shuffling feet floated from her left to her right. She wasn't certain, but she felt like breaking the glass might have worked. She could wait until he made his way to the broken beaker and make a run for it.

She stood frozen and listened for an eternity. She held her breath, held her body taut. Every muscle was poised. No sounds. No movement. She tried hard to remember the lay-out of the barrel room. She had only been in it a few times since the new arrangement. She had to choose her path carefully. A life-or-death choice she realized in a gulp of terror. Was he in the other aisle?

She raced through her options, paralyzed by the choice in front of her. This man was certainly going to kill her. She was going to die if she couldn't get out of here. She had no weapon and she couldn't fight with her left arm in a sling. There'd be no one to help or hear her if she screamed. A chill ran up her spine, filling her with an icy resolve.

Run! she screamed in her head and her feet accelerated into darkness.

She hit her slung arm hard on a metal barrel head stave and cried out. Her right arm reached out frantically as she ran into hard, invisible obstructions. Her ears roared with raging waves of fear. She made for the distant green glow, barely visible from the barrel room. Her right arm felt along a wall as she neared the glow. She shuffled harder and bounded off of a shorter stack of barrels she had forgotten about. She spun toward the glow of light and stumbled to the ground. She used her right arm to push off of the floor and re-gain her footing.

She was a yard from the barrel room door when her head jolted back with searing pain. She fell back onto the ground and into the man's legs. She rolled slightly over to her left side and freed her right arm. He held her hair in his hand and jerked her up, sending searing pain through her scalp. She hit back hard with her right arm, grazing his thigh. She threw another punch that landed in the soft tissue of his groin. She reached up again and grabbed a fist of whatever she could. She squeezed, punched, and wrung it violently. Suddenly, his screams were mixed with hers as her hair was pulled from her head. She thrust viciously with her hand again and felt a sudden relief of her searing scalp. She pushed off hard, wrenching her wounded arm as she tried to stand up. She stumbled and he leaned down over her, frantically grabbing at her with both hands. She swiveled on her butt and kicked his thigh as hard as she could. She kicked again and landed her foot in his groin. He stumbled backward and she crawled like a crab with one arm, scurrying several feet away. She rolled to her right side and bound up on her feet.

She sprinted out the door and into the big room of the winery. The cold air rushed into her face like a beacon, and she forced herself out blindly into a fermentation tank. She spun around the tank and made a path through the other tanks. She could see the door twenty feet away.

To her right she saw a dark figure and the flash of a long metal object. She paused for a split second and turned as she registered the sight. She sprinted forward again, only to stop suddenly as she was struck with a hammer of force on the back of her head. She fell like a bag of rocks to the concrete floor. Darkness filled her head, overtaking her with frightening coldness. Only one thought coursed through her fading consciousness – *Olivier.*

Chapter 36

He pulled the truck up the gravel drive, lost in thought. He would have to tell Sydney everything. He and Jim had decided it would be best coming from him, considering her recent outbursts toward Jim. Secretly he thought Jim was showing surprising cowardice for a sheriff, but he also understood. Jim was defeated in a way that men of his fortitude rarely were. He turned off the headlights and sat in the truck, contemplating the nightmarish day: Sydney getting shot, his helpless terror and anger, the guilt of having treated her so badly, and his pursuit of Rosa. And then it got much worse.

He drummed his fingers on the steering wheel, formulating some kind of plan in his exhausted mind. He knew she had lost almost everything. She would be grateful that he found Rosa. But the guilt of having missed her absence – of having known that her disappearance was odd but ignoring the nagging in the back of his mind – was unforgivable. Deep down, he feared it was a product of his own Argentine class snobbery; his father's gift to him. Rosa was the Mexican help. Did he ignore her absence because of his own classism? He shook his head. It was useless to blame himself. After all, he wasn't the one who tied her up without food or water for days, beat her, and left her to die. He wasn't culpable. But the man who did this to Rosa wasn't sitting in a jail cell either. He shuddered and got out of the truck. He would sleep outside of Sydney's door himself if he had to.

He moved across the drive under the clear night and paused to gaze up at the night sky. The tendrils of the Milky Way striped the black sky in muted celestial clouds. It was beautiful. A different night sky than the one he was used to in Argentina. But he wouldn't have to work hard to love this celestial offering. He could stay here indefinitely. His heart beat a little faster at the thought of seeing Syd, with her arm in a sling, still belligerent on her pain meds. He inhaled deep cool breaths and steadied himself as he thought of what to say to her. It wasn't over. He scanned the drive and the road for the cruiser that should have been parked outside the house. The sheriff cars had all been called to the shed where he found Rosa, including the one Jim had posted here. He was glad that he was back at least. He shuffled toward the house but stopped when a light caught his eye.

The motion light flared on up in the winery. A moment later, just as Olivier looked up to the winery, the inside light shut off. He stared, trying to see who was coming out of the doors. He could hardly make out the doors from the distance, so he strode quickly up the drive. As he moved up the drive, the hair on his neck stood up and he began to step softly. He quickened his pace to a sprint on instinct. Something wasn't right. No one left through the doors. No one was leaving the winery. Someone *went inside*.

He heard her scream as he reached the doors. He ran into the cavernous dark room and stared toward the sound of a struggle. She gasped and screamed again, her sounds punctuated by the grunts of a man struggling too. He strained to see in the darkness. He stepped lightly around the fermentation tanks to see Syd rushing blindly into the room, hitting hard against a tank and crumpled back. He grabbed the punchdown tool and raised it into the air to strike her assailant, who bound into the room a few feet away.

A flash of metal caught light, and Sydney collapsed to the ground. A flash of light from the punchdown tool momentarily lit up the attacker's face. It was a face tinged with focused triumph as the man watched her fall. Olivier cocked his arms and swung with all his might in a violent, bone-breaking strike at the man's triumphant eyes. He fell back to the sickening sound of crunching bone and metal. It echoed as the man slumped onto the concrete. A deep scream bellowed from his lungs, echoing in his ears as he raised the metal tool to strike the prone and motionless figure again. But he heard a guttural whimper that ran a cool shiver through him and he lowered his weapon. He looked down at Syd, scratching her nails pitifully on the concrete. His weapon fell to the ground in a clatter of metal.

Olivier fell to the ground next to her and turned her over onto his legs. He pulled her up to his chest and shushed her whimpering with frantic consolation. Her breath was labored and a gash in the back of her head bled freely. Blood pooled and congealed on the floor, mingling with that of the man lying next to them. The dark pool from his head was larger and seeped ominously from the other side of his body. Olivier held his left hand to Syd's scalp and felt the warm blood oozing between his fingers. Her skull was unnaturally soft under his fingers and his heart seized up in absolute terror. The room grew quiet, and he realized that she had stopped whimpering. Desperate, he remembered that his phone was in the lab. He gently lay her head against the cold floor and tried to rise on legs of mush. He cursed himself when his hands slipped on the floor, covered in blood as he tried to get up. He glanced at the man's lifeless body as he crawled past him and shuddered. His head was twisted at an unnatural angle.

He quickly found his phone inside the dark lab. He made his way back to the two lifeless bodies and called 911. Then he called Jim and Charlie. Then he lay his phone down and slumped on the floor.

He held her head with both hands, desperately trying to stanch the bleeding. He faced the lifeless man in such a way that his foot was ready to strike if he got up again. But he never did.

Chapter 37

Rosa sat day and night next to Sydney's bed for a solid week. Although she had a broken finger from the nefarious attempt at extracting information via torture and quite a few bruises of her own after taking a substantial beating, everyone at the hospital knew the best medicine for her was to nurse Sydney. They put her up in the bed next to Sydney for several nights until the doctors released her. But she never left. Someone in the hospital had the good grace to keep the bed next to Sydney empty.

Charlie stayed all day long each day, but left at night with Olivier. He kept his vigil outside in the waiting room, pacing a path in the purple Berber carpet. He left to work at the winery but always returned to pace in silence. Jim was busy tying up the loose ends of his case, but he came morning and night to see Syd and whisper details to Olivier. Charlie alone kept the men fed and cared for, making sure Rosa showered daily and brushed her teeth. She retrieved tea and coffee for everyone, always in a constant state of motion.

Syd lay in an induced coma. She had sustained a brain injury that the doctors were confident was mild. Her skull was fractured in several places, but the blow to her head from a heavy wrench was flat and dispersed over the area of her skull instead of through it. Still, she had a mild depressed injury and she wasn't out of the weeds just yet. The potential swelling of her brain could bring on clotting and more serious brain damage. She had been in the hospital for eight days since her attack. Eight days since Olivier had killed Joe Donner with a single blow.

On a crisp autumn Monday morning, Charlie, Olivier, and Rosa stood at the foot of the hospital bed and stared at Syd. The barbiturates used to force Sydney into a coma were wearing off, and Syd was expected to wake at any moment. Jim and Alejandro sat in the waiting room on plastic orange chairs, sipping terrible hospital coffee. Jim's phone rang.

"Yup," he answered impatiently. "Nope. Not yet. Nothing yet. I'll let you know, Jack." He sat quietly and nodded "Yup, okay. I'll let her know when she wakes up."

He took the phone from his head and touched the screen. Alejandro looked over at him with raised eyebrows. A nurse walked by and scowled at him. She nodded at the sign on the wall. *No Cell Phones*.

"Life insurance funded. Somehow Jack thinks that'll be good news to Syd," Jim said, shaking his head.

"*Pinche cabrón.* Lawyers!" Alejandro smiled wryly at Jim, realizing they had forged an unlikely friendship in the past few weeks.

Jim's phone rang again. He swore under his breath, retrieved it from his pocket, and squinted at it. "District attorney. I've got to take this one," he said to Alejandro. He got up to walk outside onto the wet and blustery balcony where cell phones were allowed.

Alejandro took the moment to peek his head inside Syd's room. From the crack in the door he watched the three friends keeping vigil and holding their breaths. Syd lay motionless, but her eyes fluttered and opened slightly. They locked onto his from across the room, peering from the cracked open door.

"Hey, Allie," she whispered in a dry cracked voice.

"Hey, Siddy," he said. He entered the room sheepishly and sat down next to Rosa. She gasped and wrung her hands. "*Dios mío*! *Dios mío*!" she said, holding back her tears. Charlie grinned back at her when Syd panned the room. Olivier took a deep breath and let it out in a slow heavy sigh. His face was implacable. Syd was annoyed.

"You've got nothing to say?" she croaked out, her mouth unfathomably dry. Her eyes were locked on Olivier's. "I've been in this bed for god knows how long and you don't even come visit? What kind of man are you?"

They all looked at each other uncomfortably.

"Olivier's been here the entire time, Sydney," Charlie said.

"Oh," Syd said, closing her eyes against the confused faces staring at her. She fell back asleep for a while, falling into the warm watery place where she had been. Voices emerged and faded around her. She could make out a few words and tones. She felt comforted to know that they were right outside her pool, or whatever this place was. She felt herself rising to the surface now and then and listened to her loved ones banter in worried whispers. She smiled to Rosa to let her know that she was alright. She floated at the top of the water, arms and body splayed out face down. Her eyes opened and she made out the dark figure at the bottom of the pool, blood swirling around his head. She gasped for air.

"What happened? What happened?" she said, choking back the water in her throat but finding that her mouth was dry and sore.

"Okay. It's okay now," Charlie said. She was sitting on the bed next to her, caressing her right arm. Rosa jumped over to her other side. Alejandro stood up at the foot of her bed. There was no sign of Olivier.

"What happened?" Syd asked again. She said *water* in a desperate plea that seemed comical to herself, like a cartoon character on a deserted island. She smiled as she sipped from a cup offered by Rosa.

Charlie mouthed something about a coma and a head injury. *Blah, blah, blah.* Syd pursed her lips and refused Rosa's ministrations.

"What happened in the dark? The winery?" They glanced back and forth in collusion. Syd grew more annoyed.

"Fuck," she muttered. Rosa clucked her tongue and offered more water. Charlie got up and left with a smile. Syd sipped to appease the burn in her throat, but mulled over her confusion. Was no one going to talk to her?

A few moments later Charlie returned with Olivier at her heels. She beckoned the others to leave and they paraded out of the room. Olivier stood stiffly and clutched a bed post.

"Do you mind if I sit?" he asked politely.

She shook her head. "Nope, Ollie. You may sit." He sat down next to her and avoided her eyes. His hand darted out and he grabbed her own, squeezing it too tightly. His face hardly registered any emotion but she knew him well enough to know that he was tortuously mulling over the words he needed to say to her. Syd waited for him to say something while she tried to piece together that night in the winery. She managed a flood of shattered memories. She thought of her face pressed against the cold concrete floor, the whiskey, and his caresses while she surrendered to her grief and sobbed in his arms. She thought of his hands on her skull while the life bled out of her. She remembered the tangle of his fingers and her hair holding her life hard against her skull.

"So you're capable of murder, aren't you?" she asked. He stared at her blankly for what felt an eternity.

"It appears so," he finally said. His face slackened and he dropped her hand.

"Well, I'm certainly grateful for *that,*" she said, taking his hand back. She smiled wryly at him. He grinned back at her with a toothy smile that melted her. His eyes shut back forming tears, and he worked to collect himself before he spoke again. And then he told her *almost* everything.

Chapter 38

Joe Donner would stop at nothing to prevent the truth from coming out, or so it seemed. Of course, in the end it did all come out in the horrid tabloid style of intrigue and murder. And, of course, Sydney McGrath and her arsenal of defenders were right in the middle of it. She had the indispensable protection of the Sheriff's deputy at her door for weeks, a lawyer ready and waiting, and friends who buffered her from the outside world. Still, she was the subject of many articles, news stories, and blogs gone viral. Somehow the romance of her uncle's murder took hold of the hearts of the public, eventually running amok. And she was the heroine in distress, saved by the love of her life in the eleventh hour. Truth was often the seed of the story, but time and age-old archetypes made for better reporting.

The District Attorney never released the entire story, nor did he reveal any notion of the intrigue that really went on. It was a story greater than fiction, best kept to the minds of the parties involved. Although it was an election year and he could perhaps garner some political traction from it – after all, it was the juiciest conspiracy to hit the Columbia Gorge since the Rajneeshpuram cult's water poisoning – he showed considerable grace in leaving it alone. Jim Yesler was duly impressed. Charlie, however, was not swayed with his grace. Charlie knew it was bad business to uncover something so big when running virtually unchallenged. She suspected he might save it for later.

Charlie had left Seattle for good by then. She had no job left anyway after having taken such a long leave of absence. Syd promised her a job at the winery in sales or something. Whatever Syd needed, Charlie would do with a smile. She was really quite finished with the part of the wine industry that built rockstar careers out of nepotism and mediocrity. The subtle collusion it took to create the Frankenstein of Joe Donner's career – all perpetrated by her friends and colleagues –sickened her to the core. They all helped make a giant of a little man sick with narcissism and sociopathic tendencies. It was an exercise in building alliances that created a ladder to better field their own rises to stardom; most of them having no talent or scruples. Nepotism with the wrong sort can quickly sour a relationship, especially if the person with whom you are colluding is willing to kill people to protect a reputation.

Of course, Marcus was out of the picture as soon as Charlie understood what happened that night. He had been texting Charlie when he found out that Syd was shot. He had texted when she was in the hospital and texted again while she was making dinner that night. He was desperate for information, and Charlie had refrained from responding for reasons she couldn't explain. Except maybe it was a kind of clairvoyance. She returned his call at three in the morning, in the hospital waiting room for the second time that day.

"Hullo," a sleepy voice answered after five rings.

"Marcus. This is Charlie. Sorry to wake you. Syd is back in the hospital from a head injury. They're not sure if she'll pull through. Your friend Joe Donner shot her yesterday morning and went back later to finish the job last night. He's dead, by the way."

"What?" he stupidly answered. Charlie hung up.

He hadn't tried to call since. Later, she found out that he had been calling Olivier who dutifully delivered updates.

Charlie kept the news about Marcus to herself. Olivier asked her once if Marcus was ever going to come visit Sydney. He was perplexed. But Sydney remained uninterested in finding closure with Marcus. The thought of him made her shudder with disgust. Alejandro took the perspective that Marcus was a threat to Sydney. Charlie was undeniably involved in these conclusions. Marcus became the ghost of Sydney's past, a ghost who haunted a life that no longer had meaning to the Sydney they knew and loved. Charlie felt little guilt for being responsible for excising Marcus out of her friend's life. But she suspected that Sydney never missed him anyway.

Of course, Sydney wondered how Marcus would take it all. He wasn't culpable in the least. But still, she didn't want to see him or talk to him. His worse offense was being a very poor judge of character. She often felt sorry for Marcus and knew he felt cut off from her. But so much had changed since her life in Seattle.

Syd had long hours to think through the details of the past months. She stayed in the hospital for nearly three weeks, which was much longer than she felt she needed. But she was not the only decision-maker in her recovery. A battalion of friends barraged the doctors for information on a daily basis. Her recovery was quick enough, but there was some concern that she might suffer a blood clot; a particular hazard to the kind of injury she sustained. The induced coma had sped up her recovery, but blood thinners had slowed it down again, especially when her gunshot wound became infected. And although she was anxious to get home again, she was also grateful for the time to lie down and do nothing but heal. She no longer trusted her judgment under the weight of guilt and remorse.

Her healing was as much emotional as it was physical. She lay for hours talking to Clarence's ghost and working through their problems. Olivier helped by telling her stories of his own childhood, his mother, and Clarence. Olivier would show up with the chessboard, replete with the queen bequeathed to Hans Feldman returned to her mates. They would play in silence for hours. She might ask a single question and he would answer with economic terseness, measuring out her healing in teaspoon-sized doses. She would often grow angry at his cryptic answers and beat him without mercy in just a few moves. But more often she sensed tenderness in Olivier. At times it felt so much like her uncle talking to her that it hurt sometimes to sit near him. During these times she let him win. Unlike Clarence, however, Olivier was unaware of the gesture of kindness, leaving her charmed by his youthful bravado.

On a day near her release, he sat triumphantly over a win and stretched like a cat in the light of a late autumn afternoon. Syd felt a sudden sense of alarm at the pull in her gut when she looked at him too long, an experience that had become far too frequent for her comfort.

"When are you going to tell me about finding Rosa?" she asked. She knew it was an ambush, but she was curious about why he kept it from her.

He stopped in mid-yawn and stiffened. She sighed, somehow happier in the safety of his formality.

"I told you," he said evasively.

"No, you just said you went looking for her. You left the hospital..." She looked him straight in the eye, challenging him.

He sighed imperceptibly. "Okay, I left the hospital when I watched Charlie help you into the car."

"And then?" she said, egging him on. She feigned an impatience that she hardly felt. She wanted him to stay longer and she could wait for the story to unfold at his own pace.

"And then I went to Rosa's house," he said. "She was not there, obviously. So I went inside, using the Key under the mat," he explained his foray into breaking and entering with a modest amount of embarrassment. "She had not been home for a few days. She had mail piled up for two days from a slot in the door. Her coffee pot was on and the pot was fully evaporated but the lines in the pot made it look like it was once half-full. But there was no sign of struggle. So I thought that she must have left with someone she knew. Someone she would open the door for, but maybe she left with at gun-point."

"Why did you think that?"

"Rosa? You think Rosa would take a day off when you were going through hell? She had to have been kept from coming to work. She had to have been held against her will."

Syd shook her head. She had been weighed down in the hospital bed by the guilt while thinking that Rosa had taken the day off.

"I asked the neighbors and they hadn't seen her," he said. "I was about to come home when a boy playing ball outside their complex said he saw her leave with a white man wearing a cap in a Jeep. I called Jim right away and I took off to the vineyards behind Ted's place. The direction the boy saw the Jeep head." He clipped his words as if to end the story.

"When was this? When did he take her?"

"The day after Jack's accident, I think. In the afternoon."

Syd nodded, still frowning. "And then?"

He sighed again, this time with more weariness. "Well, it took me a while but I found the little shed where he took her. I found her tied up in a corner. On some old seed sacks. I called Jim again and we took her to the hospital." He avoided her eyes.

"She was beaten?" she asked in a whisper.

"Yes. And she was half-dehydrated and frozen to death." His voice was flat and disgusted. Anger flashed over his eyes. She was reminded of his behavior in the vineyard when she was shot. She decided to steer him away from the gory details.

"How did you know where to look?"

"I didn't go straight to Rosa's actually. I went to look up in the trees where the shooter must have been when he shot you."

"Was he in the shed where you found Rosa when he shot me?" she asked, shivering. Rosa was there in the shed, held captive and beaten nearly a stone's throw away from her when she was blissfully working the vines.

"No. He had made a kind of... nest. A hunter's blind of sorts. He had built up a camouflaged place where he watched the house." He watched Sydney carefully. She winced, as he suspected she might, but she hammered on.

"Had he been there for long?"

"It looked like he had made himself quite comfortable. He had several binoculars and scope sights. He had food and cooking utensils. A bed roll. I think he had been camping there."

"Watching?"

"Watching," he said. "Watching for an opportunity to take the thumb drive from you, I think. But he could have been up there when he killed Clarence. I think he was certain Clarence was going to send the thumb drive to his publishers."

"So he killed him. And planned to remove the evidence of his writing a crooked review."

"Yes," Olivier answered. "He tried earlier too. He was at a conference for wine writers in Portland the weekend Clarence's plane was tampered with. Jim found a credit card receipt from a gas station in Hood River the day of his accident. It's circumstantial, but it points to Donner." Olivier frowned. "I came clean to Jim about your conversation with Frank."

Syd scratched under her head turban of bandages in deep thought.

"It looks like he may have just been trying to steal the evidence from you when he first came down to the house."

"I suspected that too. But then he tried to kill Jack before he came looking around here."

"I think he assumed Jack knew about it. But he couldn't let you live after Bertrand had been talking to the police. It was Bertrand's blunder that made you a victim of a murder attempt instead of robbery. Feldman baited Bertrand too many times and Bertrand lost control. Feldman and Bertrand would have stayed quiet to avoid discrediting themselves, but as soon as you learned of their complicity you would have let it out of the bag."

"But Bertrand could have blabbed?"

"Bertrand was no threat. He would never have revealed himself as a fraud. In fact, he would have colluded with Joe Donner to expose Feldman in his new venture as a shady broker with a criminal history if Feldman didn't use him as the head winemaker. Bertrand and Donner were threatening Feldman."

"So why did Bertrand attack Feldman?"

"Bertrand only attacked Feldman when he called his bluff. Feldman was forced to keep them in the loop in the new deal to keep his real identity safe. Donner was just looking for another opportunity, I think. And maybe a reason to be sticking around here. But Bertrand was clearly losing it, not a natural criminal. He was coming unglued, and I imagine Feldman began to play his own hand at blackmail with the bribery. He knew about it."

"Or he plotted it himself."

"Well, it wasn't until Feldman started talking to the police that you became a threat to Donner. I think he began to care less about being exposed as a fraud and more concerned about having murdered Clarence. He had to remove the evidence of his motive and pin the murder on Feldman while he could."

"And remove all of the people who knew about the thumb drive, that he knew of, at any rate."

Olivier nodded.

"But how did he know that the police were talking to Feldman?" Syd asked.

"He must have run to the shed after shooting you. That might be why he disappeared when Alejandro was chasing him. The shack is only visible from the top of the hill. He waited it out and then he watched the police talk to Feldman in the vineyard from a distance. And then he must have panicked. He already had Rosa, so he. . .uh. . . questioned Rosa again. He was desperate to find the thumb-drive. More motive for murder. Rosa didn't tell him anything."

"And then we came home from the hospital," Syd said, swallowing hard. "He must have been watching the entire time. And he knew that I was alone in the winery. A Jeep, you say? I think I saw him drive down the hill when Charlie was taking me home. I thought I recognized him." Her voice trailed off and she shuddered at another thought, shaking her head. "He would have had to kill Rosa after he killed me. She knew it was him."

"There is not a good deal of logic in the behaviors of a sociopath, Sydney. He was a delusional narcissist. A man who would stop at nothing for his own ambitions. From what I understand from Charlie, he hated you nearly as much as he hated Clarence."

"But he never hated Jack or Rosa? Why would he harm them?" She swallowed back the tears of guilt and regret. She and her uncle had unwittingly goaded a sick man into despicable acts by simply acknowledging his grotesqueness and dismissing it. It was the worst offense one can offer a narcissist.

"He had everything to lose," he said. "He thought Jack had seen the video on the thumb drive. He thought Rosa would tell him where it was. If he removed the evidence he would discredit possible allegation made about him."

"I know all of this, Ollie. I've gone over this in my head a million times. I understand his motives. I just don't understand how a person could do it." She held her bandaged head with her hands.

Her voice was filled with frustration she found difficult to temper in spite of his growing anxiety. His face was nearly purple.

"Kill someone, you mean?" he whispered hoarsely. He met her gaze with the hard stare of a man lost on a one-way road.

"Because he had everything to lose," she whispered.

Olivier looked down at his open hands for a moment before he slowly closed up the chessboard and walked silently out of the hospital room.

Chapter 39

Several days had passed since she left the hospital. Charlie had moved into her uncle's room without much cajoling, and Rosa was back in full force. Syd tried to ask Rosa to take on a more modest role as a mother and friend, but Rosa continued to show up as a housekeeper in spite of Syd's best efforts to keep her away. Syd tried to fire her, but Rosa just laughed when she did. Syd offered her a room in the house, but Rosa scoffed. She said she had a pending offer on a condo in Hood River.

The women settled in the house with Clarence's ghost trapped in every object. But the real haunting occurred for Sydney whenever she was alone with Olivier. He had not returned to play chess with her since he told her about Rosa. He spoke to her often enough; about the end of Crush, the last presses, and the current state of malolactic fermentations in barrel. But he continued to stay in the freezing trailer and continued to work the winery for long hours alone. He came in for dinner only at Rosa's request, and he ate silently when he did. Rosa and Charlie shot goading glances at Sydney on the night's he ate with them, but she had no idea how to soothe Olivier's growing angst. He wore the look she knew far too well; the look of a man defeated by circumstances she could neither change nor control.

One morning before dawn as Thanksgiving weekend neared, Olivier sat out on a deck chair. Syd was up early too and found herself wandering out on the deck with a mug of coffee, shivering under her quilt. He had already pulled an empty chair for her next to him. He was waiting for her.

The cool mist felt wet and cold on her face. She had covered her head bandages with a beanie. He wore his usual clean work clothes, and he held his mug with long elegant fingers and perfect pink nails. His profile was his best feature, or at least the one she knew the best. His hair was longer now than when she first saw him, which was just six weeks ago. His dark curls fell along his cheek bones, landing near his sharp nose. His mouth was set with obvious intent on remaining silent. Only the new deeper lines near his eyes revealed the weight he labored under.

She sat down and looked at him. She knew what he was going to say before he said it.

"I have to go back home soon," he said quietly.

She nodded. A hard lump lodged in her throat. She swallowed back hard. "Your mother needs you?" she asked.

He nodded quietly, still looking away.

"Is she still at your uncle's?" she asked.

"She will stay with them for now. My father is fighting it. It's one thing to live without love in a marriage in the same house, but in Argentina you don't live apart."

"Not unless you have a backbone," she whispered. The thought escaped her mouth. Her pent-up resentment toward his mother and her hold on Clarence seeped out of her. Her anger was like a sleeping dragon; a white rage of judgment and condemnation. His mother; she was the source of all grief. This small woman who kept Clarence on a leash his entire life. And now she would take *him*.

He stared at her. She felt his hot eyes blazing a hole in her, but she didn't look back at him.

"It's not like that," he said through clenched teeth.

"Are you coming back or do you want me to buy you out?" she asked, surprising herself as she spoke. The ambivalence in her voice was a mask. "You're welcome either way."

“I thought I would come back, but now I am not sure,” he said loudly. She caught a glance of his face. His eyes flashed with fury. His usual self-control was gone. He got up and paced the deck, knocking over his chair. “I am coming back. This place is mine as much as it is yours,” he yelled, storming toward her chair and jabbing his finger in the air. “And *you*. *You* will keep this vintage from harm. *You* will make sure this wine is as good as I left it.”

Syd rose from her chair, dropping the quilt off her shoulders. She stood inches from his fuming face. “I will make this vintage the best it can be,” she said quietly. “You can trust me. And I don't intend to be anything but a partner to you. I would never try to force you out of your share. I would never dishonor my uncle that way, Olivier.”

She sat down again and wrapped herself back up in the quilt. He turned to leave and entered the house. She felt oddly satisfied at having him scream at her. She had been baiting him for days, not sparing his feelings for an answer. He had shut up like a vault, and she needed to know if he was coming back.

Three minutes later he returned to fill her mug from a french press. He sat down heavy and sipped from his coffee, obviously preoccupied. She waited, and he exhaled in a controlled breathe.

“I am sorry. I am so–” he muttered, hardly discernible. “I am so ashamed.” His emotion overwhelmed his voice.

She squinted at him, confused. She didn't hate him, of course, but the alternative was terrifying. “Because you got angry just now?”

“Yes, of course for that too.” He dismissed the though with a violent wave.

“And what else then?”

He struggled. “There are no words for this. No words. At least not in English. Americans don't have this.”

“I'm pretty sure that all people have the same emotions, thank you very much.”

“This is dishonor. I caused harm by being stupid. Being a child. Not seeing. You nearly died just feet away from me while I gazed at the stars. Did you know that? A man sat hunting my dearest friend, for weeks maybe, while I was oblivious to the danger. And now he is dead. My own mother spent a lifetime in misery, making misery for your uncle in order to keep *me* from dishonor. And I sat in the shadow of my own father, afraid."

"But then you saved your friend's winery – his life's work – from ruin while you were being investigated for murder. And then you saved my life. And Rosa's."

"By taking another."

"We both know you had no choice. That's unfair."

"In the eyes of God?"

"God? Really? Do you actually believe in God, Olivier?"

"Not intellectually. But religion is a part of culture where I am from. It is part of who I am. And murder is a sin."

"So is this guilt you're feeling because you killed Joe Donner or because you didn't do it soon enough?"

He shook his head. His eyes were filled with tears and he smiled sadly.

"Olivier, bad shit happens. There are evil people in the world who do terrible things. But you're not one of them."

"Sydney, you are so much like your uncle sometimes it scares me," he said, smiling through his tears. They moved in to embrace and held each other for a long time, until each regained composure. He fumbled in his coat pocket.

"My mother moved out before Clarence died. I thought you should know. She found out that he was dying and she was on her way here. She was waiting for her visa. Clarence had sent her this." He handed her a thick leather book. It was hand-bound in tiny perfect stitches with thick, hand-cut paper. She flipped through it. Clarence's writing filled every page.

"He kept a journal. She sent it back to me to give to you. It's yours now."

Syd took the book and held it close to her chest under the quilt. She sat for a while, watching the storm clouds move over the Gorge, threatening rain and wind. She smiled through her tears and remembered how autumn storms were Clarence's favorite. She sat long after Olivier left her alone, until the rain drops were too large to avoid and threatened to soak her quilt completely.

Epilogue

Charlie poured a local sparkling wine in their glasses while Rosa carved the turkey. The table was festive and the guests were enjoying themselves, but in the quiet somber way a family gathers when they have gone through a trying ordeal. Jim's sonorous voice filled the space with the details of Olivier's reprieve, having worked closely with the District Attorney himself to ensure that no charges were filed against him for Joe Donner's death. The others listened respectfully, and the table grew quiet when Jim had finished.

"So, when are you leaving, man?" Alejandro said, breaking the silence. He sipped his sparkling wine and set his glass down.

Olivier looked up from his plate and wiped his mouth with his napkin. "Soon. A few days, maybe. I have to run some tests on the plane first. I will hit some rough weather going south and I need to be ready for it."

"You go to work your own family's harvest?" Rosa asked, completely unaware of the distinctions she raised in her question. Olivier, however, did not miss it.

"Yes. My father's winery. I may help my uncle's too. I'm not sure where I will be needed most."

"His winery is like this one?" Rosa asked.

"No. His winery is a production winery."

"*No comprendo, mi hijo*," Rosa said, raising her eyebrows.

"We make very large quantities of wine. One hundred times the size of this winery, actually." Rosa clucked her tongue at him in disbelief. "But my uncle's place is like this. Small craft wines. Blends. A lot like this, actually. *Lo mismo*." He smiled at her and took another bite of stuffing. "This is delicious, Rosa." He winked at her, apparently feeling more buoyant with the talk of home.

Syd listened with curiosity. Olivier had not mentioned much about his home or his family business and she was shocked to find that he came from a production facility. He was so comfortable in craft wines. He had a knack for it.

"Are the wineries close together then?" Charlie asked.

"About fifty kilometers apart. I often go between them in a day. Honestly, I prefer to work my uncle's Crush but my father needs me too. We are always shorthanded, always in need of experienced help." He looked at Syd across the table, but she was looking at her plate thoughtfully. Charlie didn't miss the hint.

"Syd and I should come down to help," Charlie said, startling Syd. "Be sorters or something. We can do anything. Pick fruit, or . . ."

"Yeah. *Gringas* picking fruit!" Alejandro said, sarcastically. His girlfriend Sylvia sat next to him and hit him in the arm. "Ouch!" he bellowed, but he clearly enjoyed the beating.

"Yeah, *pendejo. Gringas* can pick fruit," Charlie said, winking at Sylvia. She instantly liked her. Sylvia hit him one more time, for Charlie, and she smiled. They were going to be friends.

"You're talking about Argentina, Charles," Jim piped in. He wiped his plate clean with the homemade potato rolls that Syd had whipped up the night before. Charlie nodded wearing her best clueless expression.

"But you may need some rest. It would be good to recover this winter and, uh, heal, maybe," Olivier said to Syd, who still had not looked up from her plate.

Dinner continued with the clinking of forks on plates and the politeness of passing the salt and butter. Syd worked on her meal with sentimental devotion. The meal was important to her and she felt herself filled with emotion. Thanksgiving was always her favorite holiday and she was grateful to have all of her friends around her. At the same time she was deeply saddened at the empty chair and untouched plate set for Clarence at the end of the table. She missed his laughter, his stories, and his warmth. He loved the holiday for what it represented to him; a day of giving thanks for all of one's blessings. Of the many things that could be said about Clarence, he could be humble and grateful as the best of saints. He would toast her mother and regale the group with a story about her, telling a new one each time. It was her favorite part of the day. His nods would be directed at the empty plate set for her, the same empty chair that sat next to Syd now. As a child she would offer perfect slices of turkey to the plate next to her and bits of well-buttered bread. Today she stole glances at the two empty chairs, aching for their conversation. She gave her quiet thanks to the ghosts at the table, asking forgiveness and offering her own. She hardly heard the conversations around her but she didn't miss Olivier's invitation.

She had family in Argentina. Her father had people there. And her mother had friends there as well. After all, she was an Argentine and American citizen. She was born there. She raised her fork to her bandaged head and scratched underneath it while she pondered the prospects of travel. She knew that Olivier was watching her. She avoided his eyes while she assessed her capacity to travel down the rabbit hole of her own secret history. She had been through an ordeal and come to the other side whole, albeit battered. Still, she awoke mornings startled to find a gaping hole in her chest, alarmed at the suffocating weight of grief for her uncle. And her grief was often eclipsed in the nightmares of dark rooms and monsters in the shadows. She might need the quiet of winter to heal. But it was the quiet that frightened her the most. The noise of a busy house – the incessant chatter of Rosa and Charlie arguing over recipes – kept her tethered to reality. She ached for the usefulness of being in a group of people – all working toward a common goal – like the preparation of a meal or a grape harvest.

She had her answer.

She looked up from her plate and met Olivier's eyes, smiling.

About the Author

Rachael A Horn is a winemaker at AniChe Cellars, a small family winery in the Columbia River Gorge. She has always aspired to write novels, but gave it all up for wine making a decade ago due to various clichéd angst. However, as fate has it, insomnia provoked a story from the depths of her mind one dark and wet December in the wee hours. Little did she know that a series of Sydney McGrath novels would henceforth erode her literary conundrum into a feasible attempt at writing. No longer frightened to pen a novel, she has forsaken her dream of crafting the Great American Novel for something far more lurid and entertaining. Murder.

Rachael lives with her husband and family in Washington State. She enjoys gardening, all things Flamenco, Nietzsche and butterscotch pudding.

http://www.ataintedfinish.com